Rappahannock Review

Other Anthologies of The Riverside Writers

Riverside Currents (2001)

Riverside Echoes (2003)

Riverside Reflections (2005)

Riverside Revelations (2008)

Rappahannock Review

An Anthology of Stories and Poetry

The Riverside Writers

A Chapter of the Virginia Writers Club

All rights reserved. No part of this book shall be reproduced or transmitted in any form or by any means, electronic, mechanical, magnetic, photographic including photocopying, recording or by any information storage and retrieval system, without prior written permission of the publisher. No patent liability is assumed with respect to the use of the information contained herein. Although every precaution has been taken in the preparation of this book, the publisher and author assume no responsibility for errors or omissions. Neither is any liability assumed for damages resulting from the use of the information contained herein.

Copyright © 2011 by Riverside Writers

ISBN 0-7414-6507-8

Printed in the United States of America

This is a work of fiction. Names, characters, places, and incidents either are the product of the author's imagination or are used fictitiously. Any resemblance to actual events or locales or persons, living or dead, is entirely coincidental.

Published March 2011

INFINITY PUBLISHING
1094 New DeHaven Street, Suite 100
West Conshohocken, PA 19428-2713
Toll-free (877) BUY BOOK
Local Phone (610) 941-9999
Fax (610) 941-9959
Info@buybooksontheweb.com
www.buybooksontheweb.com

Introduction by Claudia Emerson, Pulitzer Prize Winner and Poet Laureate of Virginia

Translated from the Greek, *anthology* means "flower gathering"—and I am delighted to introduce the Riverside Writers' newest garland. For the occasion, I have reflected on the absolute importance of environment and the "room of one's own" to any writer's creative efforts—seeing the many genres and forms represented in these pages as architectures and environments in which these writers also have dwelled. Keenly aware not just of "writing process" in the sense of "composition," I have long been fascinated by the creative process within the context of where writers live their physical lives.

There's something irresistible about making a pilgrimage to the home, the actual writing space of an author you admire as part of understanding the work that was made there. The writers showcased here live near the Rappahannock River and chose to name themselves after this geographic reality. *Rappahannock*, an American Indian word, means both rising and falling, the river obeying its falling current to the ocean as well as the tides' rising to the moon. The effect is the suspense of both forces at what we call the "fall line," where the river can be placid as a lake, and as mysterious.

These multifaceted writers have found in this place and in their chosen genres a similar kind of energy: balanced—but generative, measured—but volatile. The group, like the place, has a long history, and, nearing its fifteenth anniversary, has founded what I hope will continue to be a lasting community that supports and challenges, sustaining each individual writer in what can be the loneliest of pursuits.

From their various imaginative points of view, the writers represented here have crafted poems and prose that delve into the myriad aspects of human (and animal) interactions with this world, the works ranging from the elegiac to the celebratory.

While many readers experience literature as welcome departure from reality, the Riverside Writers challenge all of us to reflect on the porous, interdependent natures of space, time, and form in our lives, and to experience the written word not only as escape from the places we inhabit, but as refreshed return to them.

Welcome to this fruitful gathering. May it sustain—and inspire.

Claudia Emerson
Professor of English
Arrington Distinguished Chair in Poetry
Department of English, Linguistics, and Communication
University of Mary Washington

Contents

Virginia's Best

Rod Vanderhoof, *Yellow Heat* 3
Anne H. Flythe, *Balefires* 5
Stanley Trice, *Summer Discoveries* 6
Diane Parkinson, *Islands* 12
Larry Turner, *Never Mind* 18
Larry Turner, *Picture of Guilt* 20
Larry Turner, *Century for Freedom, Century for Peace* 23

Love and Its Complications

Anne H. Flythe, *Something Old* 27
Kathie Walker, *For Dave* 27
Elaine J. Gooding, *It's Not Original* 29
Norma E. Redfern, *Cassie* 30
Jackson Harlem, *Yew* 31
Larry Turner, *Pajamas* 33
Chuck Hillig, *The Boy Who Had Waited* 34
Larry Turner, *Morning in the Twi-Lite Motel* 40
R. L. Russis, *Early Widowed* 41
Madalin E. Jackson, *Mature Love in Words Only* 42
J. Allen Hill, *Menudo* 44
Rod Vanderhoof, *I Send My Regrets* 55
Donna H. Turner, *A Late Romance* 64

What Was Lost

Anne H. Flythe, *What You'll Get* 69
Anne H. Flythe, *On the Wisdom of Allowing Wine to Breathe* 70
Anne H. Flythe, *Saudade* 71
Norma E. Redfern, *Brimstone* 72
Anne H. Flythe, *An Undeliverable Condolence* 73
John M. Wills, *The Nightstand* 74
Madalin E. Jackson, *The Urn* 77

Margaret Rose, *The Save Pile* 83
Michelle O'Hearn, *Blue Collar Shadorma* 86
James Gaines, *Overtime* 86
Norma E. Redfern, *Pain* 88
Madalin E. Jackson, *Poe* 89
J. Allen Hill, *Panic at Milepost 42* 90
Laura Merryman, *The Crocheting Class* 91
P. A. Moton, *I Miss You, My Friend* 93

The World of Children

Elaine J. Gooding, *The Butterfly Song* 97
Stanley Trice, *Pane Glass Window* 98
Larry Turner, *Baby in a Box: Jesus and Two Marys* 107
David Mitchell, *The Substance of Youth* 111
Larry Turner, *The Birds and the Bees* 112
Donna H. Turner, *Best Friends Forever* 114
R. L. Russis, *Closer to Scratch* 118
Elaine J. Gooding, *Memorare* 119
Tracy Deitz, *The Oasis* 126
Donna H. Turner, *A Gift of Grace* 127
Norma E. Redfern, *Fishing with My Dad* 128
R. L. Russis, *At Twelve* 131
R. L. Russis, *Favored Sayings—and Sage Advice* 132
Mr. Kelly Patterson, *Yo, Paper Boy* 133
Laura Merryman, *On Stephanie's 16th Birthday* 135

Our Animal Companions

Tracy Deitz, *Thwarted* 139
R. L. Russis, *After Fieldwork* 140
R. L. Russis, *To Me It Was Magic* 141
R. L. Russis, *Lady, King, Queenie, Max ..* 142
Laura Merryman, *For Ollie* 143
Mr. Kelly Patterson, *My Boy Rex* 145
Larry Turner, *Bomhyr's Leash and Tycy's Collar* 146
Rod Vanderhoof, *Genghis and the .55 Magnum* 151
Kathie Walker, *One Fish, Two Fish* 159
Elaine J. Gooding, *Whiplash Takes a Ride* 160
J. Allen Hill, *A Mice Christmas* 162

Seasons of Nature

Anne H. Flythe, *Manic Implications of a February Thaw* 169
Norma E. Redfern, *Spring Rain* 170
Michelle O'Hearn, *Footprints in the Grass* 170
Norma E. Redfern, *Rebirth* 171
Anne H. Flythe, *Slow Food* 172
R. L. Russis, *Our Valley* 173
R. L. Russis, *Dog Days, Snake Days* 174
Anne H. Flythe, *A Personal Equinox* 175
Dan Walker, *Land Bridges* 176
Dan Walker, *Black Spruce* 178
Norma E. Redfern, *Fall* 179
Norma E. Redfern, *Three Haiku* 179
Elaine J. Gooding, *Twelve Haiku* 180
Dan Walker, *Marks* 182
R. L. Russis, *Meditation on Winter's Solstice* 184
Elizabeth Talbot, *Whiteout* 185

On the Ground

R. L. Russis, *And Us Almost Done* 193
Laura Merryman, *There is a Sweetness in Country Life* 194
R. L. Russis, *A Question of Horse-Power* 196
R. L. Russis, *Between the First and Second Milkings* 197
R. L. Russis, *Watch! Watch!* 199
R. L. Russis, *Visiting Home after Long Absence* 200
Elizabeth Talbot, *Collateral Damage* 201
Elizabeth Talbot, *Loved by All* 204
David Mitchell, *The Fifty-Cent Tour* 213
Tracy Deitz, *Shoppers Unite* 215
Tracy Deitz, *Brake the Fast* 216
Andrea Reed, *The Stationary Family* 217
Norma E. Redfern, *Fredericksburg 1727* 218
Michelle O'Hearn, *A Night Out in Fredericksburg* 219
Madalin E. Jackson, *Eratosthenes* 220
R. L. Russis, *Appreticed to Art* 221
Norma E. Redfern, *Observation* 222
Jackson Harlem, *The Orchid* 223
Tracy Deitz, *Shades of Music* 225

Conflicts Small and Great

Larry Turner, *Punctuality* 229
Anne H. Flythe, *From Your Sweet Lips* 229
Larry Turner, *Twins Anonymous* 230
Larry Turner, *Homage to the Cardiff Giant* 232
Donna H. Turner, *A Cake for Josie* 235
Donna H. Turner, *Doris Emmit* 238
Anne H. Flythe, *A Message for Antoine* 240
Anne H. Flythe, *Nine Tenths of the Law* 240
James Gaines, *Beyond the Covenant* 241
Rod Vanderhoof, *Loaded Sabers* 252
Juanita D. Roush, *The Fountain* 256
Madalin E. Jackson, *A Time of Restlessness* 259
Larry Turner, *Swept Away* 261

For the Love of Words

Dan Walker, *The I* 265
P. A. Moton, *Cannot* 267
John M. Wills, *Words* 268
Larry Turner, *Blackmail. Noun, Verb, Adjective* 269
Donna H. Turner, *Wo Ist die Post?* 270
P. A. Moton, *In a Rush* 272
Laura Merryman, *If You Must Write* 273
P. A. Moton, *Eventually* 274
Tracy Deitz, *What Not to Do* 275
Jackson Harlem, *The Pontiff of Poetry* 275
Jackson Harlem, *Harlemese* 276

Reaching Out, Reaching In, Reaching Up

Larry Turner, *The Rainbow Pin* 281
Thomas J. Higgins, *Margaret Dillard* 283
Madalin E. Jackson, *Alexander's Legacy* 285
Margaret Rose, *Hey, Lady* 286
Anne H. Flythe, *Enlightened?* 294
Juanita D. Roush, *Imagination Lost* 295
Dan Walker, *All We, Like Sheep* 296
David Mitchell, *Inside the Bubble* 297
David Mitchell, *Magic Glasses* 298

David Mitchell, *Monster in Her Room* 299
Madalin E. Jackson, *Rambling Thoughts in Panic Mode* 303
Norma E. Redfern, *What Might Be?* 303
David Mitchell, *The Truth about Truth* 304
James Gaines, *Goodbye, Alceste* 305
Kathie Walker, *The Study of Logic in Vienna* 306
James Gaines, *Inconsistency and Remedies* 308
Juanita D. Roush, *Dancing in the Rain* 309
Diann Brunell, *The Music Plays* 309
Tracy Deitz, *Big Bang Take Two* 310
Tracy Deitz, *His Hand* 311
Jackson Harlem, *The Poet's Prayer* 314
John M. Wills, *Courtney's Miracle* 315

Contributors 317
Index 327

Preface

Writing is a passion for me whether it is poetry or prose, nonfiction or fiction. Several years ago the Riverside Writers organization welcomed me with open arms. Through this wonderful group of creative individuals, I have made many new friends and found the support I needed for writing.

Riverside is an organization open to anyone in the area who loves to write or just wishes to improve their craft. We meet the second Tuesday of each month from one to four pm at the Salem Church Library. Our meetings are free and open to the public. We often have guest speakers who represent various types of writing or the publishing industry. In addition, we have open mike readings and critique sessions.

Since 2001 the organization has published anthologies of prose and poetry by our members. In 2001 we published *Riverside Currents* followed by *Riverside Echoes* in 2003, *Riverside Reflections* in 2005, and *Riverside Revelations* in 2007. It gives me great pleasure to welcome you to our 2011 anthology, *Rappahannock Review.* This year we are proud to have Fredericksburg's own Pulitzer Prize winning poet Claudia Emerson as the author of our introduction.

We encourage you to sit back, relax, and enjoy this delightful collection of prose and poetry from Riverside Writers to you. For more information about Riverside Writers, please visit www.riversidewriters.com.

Madalin Bickel
President, Riverside Writers

Acknowledgments

We wish to thank the members of Riverside Writers who contributed their poems and stories. We also thank the following people who devoted many hours to the preparation of the book and to reviewing the submissions. Thanks also to David Mitchell for the cover painting.

Judy Hill, Chair
Larry Turner, Editor
Madalin Bickel
Diann Brunell
Greg Mitchell
Norma E. Redfern
Elizabeth Talbot
Rod Vanderhoof

Virginia Bare
Tracy Deitz
Anne Flythe
Jim Gaines
Laura Merryman
Pat Moton
Michelle O'Hearn
Diane Parkinson
R. L. Russis
Stan Trice
Donna H. Turner
Christine Valenti
Kathie Walker

Virginia's Best

Winners of the Golden Nib Competition
and the Inside the Back Cover Competition
sponsored by the Virginia Writers Club

Yellow Heat

Golden Nib Winner for Poetry, 2009
by Rod Vanderhoof

At noon I'm threatened by the flame yellows of the Devil's Anvil. The burning fireball of the Arab sun further bleaches the parched desert. Winds swirl in dirty, mustard-colored dust clouds. Canteens are empty and the heat, relentless. Sarge checks his compass then orders those who are left to suck it up and follow.

My face turns scarlet: my lips blister; hunger and thirst knot my psyche. I contemplate the death sleep. I'm a crazy man and hallucinate in a glaring yellow madness. My body doesn't walk; instead, it floats in a sulfur lake that reeks of putrid flesh. Legs are numb. If I fall I'll evaporate before hitting the ground.

The wind is the Devil's own blowtorch and blasts the scene. Hot sand sears through boots. Scorpions avoid cremation by scrambling under bile-colored, emaciated plants.

Yellow on the Devil's Anvil is the color of cowardice, the color of desperation and the color of failure.

Sarge orders us to take five, and so I collapse. Soon he hollers, "Saddle up," but I can't rise. He yanks my arms, pulls me to my feet and shouts, "You're yellow!"

"Don't call me yellow, Sarge," I say. "Call me what you will, but don't call me yellow. I hate yellow on this, the Devil's Anvil."

The trudge resumes. The Devil is testing my soul but I swear he'll not get me. I know he's hiding in the shade of a big rock somewhere. The yellow heat is too much, even for him.

Judge's Comments, "Yellow Heat"

From the poem's captivating opening to its searing conclusion, the writer holds the reader's attention by objectifying an intense and memorable glimpse into the speaker's past. This prose poem relies heavily on details to vivify the concept of yellow heat. Each image is carefully constructed to reenact a memorable experience. Generally, we think of the desert as a washed-out entity, but here it comes alive in a palette of yellows and reds. This is not just any sun. It's a mad-yellow Arab sun, alive above the "mustard-colored dust clouds." As the poem progresses, yellow takes on a sinister quality linked to the Devil. Therein lies the poem's power as we marvel at the speaker's determination to stand firm when tested. It's obvious that this writer has thoughtfully revised this piece to ensure that no word is wasted. This is a powerful poem that deserves recognition.

       Carolyn Kreiter-Foronda
       Poet Laureate of Virginia, 2006-2008

Balefires

Golden Nib Winner for Poetry, 2008
by Anne H. Flythe

She is long dead and, I hope, buried deep.
No hurricane of the same name laid waste
to more, so many, and so much.
She had a way of sussing out each weakness,
a subtler invader than a computer virus.
No Geiger counter, water witching twigs, or x-ray
could do as well; A talent? More a curse.
She'd begin by laying each of us against another:
All flammable, the young and green, the old and dry,
Driftwood, sapwood, heartwood, no matter—
Everything will burn eventually.
With all the elements in place, she'd supply the spark—
strike the steel of malice against a core of flint,
and as we self-destroyed, stand aside and watch;
the flames of our destruction mirrored in her shining eyes.
An angelic smile in place, firelight
reflected on one small eye tooth.
When she held out empty hands, her palms
at a certain and familiar angle,
I wondered at whose pain she warmed them.
Thankful that ash and char held
no further interest for her.

Summer Discoveries

Golden Nib Third Place Winner for Fiction, 2009
by Stanley Trice

With school out, every Thursday morning his sisters and Mother went to town for the weekly sale specials. They clumped together like wet clay. Jeremy guessed it was important for them to maintain a social network, but not so important for men. The first Thursday they were gone, Jeremy stayed with Papa who made a nest of tools in the garage tinkering on the rototiller. The cars had become too computerized and he took them away to be fixed. At least he could manage the simple tiller machine with the two cycle engine.

As Papa made random adjustments between four cycle engine and tines, Jeremy handed him greasy tools like screw drivers and pliers. This made Jeremy's palms and fingers greasy. He decided to avoid further fatherly direction.

"Papa, what tool do you need now?" Jeremy asked. Papa didn't answer. Jeremy guessed it would have broken Papa's concentration loosening a rusted nut.

"Adjustable wrench," he said. Jeremy thought Papa sounded like a doctor doing open heart surgery.

Jeremy gave him the wrench with one hand and a small hammer with the other thinking a few whacks on the nut would help. Papa ignored the offered hammer. Jeremy put it back.

"Hammer," Papa said.

Jeremy gave him the hammer and picked up the pliers from the floor. Immediately, Papa reached down for the pliers that weren't there.

"Why did you put the pliers back? Hand them here."

Jeremy handed him the pliers and waited for further instructions. All he got were grunts from his Papa struggling with the nut. Jeremy circled his father to see what tool he would be expecting when they suddenly bumped legs. Unexpectedly, Jeremy fell backward throwing his greasy hands behind him to keep his pants off the dirty concrete floor. The grease on his hands took hold like grease would do on concrete floors, and Jeremy slid backward fast while kicking out with his legs for balance. He hit Papa's ass who in turn lost his balance and tipped the rototiller over in his effort not to. The exposed tines looked like a laughing skeleton.

To break the silence of Papa sitting in his toolbox, Jeremy suggested they buy a new tiller. Papa spit out some distorted words which Jeremy never remembered. He backed out making sure he didn't slip on the greasy concrete floor and proud that he kept his pants clean. He looked back once to watch Papa climb out of the toolbox with grease smeared in splotches on his pants.

Jeremy took this opportunity to sneak into his sister's bedroom. Men never stayed together, anyway. At least that's what he learned every Thursday in the summer. Besides, Jeremy figured it was time to learn something about these other people he shared a house with. Maybe I'm supposed to be with them instead of Papa, he thought. I could have this all wrong, this male-female relationship, he thought.

All three sisters shared one room that was three times larger than his, but to hold three developing girls it had too many clothes and looked smaller. That was his first impression as Jeremy pushed open the bedroom door with his heart thumping as if he was running a marathon. When the floor creaked, Jeremy jumped. It was not because he was scared. He was just being careful.

He flipped on their overhead light to better see the scattering of clothes and size of the room. Wendy the youngest had clothes piled on the floor next to her made up bed. Glenda, too. The oldest Sarah had the messiest part with clothes and shoes even on her unmade up bed. Maybe his sisters had more clothes because they were shaped different from him, Jeremy thought. He did not understand the blouses with buttons on the wrong side and skirts that wrapped around their thighs. These clothes looked like it would be harder to run fast or climb things.

Their big room that looked bigger with the lights on. It looked bigger than the dining room and kitchen put together because it was. You could make three rooms out of theirs and each one would probably be bigger than mine, Jeremy thought. They even had their own bathroom. Jeremy was not going in there. He did not want to accidentally find female products that they used in places Jeremy had not figured out yet.

Standing at the doorway, Jeremy almost forgot why he entered his sisters' bedroom. He still did not know why, but he figured their bureau would be a good start. He felt pretty good about things as he pulled open the top drawer.

Jeremy could not figure out who owned the lacy underwear. He did not know why he touched the lacy things. But, the fingers on his left hand just ended up tangled in the elastic and silk. It was a trap. He shook his hand trying not to mangle the rest of the slippery material meant to cover leaky holes and support bags of flesh. He did not want to think about that since they belonged to the sister family. The material was so fragile that they moved on their own into contorted shapes that did not look like a neatly folded patterns. Why did they have a messy room and a tidy bureau drawer?

He had to get away. Jeremy could see his whole arm being dragged inside the long drawer. Finally, Jeremy shook his hand free leaving a clump of twisted, slippery material looking like a dead body. I didn't do anything wrong. "Just curious", Jeremy told the room. Shaky voice he almost did not recognize as he closed the door.

He figured he had been their too long already. Jeremy thought about what it would look like getting caught holding his sisters' underthings. He suddenly remembered that some of the under clothes touched body parts that were alien to him. He did not want to catch anything. They talked about cooties when they talked about boys. Jeremy did not know what cooties were, but they sounded like something girls gave to boys who touched girl things.

Later, while pretending to read in his room, Jeremy he heard the threesome and Mother come home. Among the spill of chattering and a chaos of shopping bags, he suddenly remembered that he had left the bureau drawer wide open. Panic feeling came right into his throat. He felt like an idiot and a fool.

Jeremy heard them pile into their bedroom still chattering away like a flock of crows cawing at each other for attention. With a glass cup shoved so close to his ear that it hurt, Jeremy heard someone shove the bureau drawer closed without breaking stride in their chatter. He swallowed that hardness in his throat and vowed not to go snooping again.

The next Thursday, Jeremy made it back into his sisters' bedroom after they and Mother left for town to shop. At first,

Jeremy approached Papa in the garage, but his father's look told him to get lost. In his sisters' room, Jeremy stayed away from the sinister bureau drawer with the dark, unspeakable secrets that had it out for him. Instead, he stood near the beds smelling sweet perfume and surveying Sarah's vanity at a distance.

One thing Jeremy learned from Sarah's vanity was that she was the first to use makeup. He studied the tubes, canisters, and brushes without really seeing them. Somehow, this world of his sisters contained fragments of a society he had yet to fully understand one day. They had connection with each other made by the makeup and pieces of clothing they used to create an attraction. Jeremy wondered what it would feel like to fix his body so that people noticed and liked him. But, people might see something I didn't want to show them, he thought.

Jeremy walked out of the room slowly and steadily knowing that he wouldn't be found out. There was no one to see him come or go from this adjoining room to his. He regretted that he had not found something to prove that the sisters had been in his room and been just as curious. There was no evidence that they had any interest in who he was. Until the next month.

In July 1983, Glenda hit sixteen like a locomotive smashes into a car stuck on the tracks. Jeremy saw more of her skin than ever before. On the night of her birthday party, the house filled with giggling and gaggling girl chatter.

"You're a boy. You think boys will be attracted to this body and love me?"

Glenda had pounded on his door with her foot and Jeremy wondered why she did not feel pain. They stood facing each other on the threshold of the door. Jeremy only hoped one day to be taller than she.

"What about your party?" Jeremy could hear people singing 'Happy Birthday' in the dining room.

"They don't need me. They know the words. Are boys going to love me?"

Predictions like this had no meaning to him at his less than mature age. "Yeah, of course boys will like you. Why wouldn't they? You didn't get a tattoo, did you?"

"No, stupid. Why would I get a tattoo? Will boys like me if I had one?"

Jeremy did not like this situation. Glenda sought his brotherly advice on a topic he still did not understand himself.

"You're a girl. You're not fat. Your face isn't scarred. You got hips and breasts, so you got all the right equipment. And, your skin is hairless and smooth and fleshy."

"I know what I want. It's to get laid before I get out of high school. If I can't do that on my own, I expect you to help me when you get older."

She spun around and left as the singing died down. Jeremy shut his bedroom door trying not to picture Glenda having sex with someone he knew.

That evening, Jeremy saw her reading *Christine*. Jeremy imagined the evil car driven by a maniac Glenda running him down over and over because he could not provide her a suitable suitor.

To avoid Glenda's presence for the next few days, Jeremy stayed outside pushing the vibrating rototiller between plant rows. A hot humid sun pushed sweat from his face that fell in a spiral and bounced off the hard clay. Through his salty haze, Jeremy scrutinized tomato vines slipping through wire mesh and green leaves that dangled pea pods from narrow stems. He puzzled at the onion sprouts and cabbage balls and wondered at how living things could creep up from such inhospitable clay. He admired his Papa's talent to mother plants into living things from this incompatible soil. Why couldn't the edgy moods of his sisters be put to greater use and come out to witness life's growth?

Papa had placed the plants with enough space for Mr. Rototiller to breeze through. Jeremy just had to keep the machine from running away and taking him with it. He hit as many rocks as he could so that fixing a jammed rototiller engine would make Papa happy. Sometimes Mr. Rototiller hit the rock Jeremy meant for it to hit, spun in a non-straight direction, and took out one of those precious plants. Maybe his duty out here on the hard clay tundra of Papa's farmland included hope that life would spring up despite loss. At least the tines would need sharpening so Papa would be happy with something to do.

Whenever Mother took the sisters in tow, Papa did not take his son. Papa had the clay soiled farm to hunt for spots to grow eatable plants that only he could do right. It was a question of communication. Jeremy thought that Mr. Rototiller clipped down those plants on purpose to bring about communication with Papa that didn't happen.

At the end of July, Papa divided the girls' bedroom into three. This caused a major renovation to one side of the house that ended with a reduction to Jeremy's room. Another question as to why being the son was so good. Outside, Jeremy pushed Mr. Rototiller feeling his brain vibrating in his skull while inside his house the world got smaller.

In the heat of summer and under the solitude of a hot sun, Jeremy felt the ground beat back. He watched the clumps of clay get smaller with each churn of the tines; he imagined the same thing happening to him and his bedroom. Maybe Papa did not realize this. Jeremy pretended he did not, anyway.

Islands

Golden Nib Second Place Winner for Nonfiction, 2008
by Diane Parkinson

The Cataño ferry skims over the bay. Blue water shimmers in the humid air and I tug my sticky blouse from under my arms. The bastions of Old San Juan rise up, stark and ancient. My mother and grandmother sit huddled together on an undulating deck bench, their glares just as severe.

The ferry glides into dock. People rise and shuffle in a line to disembark through a creaking turnstile. My mom stands before the rotating doors as if afraid to move.

"Come on, Mom. I'll help you." I take her arm to guide her. She jerks away from me and smacks me twice with her oversize purse.

Stunned, I back away. We leave the ferry in strained silence. I fight tears and walk beside my grandmother up the winding path into the old city.

"Your mother is having a lot of problems with your brother," she whispers.

"Why is she angry with me?" I ask, frustration pounding in my head, but my grandmother just shrugs.

We enter a courtyard called *Parque de las Palomas,* where several pigeons squabble from nests in niches cut in a stone wall. Opposite, over the low city rampart, the bay stretches before us, lapping around El Morro, the Spanish Fort, a grim citadel close by. The breeze carries a lush tropical scent mixed with decay.

My mother stands stiff and indignant, ignoring the beauty of this white colonial town with its narrow, blue-bricked streets and lacy wrought-iron balconies. I try to ask what's wrong, but she turns a frozen shoulder—always staging her private play where I'm not allowed a speaking part. I feel to suffer the punishment, one should at least understand the crime.

After desultory sight-seeing, we return on the ferry and catch a taxi back to the navy base. Before I moved here, I'd naively pictured myself residing in a hut on a white sandy beach with swaying palm fronds, not in a military compound with square, cinder-block houses all the same—cold conformity in a humid climate.

"The baby is sick again," my husband says when we walk in.

I pick up my one-week-old son, hearing his little chest rumble with congestion. I press his warm cheek to mine. At the same time, my toddler hugs my knees. I trail my fingers through his golden hair.

My mother mutters something and goes to her guest room. I'm too tired and sad to be angry with her. My grandmother shakes her head.

Mom comes out with her suitcase. "Your grandmother and I are going to St. Thomas."

"Why? You just got here." My confusion makes her more self-righteous. "Fine, then go."

We drop them off at the airport on the way to the hospital. My mother and grandmother had flown to Puerto Rico to help me after the birth of my second child. Mom arrived and left again with baggage she refused to unlock.

In our dilapidated Mustang, we rattle the sixty miles of back roads—through steaming jungle bordered by kiosks advertising pineapples and mangos in every form possible—to the naval hospital.

"Your son has a hole in his heart. But he's too young for surgery. We'll have to wait and see," the pediatrician says.

At home once more, I care for my frail child while my husband works shift-work, back to back night shifts, sleeping days, double-backs, no time for exhausted wives. My hyper toddler fills my days, my wheezing infant cries all night. His clothes cling to his wriggling body, damp from the humidifier that adds to the sultry island air.

"I feel really sad, doctor, so tired." *Afraid, alone, depressed!* I tell the OB/GYN on my next checkup.

"You're young, you'll be fine," the unsympathetic Lt. says with a dismissive smirk, one of many; hysterical wives weren't issued with his seabag.

Who knew that post-partem depression would become a recognized medical condition many years later? I thought I'd lost my mind.

A post card from St. Thomas extols the beauty of that island, and a hint of wishing for forgiveness for my mother's eccentricities.

I read somewhere that eccentric is just a frivolous word for insanity. It must gallop through my family.

Still not one word on these "problems" with my brother. But my grandmother had whispered something about drugs.

I buzz on the outside of my family, trying to squeeze through like a fly, ramming my head against the screen of my mother's silence. Four years previously my brother and I had unrolled green mesh like new sod and nailed it to the shutters of my house in Greece to keep out the insects. Those flies managed to burrow their way in, welcoming themselves if unwelcomed by us. I just splatter.

In fitful dreams my brother and I remain children. I roam inside the house I grew up in, still dressed in its hues of orange and avocado. I see my father sipping his spiked orange juice to drown out failures kept secret by my mother.

I climb our backyard tree, not the stump my mother reduced it to because she tired of the apples, but still tall with spreading arms. Branches that grasped toward our tarpaper roof, heavy with green fruit, tart and crisp to bite. My brother scuttling to the top, his high-top keds just out of my reach—a blond, buzz-cut boy with an impish smile.

He climbs to the roof where "tuck and roll" pigeons flutter in cages; below a chicken squawks and kittens frolic among the perfume of gardenias. The orange stucco wall, rough to the touch, doesn't stop me from floating through, into my past. My mother locked in her room, taking valium "naps," out of my reach in her shadowed corner.

The house deteriorated as I grew, as did my parents, a job lost, plumbing neglected, a toilet ripped out, holes in plaster to chase leaks, wiring that sprouts from walls like angry worms. My father, once so adept, grown fat, an atoll surrounded by a sea of alcohol.

Growing up, I never thought my family wasn't normal. We were dysfunctional before the trend.

****

A knock on the front door.

"I have a phone call at the quarterdeck," my husband says after speaking with someone on the front stoop. In Puerto Rico, it's too expensive for us to have our own phone.

Seven months have passed since my mother's visit. My son is better and never needs the surgery. His own body repaired the hole, a miracle.

My husband drives off. The wall air-conditioner whooshes and drones. I pat medicated powder over the back of my oldest son's heat rash, little bumps on his fair skin.

The mee mees buzz outside. Tiny mosquito-like blood suckers.

My husband returns, his expression strange. "Your mother will call back. She wanted to speak to me first. Your brother has died."

"What?" All the usual questions bubble up, but most of all disbelief. No one in my family has ever *died*. Well, my dad's parents, but they were old when I was born.

It's April Fools Day, yet I know it isn't a joke.

"How?" is all I can ask. What a simple, stupid, inadequate word. Of course, it's a huge mistake.

"He was on drug treatment for heroin. He overdosed."

"On the treatment? How is that possible?" I want to scream, but I'm still in denial.

"Let's go to the front gate. She's calling back."

In a daze, we pack the boys into the car. The mee mee's splatter against the windshield. We rattle through the darkening cookie-cutter houses.

Why didn't she give me the dignity of calling me first? More of my mother's bizarre behavior. Her voice on the phone is more distant than just the thousands of miles that separate us. "We'll have him cremated. We don't want to be tied to a grave."

She's indifferent, cold. I knew virtually nothing of my brother's addiction, thanks to her secret-keeping, and now I must deal with his unexpected death.

I'm furious at her, though all I do is cry. She seems to resent my tears.

Her silence is a torment, an insult. I scratch at mee mee bites and want to smash the receiver against the plaster wall.

I slide back into the car. I cuddle my children and mourn my brother and the relationship I'll never have with my mother. No emotion is allowed in her world. She stews privately on whatever demons she harbors. Am I not entitled to feel bewildered by any of this?

I look to my husband. "If I'd known, I could have said goodbye."

"I know, I know." He tries to comfort me.

"They don't want to be tied to a grave?" My childhood playmate tossed to the wind. When did my parents become this odd couple, apathetic, dull?

As a little girl, I remember Mom as nurturing to me and my brother. Always there for us, active in our school, making Halloween costumes, caramel apples, cookies for Christmas; Brownie leader and Cub Scout den mother. Was this all a façade? What hopes had she once envisioned that were never fulfilled?

I smell the sweet, baby scent of my sons and vow never to become like her.

****

My children are grown and healthy, my marriage thrives.

Fifteen years after my brother's death my father passed on, cirrhosis. Mother is still the grim citadel beyond my shore, refusing to be close to me or her grandsons, unwilling to give up her secrets, to come down off her stone perch. She insists that she loves us, at a distance, on the surface. Maybe that's why in dreams I keep haunting the house of my youth, searching for an explanation.

In dreams I still laugh and romp with those I've lost, and awaken fuddle-headed, pondering their stumble through pungent leaves, spirits, white powder and disappointment.

Looking back from just as many years, I know we could have handled it better. As I struggle with the rough turns of life, I strive to make my own warm. Her neglect has made me strong, not weak. My children are secure in my love. I've come to realize I may never understand my mother's limitations. I just strain not to be damaged by them.

A friend once told me that a psychiatrist advised her "she would never have the mother she wanted, only the one she had."

As I pursue my own hopes in the second half of my journey, I try to reconcile myself to this woman on her arctic atoll, and the part of me that is missing because of her rejection.

Long ago, I realized you can't let your childhood define you if it holds you down. Remember the caramel apples, the warm holidays of my youth, my father's reading from *The Wind in the*

Willows; *Peter and the Wolf* on the phonograph. My brother and I laughing at the follies of the adults. Don't look too close at the edges, where it's darker, and deeper, in the sea of memory and dreams.

Never Mind

a simultaneous poem
Inside the Back Cover Competition Winner for Poetry, 2009
by Larry Turner

Losing My Mind

I search the woods.
Is that a small golden ball
half hidden by leaves in a ditch?
The ball is my mind.
And I've lost it.

Gold. They say these should be
my Golden Ears. I look in the mirror,
there's no hint of color change.
I touch them. There is no metallic feel.

Perhaps it's not a ball.

Perhaps it's a Moebius strip

with no top, no bottom.

Out of My Mind

Maybe my mind is a bathtub,
an old-fashioned kind standing
on four claw feet. Easy
to get out of. Hard to get back in.
The bathtub is my mind. And right now,
I'm out of it.

Is it a tub or something else?
I'm of two minds about it.
Yes, two minds.
Two bathtubs, side by side.
One on the right, one on the left.
I hope soon to be back in my right mind.

Perhaps it's not a tub.

Perhaps it's a Klein bottle

with no inside, no out.

Picture of Guilt

Inside the Back Cover Competition Winner for Fiction, 2009
by Larry Turner

When Lambert heard the rapping on the classroom door and saw the two policemen through the glass, he walked over with resignation and opened the door. His shoulders fell as he saw the sketch they carried; anyone could recognize him from it.

"Okay, Lambert, come with us," said the older policeman, round-faced and round-bellied.

"Have a heart, guys," Lambert said. "This is the sixth time you've picked me up this year." He laid the chalk on the groove under the chalkboard covered with chemical symbols and formulae. "How are these kids ever going to learn the difference between an ether and an ester?"

"You should have thought of that before you exposed yourself in front of those two schoolgirls this morning," the younger policeman said in a high-pitched voice, looking down at the sketch. He appeared little older than the students sitting in rows of school desks, some relieved that class would end early, others irritated, but none surprised by another visit from the police.

"Now, Tom," chided Al, the older policeman. "Even a pervert like Lambert here is innocent until proven guilty."

Experience had taught Lambert it was pointless to resist. He stuck his head into the principal's office as they went by.

"The police are taking me downtown again," he said. "You'll have to find someone to take my classes." He knew the principal was getting tired of finding substitutes every time the police picked him up.

Lambert followed the others into the dimly lit room. Then a light blinded him, and he realized he was in a police lineup with a teen-aged pizza delivery boy, an old woman, and a uniformed policeman.

"You can sit down, Tom," Al told the younger policeman. As he did so, Al told Lambert, "It's his first lineup." When Lambert didn't acknowledge the honor, he added, "We've been criticized for not following proper procedure."

The delivery boy turned to the old woman and muttered, "The things you gotta do to get a tip here."

"I don't know why you're complaining," she hissed back. "I just came in to report my cat was lost."

The light had slowly tilted down on its clamp, and Lambert could see the venom in the faces of the four parents, each grasping a copy of the sketch. He recognized Mr. Venuti, the butcher, and shuddered at the thought of being alone with him in the butcher shop some time.

The other father was Mr. Fortner, editor of the local newspaper; his retaliation would be less dramatic, but more public.

The two girls sat in chairs in front. Angela sat stiffly, her hands folded over the sketch, wondering what was expected of her. Vicki sat in boredom, swinging her leg and every so often thrusting out her lower lip to blow her blonde bangs off her eyes. She had added a mustache, goatee, and cigarette to the sketch and then turned it over to draw horses on the back.

Al Parker stood behind Lambert and put his hand on his shoulder. He asked the girls, "Do you see the man?"

Angela looked at Lambert, then quickly looked down. She licked her lips nervously and said nothing. Vicki stared at his face steadily for ten seconds, and then turned her gaze to the policeman and said, "That's not him."

"Are you sure?" Al asked her. "He sure looks like the drawing."

Vicki scarcely looked back at Lambert and answered, "No, that's not him."

Angela repeated softly, "No, that's not him."

Back in the squad room, Tom asked, "Can we drive you back to the school, Mr. Lambert, or would you like to go home?"

"To the school, please. My car is there."

"Sorry about all this, Mr. Lambert," Al said, "but we were only doing our job."

"Yes, I know, I know. But the police artist—"

"He's doing his best, Mr. Lambert."

"Yes, but dammit, just because I modeled for that drawing class he took, can't he draw anybody's face but mine?"

"Like I said, he's doing the best he can," Al replied. Then he looked at the sketch and chuckled. "It sure does look like you, though."

Century for Freedom, Century for Peace

Inside the Back Cover Competition Winner for Nonfiction, 2009
by Larry Tuner

It is 1809.
    I will not write about the devotion of slaves to their masters, the benevolence of masters toward their slaves, the culture that leisure has allowed the masters to develop, the habit of hard work that has been instilled within the slaves. I will not write about the widows and orphans who would be destitute were it not for the slaves they own, nor of the morality that the religion of their masters has instilled in the slaves. In the cause of a greater good, I must reject both the half truths and the claptrap.
    I will not esteem a human on the basis of how many other humans he owns.
    I will not accept as "honor" the notion that a white man is better than a black man and the laws and codes of conduct that enforce that notion. And if the father has done wrong, the son gains no honor by repeating it.
    I will never accept that I have a right to own another human merely because his skin color is different from my own.
    Then by the end of this century, slavery will be rare, and the world will find slavery and slave owners repugnant.
    And if anyone argues that these changes will come about not through any advance in human morality but through economic forces that have made slavery unprofitable and obsolete, I will not argue; I will only applaud the consequences.

It is 2009.
 I will not write about the camaraderie of a group of men thrown together to kill or be killed. I will not write about the sacrifices of our ancestors as they fought so that our country could prevail over another. I will not watch photographs, paintings, and films that glorify war. I will not watch parades or listen to speeches that extol the virtues of those warriors. I will not reiterate the advantages that combat brings to our rural and urban poor, opportunities to see other nations of the world and to develop the habits of discipline, obedience and respect for their superiors. I will not reiterate the benefits to the peoples in the lands we conquer, the presence of our young people and the plans our leaders make for their nation's future. In the cause of a greater good, I must reject both the half truths and the claptrap.

 I will not esteem a human on the basis of how many other humans he can kill.

 I will not accept as "honor" the notion that a person should journey across the globe to kill people he has never met in the cause of lines drawn on a map. And if the father has done wrong, the son gains no honor by repeating it.

 I will never accept that I have a right to kill another human merely because his nationality is different from my own.

 Then by the end of this century, war will be rare, and the world will find warfare and warriors repugnant.

 And if anyone argues that these changes will come about not through any advance in human morality but through advances in weaponry that have made warfare unprofitable and obsolete, I will not argue; I will only applaud the consequences.

Love and its Complications

Something Old
by Anne H. Flythe

Time as elastic as a bride's garter
to encircle a thigh, virgin or not.
In any case temporary cincture
off by bedtime in Bermuda.
In the local, the nearest motel,
how long would they wait
to consummate the marriage?
Three flutes? Two cigarettes?
Already yet.

For Dave
by Kathie Walker

for you, a poem?
I hesitate.
I'm somewhat afraid
to fix in ink or pixels
your name.
to set you in words
on a page
is to set in stone
in time and place
what was only yesterday.

When that is not
what I hope.
I look to the we,
the future,
more than ink,
more than paper,
or pixels in space.
more than merely
a beginning.

and so I write
tentatively,
putting your name
in this space
where nothing existed
before.
I write your name
as I would whisper it,
softly, letting the
breeze carry it
into tomorrow.
letting it land upon
the future
like a moth
fluttering its
wings in the shadows
of the sunlight.
I hold my breath
and hope
that ink
and pixels
won't hinder
its flight.

It's Not Original

by Elaine J. Gooding

It hurts when I try to say, "I love you,"
The pain lies in my loss for words.
I would do anything to please you,
I need inspiration, not words.
>Why can't I sing like Barbra Streisand?
>Why can't I paint like Norman Rockwell?
>Why can't I copyright this feeling?
>It's one I know so well.

Chorus: It's not original to say, "I love you."
>It's been said inside and out,
>So I'll show you now and forever;
>Listen to my eyes and hear them out.

This song is written for my husband,
A Grammy winner it won't be,
But in my way I need to show him,
He means the world to me.
>Why can't I skate like Peggy Fleming?
>Why can't I speak like Martin Luther King?
>Why can't I copyright this feeling?
>It's one only you can bring.

Chorus

Cassie

by Norma E. Redfern

Dark eyes and hair like night
You stepped through the door
Dressed in black leather
Walking in like you owned my soul
Cassie, my brown-eyed woman
I want you bad
I'll play music just for you
Down in the Pool Hall on
Saturday night

Cassie, look at me
I want to see you smile
Won't you look at me and
Stay with me a while
I'll play music from my soul

Can I change your mind
With the music I make
As I watch you tonight

You came to hear me play
Your voice burns inside me
When you say my name
I'll touch your heart with mine

Kissing your lips, holding you close
Loving you through the night
I'll strum my notes upon your skin
Our souls will be one tonight
Cassie, my darling, be my wife

Yew

by Jackson Harlem

Your kisses are sweet like warm Coca Cola
There's nothing artificially preserved about you;
You're so home-grown.

My actions speak louder than birds
Conferencing about how good the bread is and when
I will belong to you like I've prayed to do
I'm in God's waiting room watching the clock for you
Checking my watch and counting tick-tocks
Like a child, are we there yetting my way to you
I'm asking yesterday for the today of you
Watching my weight for you so I safely
make a weigh for you
Praying Tuesday is paving the way for you
like I've prayed for it to do.

I'm just a sinner trying to be a saint with you
I get light-headed and heavy-hearted
feeling...rather faint with you
I'm a poet spitting pastels on the ceiling
because humans still need color
And I've been what Michel is to Angelou,
so that makes me a painter, too

And sometimes that means spitting paint in these rhythms
and consulting dictionaries to infuse them with symbolism
and although I stand clear and still like window
sills to find your heart's rhythm, I hear your heart as it breaks
apart my heart's chronochronism and it gets lonely basking
in individualism, so I'm still praying for you
like I always thought to do.

I've resurrected Hip-Hop and Elvis at the same time because
I just wanna Hip-Rock with you. You know, Left-Eye,
Aaliyah, and Tupac with you.
I wanna... ballet, square dance, and pop-lock with you.
Cybersextext and moonwalk with you.
I wanna don't stop until I get enough of you...
I wanna March down Washington and stop at *you*.

Maybe yesterdays can bring me to you.
And maybe Sarah Vaughan can sing me to you.
And maybe Sandman can just dream me to you.
And maybe God can show me what I mean to you.
I told genie that yes, *I* dream of *you*.
Fresh out of the dryer. I always seem to *cling* to *you*.

Pajamas

by Larry Turner

My girlfriend ran in, waving a newspaper.
"Look at this photo!"
A couple lying in bed.
A sign BED PEACE hanging above them.
"It's John and Yoko!"
So it was. With seven photographers
gathered around the bed.

But why was she so excited? We loved the Beatles' music,
but she never got caught up in the hysteria,
as far as I knew.
"They're on their honeymoon!
A week at the Amsterdam Hilton."

"His pajamas!"
Sure, I couldn't miss the pajamas. Rather overdressed
for a honeymoon if you ask me.
"Look! The stripes! The cuffs! The collar! The pocket!'
My face was blank.
"I MADE THOSE PAJAMAS!"
I knew she was a seamstress for an upscale pajama maker,
but still….
"Yes, there are John and Yoko, just married in Gibraltar,
having a bed-in for peace wearing MY PAJAMAS!"

She's never been the same since.

The Boy Who Had Waited
by Chuck Hillig

They were coming home today, and he had been sitting on the curb watching for their car since breakfast. It was now a little past twelve, and he was getting hungry.

He wondered what he would say to her. He couldn't let her know that he'd been sitting there for hours just waiting for her. She'd probably laugh at him. He knew she would, and he just couldn't stand that. Not her laughter.

He sighed deeply. This wasn't at all the way he would have preferred it to be. It would have been so much better if she had seen him working on his father's old car. His hair would be mussed and there would be grease smudges on his cheeks, and his shirt would be open, revealing his tan chest.

And he would look up from under the hood and flash his white teeth and wave and say "hi." And she would say that the car was "very cool," and she wished that she could take a ride with him sometime when he got his license. And he would say, sure, anytime, and flash his smile again. And she would be very impressed that he knew so much about cars and motors and things, and he would feel good that she had noticed that.

Or maybe her house would catch on fire today, and he would turn in the alarm and keep on going back into the burning house again and again to save what he could. He would try to save *her* things first, of course, because he knew where her room was. And then, when he was just about overcome with smoke, he would collapse on the lawn. And she would find him lying there and would wipe his face with her handkerchief and tell him how wonderful he was and how grateful they all were. Then she would kiss him and cry, and he would hold her very tight.

A green car turned the corner and came down the street, and he looked up to watch it pass. He sighed again and gathered up a handful of pebbles along the curb, shaking them in his hand until the smaller ones had run out through his fingers. He tossed one of the pebbles at an oak tree 50 feet across the street. It hit about four feet up and then dropped onto the grass. He wished that she had seen that. He threw a second stone, this time aiming at the corner line where the curb meets the street. If you threw it just right, it stopped dead as soon as it hit. It was a difficult shot. He flipped it across the street, and it stopped stone dead against the curb. He smiled to himself and wished even harder that she had been there. He took the largest stone and threw it sideways at the nearest tree on *his* side of the street. It missed badly, skipping on the sidewalk and up onto their front lawn. He was very glad that she didn't see that one.

He began to crack his knuckles. It wasn't until he was almost finished that he remembered that she didn't like the sound. "How can you do that," she had asked. "Doesn't it hurt you?" He had never really thought about it before but after she had mentioned it, he had tried to stop. It was hard, though, because he could never remember until after he had started and someone had once told him that, if you cracked one knuckle, in order to keep them all even, you then had to then crack them all. It had always sounded reasonable. Feeling justified this one final time, he cracked the last two knuckles and sighed. Someday, he'd really have to break that habit.

He began to think again about the last time that he had seen her. It wasn't actually the last time, but it always came to his mind first. It was the day before she was to leave on vacation, and he had walked over to her house. Their car was gone, and nobody answered the doorbell. When he walked around to the side door, he saw her sunbathing alone on one of the lounge chairs in the backyard. She was wearing a small white bikini that he had never seen before, and she was lying on her back facing the sun with her hands behind her head.

She was asleep, and he didn't know whether he should be there or not. The sun was hot and her body glistened from the heat and from the baby lotion that she had been using. The bottle lay flat on the grass beside her. He remembered that he was surprised at how thin she looked because her stomach was drawn down, narrowing her waist and stretching the skin over her ribs. He didn't mind at all that she was thin because it was always better to be thin than fat. She looked very white and shiny and a lot like the porcelain figurines in his mother's cabinet.

And then he began to wonder what it would be like to touch her bare stomach with his hand. He never did, of course, because, as soon as he thought about it, he began to feel guilty about spying on her, and so he turned and quickly walked out of the backyard, hoping that none of the neighbors had seen him. And he knew even more that he loved her so much that it hurt.

And now, sitting on the curb, he tried to imagine how beautiful she would look with a golden summer tan. And then he wondered if she had ever worn the white bikini in front of everyone at the lake. Well, he'd probably never know because he certainly couldn't ask her.

Throughout the summer, he had written letters to her, and he had tried to be clever and interesting, but he just wasn't used to writing, and they always ended up sounding stiff and not at all like what he wanted to say when he read them aloud to himself. But he always double-checked them for spelling and then made a final copy for her so that there wouldn't be any smudges on the paper.

She had written, too, but only a few postcards. They didn't say very much except that she was having a "wonderful time" and things like that, and on the other side were glossy pictures of sailboats and people swimming and water skiing. He had wished that she would have mailed the postcards in an envelope so that they would have been more private and just for him.

Another car passed. He figured that it must be after two. He still didn't know what he was going to say to her. How could he explain what he was doing there, just sitting on the curb? Then he thought he could say that he had just walked over there a minute before they arrived and wasn't it lucky that they had just gotten there and maybe he could make some joke about mental telepathy telling him when to come. And then she would smile, and he would help them unpack the car, and her mother would call everyone into the house for lemonade or something.

And he would ask her how she was and she would tell him everything and say that she had had a wonderful time but that she was glad to be home again. And he would say, yes, he knew what she meant, and they would smile and her mother would pour them some more lemonade or something.

He smiled and cracked all of his knuckles at once, and another car passed and it was getting later.

He twisted around so that he could see their front lawn. He had been cutting the grass there every week because he had promised them that he would. That was on the morning that they had left, two months ago. The morning after he had seen her sunbathing in the backyard.

He had helped her carry her suitcases out to the car. She was wearing shorts and a large gray sweatshirt with the sleeves pulled up. He noticed that her face and arms and legs were red from sunbathing, and he wondered if her stomach was red, too. He hated to see her go, but he couldn't think of a thing to say to her.

Her father was upset to learn that his wife had forgotten to arrange for someone to mow the lawn. He quickly volunteered and said that it was all right, and that he would take good care of it for them. Her father smiled and winked at him and said sure go right ahead and that they would pay him when they got back. She thought that it was nice of him too help out and she said so, and he appreciated that

He had worked hard, too, especially yesterday. He had come over early and had cut both the front and back lawns twice, criss-crossing the second time. And he had swept the sidewalk and the driveway, too, but that was only because they were coming home today. He enjoyed cutting the backyard best because he liked to remember her lying on that lounge chair in the white bikini. For some reason, he always felt funny when he mowed over that spot.

Today, the lawn looked green and smooth, and he looked proudly on his work. Then he remembered about that large stone that he had accidentally tossed up onto their grass. He'd better find it because it could chip the blades of the mower. And besides, his legs were getting stiff. He got up and crossed the lawn up to where he thought the stone should have landed. He didn't see it right away, and he stooped down for a closer look.

A blue car turned the corner, cruised silently down the street and turned into the driveway. He saw it and quickly stood up, brushing his hands and not knowing quite what to do. The car horn beeped and both doors opened at once.

"Hi. How are you," her father said. "It's good to be home. The place looks great" *She wasn't with them. Where was she?*

"Uh, the lawn?" he stammered. "Uh yes. Thanks. I...I just did it yesterday. Glad to do it." *Why wasn't she with them?*

Another car turned the corner and came down the street, somewhat faster than the first, and turned into the driveway, radio blaring loudly on some heavy metal station.

And then he saw her.

"Oh, what a totally cool car," she said. "We had the top down all the way." He looked at the strange boy behind the wheel.

He had lots of hair, his shirt was open, and he was wearing sunglasses. The strange boy flashed a big toothy smile at her parents and then, in turn, at the boy who had waited.

"Hi," she said to him. "Thank you for your letters. Here I want you to meet..." He didn't catch the boy's name, and so he mumbled something in return. The Smile flashed and a bronzed hand shot out to grip his, maybe a little too long and little too hard.

"He's a new senior," she said, "and his family just moved in down on Dover Street, and he's going to school here, and he's just moved from California and..." She caught her breath. "And here's the best part: his family also bought a summer house at our lake right down from ours. Isn't that a coincidence?"

They all smiled, but only two of them were sincere. He began to feel sick.

"Did...did you have a nice time?" He didn't recognize his own voice.

"Awesome! We went swimming everyday."

"You...you have a great tan."

"Hey, I talked her into swimming in her bikini," the stranger said. She giggled and blushed and, again, the Stranger flashed his toothy smile.

He couldn't think of a thing to say.

"Just look at my tan," she said, lifting up her sweater to reveal a deep bronze stomach. He thought of her in the backyard. "We were both out in the sun almost all of the time."

"I...I just wandered over here a few minutes ago," he said. "I figured you'd be here about now." His voice cracked.

"Hey, it must have been be mental telepathy," said the Smile, waving his fingers. She laughed and her face was radiant and beautiful. And he loved her so very much.

The laughter stopped. They all waited silently. Awkwardly.

"Well, I guess that I'd better get going. I just dropped in for a minute. Uh, nice to have met you. See you guys around."

His breathing was ragged, and he knew that he was speaking much too fast. His body was turning to granite, and he had to get away quickly before they all noticed. He nodded goodbye and began heading up the street towards his house.

He didn't even turn around when he heard her mother calling everyone into the house for lemonade or something.

He was just trying to act as if nothing had happened until he got around the corner where they couldn't see him, but his mouth was dust and his legs wouldn't walk in a straight line.

A few houses down, his foot kicked a large stone, and he picked it up and threw it hard at the nearest tree. It missed badly and skipped out into the street. He felt angry and betrayed and very, very foolish.

And by the time he got home, he was having a hard time keeping his cheeks dry.

Morning in the Twi-Lite Motel

by Larry Turner

I
wake first
don't move
don't want the night to end.

She
moves on the bed
gets up.

I
open my eyes a crack
watch her as

She
walks sleepily toward the bathroom
knocks the room key to the floor
picks it up with her toes
returns it to the dresser.

God!
The things you don't know
about a person until
you spend a night with her.

Early Widowed

by R. L Russis

Things were home-grown or home-made then,
or mostly so, with rare exception. We couldn't
afford much, not that was store bought, aside
from staples. Even when we had a dime or two
to spare we bought essentials and not much else.
And though the peddler's wagon always stopped,
it was always more to rest and water his team
than at any thought of making a sale, as Mother
seldom bought much at all, other than needles
or thread, a skein or two of yarn, a bolt of cloth –
cotton or wool, depending for when she sewed.
And all bought with her frugal savings – egg
money mostly – which came largely in change,
in that supply of loose coin, of nickels and dimes,
left in exchange for eggs and butter, for milk
and cheese, or in the rare silver dollar from sale
of an occasional stewing hen, a bird gone past
fruitful laying and now better-off boiled and served-
up in a pie. But, all that history aside, whenever
his wagon came, she was always quick to spring
from whatever chore her hands held at the time.
And she always carried a smile with that ewer
of tea she brought, she said to slack his thirst
and to whet their conversation in anticipation
of the bartering, for the dickering they'd do,
for the things she'd trade or the price he'd pay.
Thinking back on it now, on those days back then,
there might have been a brighter twinkle in her eyes
and something different in the tone of Ma's voice,
in the way she told us kids, *"Run off now, go play."*
And I remember the young peddler always said,
"Yes," to her invite to stay for supper... and more
than once I dreamt I'd heard his horses' hooves
go clopping off toward dawn, their harness bells
jingling and the peddler whistling a carefree tune.

Mature Love in Words Only

by Madalin E. Jackson

Age forgotten,
Love pursued,
Optimistic belief
That love is obtainable.
Miscarriage of thought,
'Tis only for the young
When lies are less meaningful.
Experience clarifies.
Questions are asked
The truth becomes real.
Fearing commitment,
Inflicting pain.

Man so insecure,
Sexually based.
Woman warm,
Trusting, loyal and
Naive.
Does not the poet say
Love deserves truth
Openness, honesty?
Is it true
Love is the greatest of all?
Or just words written
And allusive.

If she loves you,
She loves you.
If she wants you,
She wants you.
Trust in the strength
Know it is real
For only a fool would consider
How it is, was, will never be.

Life is not infinite
Death is inevitable.
Why end it alone
When love waits?

Menudo
by J. Allen Hill

On the last day of March of his fifth year in Mexican Jay, Kansas, Jesús Campos clocked out of the Wonder Fields Winery and walked into town. He was tired and hurried to get to Pepe's Bar where he could order a cold beer and a sandwich, and where no one cared that his boots were muddy and his shirt sweat-stained. Crossing the town square, he spotted a bright gold poster tacked high on a light post, and hunger and fatigue were forgotten. In bold red script, the poster invited, **Come Celebrate *Cinco de Mayo*.**

Stretching to the limit of his five feet four inches, Jesús Campos eagerly tore the paper from its post and ran into the corner barbershop, shouting, "Hey, Jorge, look at this! *Cinco de Mayo!* Right here in the USA!" Together they read the flyer.

Come Celebrate Cinco de Mayo
The First Annual Mexican Jay Spring Fair

Talent Contest
Brahma Bulls * Tractor Pulls
Greased Pig * 3-Legged Races
BBQ, Hot Dogs, Corn Dogs, Bratwurst
Blue Ribbon Pies, Cakes, Pickles, Jellies

Bluegrass with the Franklin Brothers Fabulous Four
Main Stage in the Square

Contact the Chamber of Commerce for booth information

"Jesús, you never read beyond your nose."
"What? What you mean?"
"Think about it, Jesús. Does that sound like *Cinco de Mayo* to you?"

Well, no, of course it didn't. Wrong sounds. No mariachi to lift the heart and stir the feet. Wrong foods. Brats and BBQ tasted okay, but they did not make the tongue weep and the nose gasp. Without these, this thing was just a country fair.

Jesús Campos sighed deeply, his joy at the promise of *Cinco de Mayo* fading. It was his nature to jump first, ask questions later. This habit had gotten him and most of his friends to Mexican Jay in the first place.

Jesús Campos once believed that all places he had not visited were better than where he was. If he had not exactly believed it, he had wished it very deeply. So when he had seen the advertisement for vineyard workers in Kansas, USA, he had painted a glowing picture for his friends and neighbors: bounteous harvests, luscious fruits, good wages. The vineyard owner offered sponsorship. They would be legal and their children could go to good schools.

And then there was the name. How could any place named Mexican Jay be a bad place? Forty-six citizens of his village – forty-six! – abandoned the old barrio and walked, hitchhiked, and drove, to answer the call for working hands and backs in the vineyards of Kansas, USA.

The change was hard; English was difficult. Soon many could not understand their own children who found it easy. They could buy beef and pork, corn meal, garlic and spices in Kansas markets, but the old recipes made in the new kitchens never tasted quite the same. As their clothes wore thin – clothes often crafted by the hands of their grandmothers – they replaced them with shirts and pants tagged with names of people they did not know, like Tommy Hilfiger and Jaclyn Smith.

They missed the pink and green and lemon yellow of painted adobe, the rainbow mosaic tiles of church walls and courtyards. They missed the fountain in the center of the village square where the women gathered for gossip and the men for smokes – just as their mamás and papás had done; mamás and papás whose graves they could no longer visit. There was a square in the middle of Mexican Jay, but it had no fountain, not even a general on a horse in its center; only a small patch of green and a large spreading maple tree.

They had been here for almost five years now and his friends still spoke to him in public, but he knew many were unhappy and longed for home. Good or bad, Jesús Campos was to blame.

"You know, Jesus Christ," Jesús Campos addressed the Lord who sat always on his right shoulder. "If you are going to have me use your name, you need to make me smarter. Why you let me do dumb things? I am nothing here. My sweet Doña Maria don't want to come here. I never even seen my little Benito learn to walk. Why you treat me this way?"

Jesus Christ as usual, was silent.

Jorge Perez watched his friend mumbling, as he often did, into his shirt and said to him, "Come, we will sit here on my porch and talk." They sat together on the edge of the low, wide veranda which fronted on the town square. "Why you think this fair thing is anything different? They steal our *Cinco de Mayo* name. Big deal. They don't want us to be in it."

One thousand eight hundred and three days ago – he had counted every one – Jorge had packed up his belongings, his jolly wife, Christina, his quiet son, Little Louie, and his sweet, fat baby daughter, Olivia, and moved. Jorge hated field work but Jesús Campos was his friend. Jesús Campos needed him, so he came. Jorge knew how to cut hair so he opened a barbershop. Life was not so bad here.

"Mr. Michael Saunders, my boss, is in charge of this fair," said Jesús Campos. "He is very nice to me. Always wanting to know about my country – about my *culture*, he calls it. *What kind of soil you got down there, Campos?* he says."

"Just talk. He don't really care. He ever ask to meet your wife? Ever ask how your boy doing in school? Ever ask you to sit and have a meal with him?"

"I never tell him I have a wife," Jesús Campos said. "Maybe I don't." He leaned his back against the old striped barber pole. "*I come later. I come later*," she says. I used to think it was the place she didn't want to be in. You think it's me she doesn't want to be with, Jorge?"

Jorge never knew how to answer such questions. A good devoted wife would never refuse to follow her husband wherever he chose to go. Jorge secretly thought it might be true that Doña Maria no longer loved Jesús Campos. But he could not say this to his friend, so he spoke of other things. "You think maybe we could join this *Cinco de Mayo* Kansas fair?"

"No. They never invite us to anything before."

"Maybe we never asked," said Jorge.

"It would not be like home."

Jorge snorted. His friend was like a mule.

"Maybe not. But it could be just a little bit okay."

Always the strategist, Jorge continued, "But if we want to ask this thing, we got to have a plan. We cannot just go to these Chamber of Commerce people and say we want to do something, but we do not know what. That would be dumb. So, what do we want to do?"

"Well, I don't know, Jorge. What do you think?" Jesús Campos traced a spiral in the dirt with the toe of his boot sending a cloud of yellow dust into the air. Jorge watched it form. Drifting slowly. Round and round. Higher and higher. Not so different from the dust of home.

The silence and suspended dust filled the air.

"Menudo. I sure could eat some menudo," said Jorge finally.

"Oh yeah," breathed Jesús Campos. The two men dreamed of the rich, red, fiery stew, sliding like a steamy river down the throat, soothing the stomach, warming the limbs, kindling the wits.

"You know how to make it?"

"No, I do not. My Doña Maria makes the very best." Jesús Campos' throat ached at the thought of her. For the taste of menudo, he must be brave. "I will write her a letter tonight." And he would cover the letter with kisses knowing she would touch the paper. He growled and hacked to clear his throat and made a show of scrubbing his face on his shirt sleeve to hide his moist eyes.

Jorge pretended not to notice. "Know where we can get some honey guts? Very important ingredient."

"Honey guts?"

"Yeah. They got that in Kansas?"

Jesús Campos thought for a while about the market on the corner near his old house. Dark and cool inside, it offered a haven from hunger and comfort for a hot tired laborer. Nothing was wrapped in plastic there. "Yeah. I know a farmer. Slaughters couple of beefs every spring. He will sell me the tripe cheap. Calf's feet too."

"So. Good. We will make a huge pot of menudo, enough for every one of us. I s'pose we could make enough for the town people too, but I don't know. Gringos are picky about their food."

"Huh! If we ever figure out how to make it." Jesús Campos was discouraged again.

"You give up too easy, my friend. You will talk to Mr. Michael Saunders about this. Ain't he a bigwig in this town?"

And so he was. The owner of Wonder Fields Winery was also the President of the Chamber of Commerce. "And, Jesús Campos," added Jorge. "Do not forget to ask about a booth. We will need a place to ladle out the stew into cups with little spoons and napkins and such."

Later as he was eating his sandwich in Pepe's Bar, Jesús Campos spoke to Jesus Christ. "I don't mind you didn't give me a pretty face, Lord, long as Doña Maria don't mind. And I thank you for my good strong back.

"Now I am not so good at talking to bosses and bigwigs. And I know you usually give out all you got when we are born from our mamás, but don't you think you could spare a little something extra for me now?"

The next morning, Jesús Campos cornered Mr. Michael Saunders in the grafting shed and, standing hat in hand, polished his boots on the back of his jeans and blurted, "We want to cook my wife's menudo for *Cinco de Mayo* and we need a booth."

Mike Saunders had learned to translate his employee's spare speech into layers of unspoken meaning. His interpretations were often correct. So when Jesús Campos reported that the noon sun was *very blistering* and that he and his crew *needed to plan*, Mike Saunders knew the field hands would be taking siestas. And when Jesús Campos said to his boss, *The Lord sits on my shoulder*, Mike Saunders was glad to hear that his foreman was a religious man. He failed, however, to realize that the Lord's position on the right shoulder of Jesús Campos was often a contentious one.

"Didn't know you had a wife, Campos," said Mike Saunders. We should look into gettin' her up here. I don't know 'bout this Mexican stew you want. We got the fair pert near organized. Booths on Square East and West for the ladies with their hot dogs and jellies and stuff. Races on the library lawn, bulls and tractors on the school grounds. Band and talent on the main stage. Runnin' outta room. Worthington Ranch boys are settin' up their barbecue drums on Square South; tables up and down Maple Street. Maybe you can sell your stew on the barbershop porch. Best I can do."

The menudo was working its magic or maybe Jesus Christ had answered his request for a *little something*. Jesús Campos felt bold. "Music. We also got to have Mexican music."

"We already got music. Contracted for the Franklin boys to play all day. If you want to get a couple guys together, maybe they can play when *The Fab Four* take a break. Ten minutes every hour. How 'bout that? Now, today I need your crew in the River Bend section."

Jesús Campos knew when he was being dismissed and worked the rest of the day with a heavy heart. He had asked Jesus Christ for a little courage, and he had asked Mr. Saunders for an invitation to the fair, and both of his benefactors had provided. Jesús Campos had no idea how to make it all happen.

That evening he stood in the barbershop and made his report. Jorge was weary of boosting up his friend's sagging spirits but he had long believed that a person could face life looking down or looking up. Given that choice, he always said, "Might as well look up. Easier on the neck." Today he said, "So. Good. You write your letter. We eat menudo. We get some people. We make music. Now who we gonna get to play?"

Jesús Campos shrugged his shoulders.

Jorge decided. "We will do mariachi. Pepe can bring his guitar. Little Louie's violin is pretty sweet."

"Louie is fourteen years old," doubted Jesús Campos.

"So?"

"Okay. All right. We need some brass."

"My Olivia is learning the *flauta*. Don't know anybody plays brass. Tim Deanda got a harp. Pablo Perez, I think, still has his grandpapá's old *vihuela*."

Jesús Campos would not again challenge his friend about his children's musical talent. Olivia was only ten, but she was her father's angel. "Too bad we don't have anybody plays the *guitarrón*."

"The harp just got to play real loud. It will be fine."

But Jesús Campos was worried. The next day, as he walked the rutted rows of Mr. Saunders' fields, checking for errant vines and wayward pests, he spoke to Jesus Christ. "You got to help me here. What I'm going to say to my Doña Maria I haven't said so many times before? I need to see her smile and hear her laugh and smell her scent? I need to feel her body next to mine? She knows all that. Now I need her menudo."

He stopped to clip a withered tendril and tie up a fallen vine. "You got to stay out of the dirt, little fellow, so you can grow strong and your fat fruit can get sweet," he said, patting the vine into place.

"So, Jesus Christ, where were we? Ah, yes. You need to make this *Cinco de Mayo* special so everyone will stop hating me for bringing them here."

Jesús Campos! Jesus Christ answered. *You humans asked for free will and I have given it to you. Now it is up to you to take charge of your life. I cannot set the future in place for you.*

Jesús Campos, ever stubborn, retorted, "I pray to you for advice and this is all I get? You bring me here and abandon me?"

Jesús Campos, I gave you the power to do anything you want. Now use it! As angry as when he drove the money lenders from the Temple, Jesus Christ disappeared right off the shoulder of Jesús Campos and headed toward Turtle Creek, his skirts hitched to his knees, his white robes flying behind him.

That night, Jesús Campos wrote to Doña Maria. "Dearest Wife. I am trying to make this place feel like home. Please send menudo recipe. Your faithful husband, Jesús Campos." The next morning, he left the letter in the Wonder Fields office to be mailed.

April was very busy in Mexican Jay. Vines to be tended, fields to be groomed. Rotating cellars, cleaning vats, tapping barrels, buying supplies. There were tours and tastings and the coddling of the big city restaurant chefs. And then there were the preparations for *Cinco de Mayo*.

The mariachi band met in the barbershop on the first April Monday and every night after that. By the fifth rehearsal, its five members were able to start and end a song together. By day ten, it was possible to tell what they were playing. Little Louie's violin sang like a lark – one with a head cold, but a lark nevertheless. Olivia's flute fluttered behind. Tim Deandra's harp thrummed deeply, the guitar and *vihuela* were valiant. The soaring lead of a trumpet was sorely missed, but there was no lack of heart. Soon the wide porch in front of the shop was filled every evening with foot tapping crowds and laughter and teasing. It was there that the idea of being part of the *Cinco de Mayo* fair took hold of the small émigré community and began to grow.

On the second April Monday, Paco Rodriguez decided that for the fair he would produce fifty pounds of pork butt steamed in banana leaves with achiote and garlic, oranges and bitter chocolate – *Cochinita Pibil* – so wonderful. "You find no banana leaves for a thousand miles and I give you no money," said his wife. "You will make frijoles." They fought fiercely and Paco was locked out of the bedroom until on Monday of the third week, he agreed to make frijoles.

On Monday of the fourth week, Isabella Concepción stated she would sell handmade silver bracelets and Niña Gonzalez said she would sell tiny wooden table icons which she had hand painted with the image of *Madrecita de Guadalupe*. The oldest member of the community, Juan Martinez Escudero, was called in to negotiate their spat over market share, and combat was averted.

On Tuesday, the Martinez family folklorico group was selected to represent the Andrew Horatio Reeder High School in the Talent Contest, defeating the Pom-Pom Team, resulting in a mashed potato fight in the cafeteria on Wednesday.

On Thursday, Adelaide Alderson, corn dog chair lady, agreed to apologize publicly for pulling the hair of chief chalupa maker, Cecilia Delgado, during a struggle over the last keg of cornmeal at the Black Angus Market.

On Friday, Francisco Peña pledged enough mole poblano chicken for three hundred hungry celebrants, but that evening was overheard cursing his saintly namesake, after realizing he had committed to the purchase, slaughter, gutting, picking and stewing of seventy-five pounds of chicken.

On Saturday, the Charro Cowboys ran the Brahma Bull riders off the high school soccer field, and construction of the main stage began on the north side of the square.

On Sunday morning, Jesús Campos stayed in bed until noon. He had received no letter from Doña Maria. Jesus Christ was still absent from his right shoulder.

When he arrived at Wonder Fields Winery on Monday morning, Jesús Campos was called into his boss' office. "See here, Campos. Your group was s'posed to sell some stew and fiddle around on stage for a couple of minutes. That's it. I'm hearin' all kinds of things are goin' on. You got no permits. Where you gonna locate? You're a good man, Campos and I'm countin' on you to fix things."

That evening at band rehearsal, Jesús Campos addressed the gathering on the porch. "Mr. Saunders says we can only sell menudo from this porch and play the mariachi when the band breaks. The crowd began to rumble, then shout. Angry words

Riverside Writers

could be heard. "...does he think he is?" "Damn gringos." "Shit my hat." "Madre de Dios," and other words so shocking that Jesús Campos was glad Jesus Christ was absent.

What we gonna do? he thought. The *Cinco de Mayo* fair was five days away. He had lured his friends to this place so far from home and they had not been happy. Now he had gotten them involved in the fair, and for the first time, this place had begun to feel like home to them. Was he going to let them down again? Something had to be done. Since Jesus Christ had not yet returned from Turtle Creek, it looked to Jesús Campos like it was up to him.

Jesús Campos had heard about this thing called 'leave.' It seemed it was time you could use and still get paid. What a wonderful idea. When he looked into it, he found he had accumulated over ten weeks of leave. For the first time in his life, he did not report for work on Tuesday morning.

Jesús Campos was a thrifty man and could not waste a minute of this gift of time. He visited permit offices, negotiated with booth owners and race judges, filled out forms, discovered bureaucracy, learned how to read plat maps, helped to build a grandstand, delved into small town politics in action, and shook hands with the Mayor.

He convinced Father Sean Carroll to ring the church bells on fair day. "On *Cinco de Mayo* in my village," Jesús Campos assured the good Father, "bells ring all day. Jesus Christ, he loves it."

He recruited idle teenage boys to build tables and girls to paint signs and their mothers to make paper flowers and cotton bunting. In every household, the contents of old trunks were searched for *sombreros, serapes* and *chalecos*. He tried but failed to stop Juan Cortes from painting a mural on the side of Jorge's barbershop. When it was finished, Jesús Campos was happy he had failed. Juan had painted the old village streets, the rainbow houses, the pottery market, the fort with its red tiled roof, the *Catedral Nuestra Señora de la Inmaculada Concepción*. It looked just like home.

By Saturday morning – May 5, *Cinco de Mayo* – Jesús Campos had found a place for everyone and everyone had an official permit. Every friend's house was draped with bunting, windows sprouted red, green, and bright yellow paper flowers. Every little Mexican girl wore a long swirling skirt and a flower in her hair. Every little boy sported a *serape* on his shoulder or a silver buckle on his belt.

Painted icons and silver bracelets sold side by side from blankets in the generous shade of the spreading maple at the center of the square. The barbecue drums made room for the pots of mole. The frijoles squeezed into a corner of the hot dog stand. The chalupas found a place with the bratwurst.

Little Dolores Concepción confessed that she had secretly made several pounds of *camotes* and *cajeta*, her favorite *dulces mexicanos*. The jam and jelly ladies quietly made room for her and did not ask about a permit. Juan Cortes, idle after completing the mural, set up an easel next to the library, where he offered to sketch the winners of the races or anyone who asked. The judges re-scheduled the Brahma Bull riding for the morning so the Charro Cowboys could show off their roping and saddle skills in the afternoon. The Tractor Pull moved to a field behind the Free Clinic.

The mariachi band planned to perform on the porch of Jorge's barber shop as they were afraid if they changed location, they would forget how to play. But at 9:30 in the morning, the Franklin Brothers Fabulous Four sent word that their bus had broken down outside of Kansas City, and they could not arrive in time to perform.

Emboldened by the opportunity, the violin, flute, guitar, harp and *vihuela* took their places on the main stage at 10:30, and bravely began to play. After listening for an hour to this new music that excited him, a tall blond boy wearing a white Texas cowboy hat joined them on stage, put a trumpet to his mouth and the mariachi found its soul.

Crowds came from Topeka, from Wichita, and all the small surrounding towns and ranches. As Jesús Campos helped his friends get organized, he was pretty sure he felt Jesus Christ again on his shoulder.

A very strange thing was happening, though. He dreamed he could smell menudo, the aroma making his nose tickle and drip, his mouth water. No. Could not be. The long awaited letter from Doña Maria had never arrived and there was no recipe. No one here could make the delectable stew. Still . . .

His friends were happy. Many remembered to thank him for their good fortune to be living in this great little town, with the great name and the great fair. His boss came to him during a break in the music and shook his hand. "Jesús Campos, you sure pulled this one together. How 'bout you and me, we do this again next year."

Then Mike Saunders grinned slyly and said, "Don't know what's in it, don't think I wanna know. But I even like that stuff you call menudo. Did you have some yet?" Then he walked away into the crowd.

Frantically, Jesús Campos ran through the square. He searched the library, the school grounds, up and down Maple Street. His nose had not lied to him. When he found it, he also found a vision. There was his Doña Maria watching over a steaming pot of rich, red stew, smiling her radiant smile. She held out her ample arms to welcome him. Of course, it was the spices that made his eyes water and his body flush.

A shy little boy he hardly recognized ladled a small cup of soup from the pot, handed it to his father and softly kissed him on the cheek. "*Hemos venido a vivir contigo, Papá. Te amo,*" [1] whispered Benito.

"*Has crecido muy alto, Benito. Te amo también,*" [2] answered his father.

Jesús Campos was not sure who was responsible for this miracle – Michael Saunders or Jesus Christ – but it felt good to be at home and to have two such wonderful friends.

[1] *We have come to live with you, Papa. I love you."*

[2] *You have grown very tall, Benito. I love you, also."*

I Send My Regrets
by Rod Vanderhoof

*Once on a high and windy hill,
In the morning mist, two lovers kissed,
And the world stood still...*

Paul Francis Webster

  I was alternately reading the newspaper and watching the Late Evening Show on TV when Emcee Johnny Jeffers announced, "Please welcome the internationally famous singer and actress, Debbie Donnelly. She will sing, 'Love is a Many-Splendored Thing.'" As the applause subsided and she began her song, bittersweet memories flooded back.
  Twenty-five years earlier, as a senior at Seattle's Nordlund High School, I examined a coffee table book of Florentine art while awaiting the start of my literature class. The principal entered with a new student.
  "Class," he said, "meet Deborah Donnelly. Debbie just moved here from Laramie, Wyoming. Please say hello and make her feel right at home."
  Debbie was slender and elegant with lots of freckles, golden hair, cobalt blue eyes and a cute little ski jump nose. Her smile enraptured me. Just looking at her made me smile too.
  I stepped up and said, "Welcome to Theattle, Debbie. I'm Thteve Thimpthon."
  I wasn't aware that I talked funny...until I met her. I didn't hear myself the way others heard me. When I spoke, I sounded either comical or pathetic, depending on the listener's frame of mind.
  I looked directly into her eyes, and discovered that my heart couldn't hold still. I choked up. So I blurted, "You are ath beautiful ath a Botticelli angel." I had just seen pictures of these angels in the art book.
  She seemed annoyed and turned scarlet. "What's a Botticelli angel?"

"A Botticelli angel ith very beautiful. Here, let me show you." I picked up the art book, "Thee, there'th a definite rethemblanthe."

"What did you say your name was?"

"Thteve Thimpthon."

"Oh, Steve Simpson."

"That'th what I thaid."

"You did not! You thaid Thteve Thimpthon!" She paused. "You thtupid idiot! Now you've got me doing it."

So we got off to a rocky start. I was trying to impress her and she called me an idiot. After that, I was reluctant to talk to her. I was afraid she'd call me an idiot again, or laugh at me in front of the other kids.

Anyway, she was very talented and was being trained as a professional singer and actress. She sang in the school choir and her soprano singing voice was full and compelling, and made the other singers sound much better. The choir sang for the parents at several of our school open houses that year. As the highlight of the evening, Debbie sang popular tunes made famous by the likes of Judy Garland and Jo Stafford.

I was a pretty fair trumpet player, if I say so myself. And I do say so myself. My classmates referred to me as the next Harry James. I practiced by the hour developing my embouchure, which, if you don't know, refers to the use of my lips on the trumpet mouthpiece. With long hours of repetitive practices day after day my lips became strong, and my tone evolved into a nice brassy sound.

I used my allowance money for sheet music and played the Harry James theme song, 'Ciri Biri Bin,' like a professional. Also, I played 'Sleepy Lagoon' which I called, 'Sleepy the Goon,' a little joke that nobody else appreciated. For my *pièce de résistance*, I often played a dazzling rendition of 'Two O'clock Jump,' a flashy tune with a nice rhythm. In reality, it was a cinch to play because it didn't require triple tonguing and the *arpeggios*, the rapid succession of chord-like notes, were all downhill, the easiest kind for a trumpet player. I, too, played at school events.

In class, we were often seated next to each other. We talked some and compared notes, but when she would giggle and say, "Thay Thteve, I have a quethtion," that would shut me up for days.

During January of that year we presented the senior class play. It was a production that featured songs and scenes from famous musicals. Debbie was the singing star of this production and I was to play a trumpet accompaniment for her special song, 'Love is a Many-Splendored Thing.' The performance was on a Saturday night.

We both stood downstage facing the audience. She was dressed in a white, full-length formal gown and her presence exuded the charm and surreal beauty of a fairy-tale princess at a Parisian ball. I wore a dark blue, single-breasted, draped suit with oversized shoulder pads and a glaring red tie. My golden trumpet glistened and flashed the colors of the rainbow from the stage lighting. The audience was silent.

I raised my horn and began playing the overture: jazzy variations of the main melody that flowed over the audience. My tone became gradually more turbulent and intense until the mood was built up for Debbie. Then she took it from there. I eased a few steps back and to one side as she began singing. My playing enhanced her voice with harmonies and feathery runs. I controlled my volume so as not to overpower her. About half way through, she turned the song over to me.

I again stepped toward the audience, and played trumpet versions of the main chorus followed by a series of smooth and connected jazzy licks that ultimately segued back to her. Then, once again, I sidled into the background and harmonized. I played light, effortless bits that literally bounced off the melody and lyrics as she gave a second rendition of the main chorus. My trumpet playing was in perfect form: the tone was crisp and the phrasing seamless.

Suddenly, I sensed a shift in Debbie's voice. She was now singing to me as if I were the object of her deep love. My trumpet answered each nuance of her emotion. It was now talking to her, and responding to every trace of expression in her angelic voice. Her intensity increased and climbed toward a full crescendo. Her song climaxed on notes as clear, pure and fresh as a cold mountain lake. My brassy trumpet sound followed her up that scale in supporting harmony, almost but not quite matching her in volume, but wilder and ending in a magnificent, metaphorical, icy peak.

By now the audience, too, was on an emotional high. They loved it.

Riverside Writers

After the final number and after taking the applause of the audience, we returned to the music room with the other cast members, and were congratulating ourselves on how well we all did. Debbie rested her hand on her hip and said, "Thay there Thteve, you thounded like Harry Jameth." Then she and the other kids laughed and enjoyed the joke. They were laughing at me. My elation shattered into the jagged shards of a broken mirror. My eyes looked into what was left of that mirror and I saw myself as an absurd fool. I slid my trumpet into its black case and, not looking up, shuffled out into the winter cold and headed home. The music director had entered the room in time to hear everything.

Looking back, I think Debbie intended her words as a playful, backhanded compliment. Maybe I really did sound like Harry James. As the star of the show, she was swept up in a post-performance high, sucked into a whirlwind of celebrity and stardom that was becoming hers.

A week later she stopped me in the hall. "I want to apologize, Steve."

"Oh?"

"I was rude in teasing you and I feel awful. Will you forgive me?"

"Yeth, I forgive you."

"You did a wonderful job with our song. You made me sound terrific and I love you for it." She kissed me on the cheek and hurried away. I felt better. Maybe she did appreciate me after all.

At about the same time, the music director contacted the school advisor who enrolled me in speech therapy. The lady therapist had me open wide and, using a wooden tongue depressor, examined my mouth. She asked me to say "suffering succotash." I slopped it out as, "thuffering thuccotash," and sprayed her with droplets of saliva. She laughed at me and said I sounded like the cartoon character, Sylvester the Cat.

"Even great men like Winston Churchill lisped, so you needn't feel ashamed. The question is, do you want to fix it, or do you want to spend your life avoiding words that contain the *ess* sound?"

"I'd like to fickth it."

"Good, so let's get to work. Your tongue needs retraining."

She explained what my tongue position should be in order to speak properly. I began practicing *esses* for hours every day for over a month. Gradually, I was saying them just like everyone else. I felt better about myself and it showed.

Debbie and I had our own lives and activities in high school. She was taking drama and singing lessons, while I played in the band and was in training for the track team.

I lived two miles from school and usually caught a ride with my father or a neighbor. Occasionally, I rode the city bus. After school in early spring, I found Debbie waiting at the bus stop.

"Hi Debbie," I said. "It's a great afternoon. Why don't we walk home together, unless you're in a big hurry? We can do it in less than an hour."

"I'm in no hurry, let's go."

The trees had been in leaf only a few weeks. We walked north about four blocks through a working class neighborhood. The white dogwoods were still in flower. Robins were chasing each other and building nests, hopping on the lawns and pulling up night crawlers. Bright daffodils and blue crocuses were in bloom.

"I've been talking to the music director, Stevish," she said. "I am so thrilled. He thinks I have a future as a professional, providing I work hard enough."

"I agree with that," I said. "You have a terrific voice. By the way, I guess you know that every guy in school is madly in love with you. You'd have a hundred boyfriends, if only they had the nerve to ask."

"Oh, bosh. The other boys don't give me any attention, except you, and that's only once in a while."

"That's because you're so beautiful. All the boys, including me, go into a panic at the thought of you. Did you know that? When I asked you to walk home with me, I thought you'd probably tell me to get lost. If you had, I'd have collapsed into a mass of quivering flesh. You'd have needed an ambulance to come after me because I would have been terminal, and probably dead on arrival at the hospital."

"You're being silly, but thank you for saying that." We crossed the intersection with cars whizzing in all directions. She took my arm as we crossed and stayed close. We entered Woodland Park, an area of dense trees and brush. The trail through the park was shaded and isolated. The trees quickly muffled the traffic sounds. It was a secluded world of skittery chipmunks, clicking insects and flitting birds. After a little, the path led into a partial clearing where a dazzling shaft of yellow sun, like a spotlight, broke through the limbs of tall evergreens, creating an idyllic theater stage.

We stopped in the spotlight and faced each other. She was smiling and began softly humming, 'Love is a Many-Splendored Thing.' Without my trumpet, I felt awkward. How could I respond? I folded my hands together and placed both thumbs against my lips as if they were a trumpet mouthpiece. My voice did a corny imitation of the counterpoint that we both knew so well. She burst into full singing voice, while I provided the complementing harmonic phrases and jazzy riffs. After she hit the final note, we were facing each other and laughing, then became serious. We embraced and our lips met. Talk about a post-performance high: I laughed and waved at those Botticelli angels as I rocketed past them, and did aerobatics among the clouds that would put a barnstorming stunt pilot to shame.

An aged couple had walked into the clearing from the opposite direction and stood watching.

"Bravo, bravo!" the old man said. He and his wife applauded and both had tears in their eyes.

"We enjoyed your song so much," said the old lady. "You reminded us of our life together, all fifty years of it. I hope you two do as well." I gulped when she said that…a whole life? Could we do that?

"Well, we have to keep moving," said the old man. "This is our daily walk through the park. Good luck to you young people. Remember, always follow your dreams."

"Goodbye," we said and continued through the woods. Neither of us spoke.

Finally, I said, "So, the music director likes your voice. What else did he say?"

"Well, he was telling me about some eastern school…Juilliard. He says the best musicians go there."

We left the heavily wooded area and reached the bicycle path that circled Greenlake, another part of the city park. We'd walk up the west side of the lake for about a mile and would be just four blocks from her house. We stopped beneath a huge alder that loomed overhead and next to a vine maple bush that screened us from cars and trucks going by. We embraced and kissed again.

Kids bicycling on the path made smacking sounds with their lips and said, "Having fun? Naughty, naughty!"

We stopped at each outlook and under every tree that gave us a modicum of privacy. Finally, we didn't need much privacy...any excuse or no excuse was just fine.

The sun was low in the afternoon sky by the time we arrived at Debbie's front doorstep. "Thank you for walking me home, Stevish. I love you."

"I love you, too."

Suddenly her mother opened the door. "Debbie, I just called the police! Where have you been? I've been in a panic!"

"It's okay, Mrs. Donnelly," I said. "She was with me."

"Somehow that doesn't reassure me one little bit! I thought somebody had grabbed her!"

Well, I grabbed her, sort of, I thought. But what I said was, "I'm sorry Mrs. Donnelly. It was my fault, not hers."

Debbie smiled at me and whispered, "Don't worry, Stevish. I'll handle Mother."

Eight weeks later, we graduated and went our separate ways.

The so-called professional bands in Seattle were second-rate. I hated the way they sounded and wanted no part of these total amateurs. Besides the pay was terrible. I quit playing the trumpet.

Debbie moved to New York where she attended the Juilliard School. I attended State University, took Air Force ROTC, and after graduation, entered the Air Force. I had no choice since military service was mandatory for all able-bodied men. We corresponded intermittently while we were in school, but afterward were too busy and lost track of each other.

Then, according to the high school grapevine, Debbie met a handsome, ostensibly wealthy New Yorker and fell crazy in love. The only problem: the guy already had a wife and three kids. Debbie dropped him and moved on with her life, and had a great career in singing and acting.

The Air Force sent me to distant lands. I married once, but my wife came from a wealthy family and had led a pampered life. She couldn't cope with the hardships of having a husband in military service. I lost all contact with the high school crowd.

In retrospect, I should have pursued Debbie, but I was too much in awe of her beauty and talent. Sometimes it occurred to me that I'd like a rematch with life. Maybe I'd be smarter the second time around.

After twenty years, I retired as a lieutenant colonel and became a free lance writer, again living in Seattle. I had begun to renew old acquaintances, when one day a fancy invitation arrived. It read: "Nordlund High School's Class of '55 will have a reunion. Debbie Donnelly will be our honored guest." The note required an RSVP. I mulled the invitation for several days. Would she want to see me after all these years? After agonizing over it, I decided not to go. I penned a short note: "I send my regrets...."

The evening of the reunion, my doorbell rang and I answered. Debbie stood in front of me smiling and looking elegant.

"Debbie! You are beautiful, absolutely stunning," I said. "Come in." She raised her face to mine and I kissed her long and hard. My feelings burst from inside out, as if I'd stepped on a live power line.

"You bet I'm coming in. Where have you been all these years, Stevish? I tried to contact you through our high school friends, but everyone lost track."

"I've been in Saudi Arabia, Vietnam, Greenland, the Arctic circle, Europe... It's almost easier to tell you where I haven't been. I retired from active duty so I could write. How'd you find me?"

"The chairman of the reunion committee gave me your address just last week. She didn't think you were married, so here I am. Everyone at Nordlund knew we were wild about each other. How did we drift so far apart?"

"I wasn't about to hold you back, Debbie. I'd be in the way. Your great successes prove me right."

"Wrong, Stevish. All my successes and two divorces prove that all the money in the world is nothing without love. I learned that the hard way."

"Me, too," I said. "I've never stopped loving you. I thought you'd forgotten."

"I've been trying to locate you for several years, but nobody knew how to reach you. You should have written."

"Perhaps, but I'll tell you something I've never told anyone. After I was shot down in Vietnam and was struggling to stay alive as a prisoner of war, I thought of you every night for nearly four years. You appeared in my dreams as a Botticelli angel and told me not to give up. Sounds loony doesn't it?"

"No, it sounds fine," she said. "Look, you dope, I still love you. Get your coat and tie. We'll go to the reunion because they expect us. I'll even sing our special song, but after that we'll get to know each other again. We might go for a walk in Woodland Park. We won't drift apart this time. From now on we're together."

"Together for real? Forever?"

"Yes, forever."

A Late Romance
by Donna H. Turner

I was sitting in a chair with my walker next to me when a gorgeous, sinewy, tall young man fell from the sky and landed on a paved street in full view of my two surprised eyes. He was dressed in absolutely nothing, not one stitch of fabric covered anything. I thought, *He's for me!* Never mind that my husband of forty-six years was sitting on a couch near me. I was in love with a naked, beautiful David Bowie, looking just as he did in the movie "The Man Who Fell to Earth."

I imagined the two of us walking arm in arm down a French boulevard on our way to the best restaurant in town for the meal of a lifetime or better yet relaxing in the back of his limousine as it pulls up to the restaurant. "Your table is ready, Mr. Bowie. A rose for Madame," says the doorman as he helps us from the car.

The headwaiter walks us to a table in an alcove. Three waiters are there to greet us and attend our needs. In addition to the one rose I was given at the door a vase with eleven others sits on the table. "May I put your roses together?" Pierre asks. "Would Madame care for her American iced tea?" Even before I know I have a need, someone is there to fill it. David orders the meal in French—Doesn't ordering in French always seem more elegant? Until the first course arrives, we are alone to talk. I smile and shake my head and look at his naked body.

David pulls a small box from under the table, opens it, and says, "Will you marry me?" He pulls a nine-carat diamond out of the box and places it on my finger.

"I'd love to David, as long as you promise never to wear any clothes."

"Yes, darling, I promise. I would do anything for you."

I am the happiest person in the world. A gorgeous forty-year-old with all the money anyone could ask for and a flawless body. Travel anywhere I want to go. Is there anything else a sixty-something could ask for?

Then my vision returned to a room untidy with books. I heard sentences like, "I love the way you smile. I'm glad you never remember jokes; it means I can tell you the same joke over and over." I didn't know where all the images were coming from, but now I remember how much I enjoy the home I already have, the times we go out to eat at McDonald's or Wendy's, the meals with our own children. Beautiful as David Bowie is, living with someone I've known for forty-six years seems even better than trying to start fresh with a young man.

What Was Lost

What You'll Get
by Anne H. Flythe

When you've outlived the eulogists, don't linger
amorphous on the evening air
expecting tented throngs and limousines.
Don't wait for hymns and hot-house flowers.
All you'll get is a solemn man in a cheap black suit
with a large umbrella and one folding chair
set up on a scrap of Astroturf,
that lurid insult to all natural grass,
and the traditional empty neatly squared 6 x 6 x 3.
Raw earth piled by the gravesite waits
to return with you to fill the void.
Hope someone cares enough
to name and date a stone for you,
heavy evidence that you lived,
lasting proof of your existence.

On the Wisdom of Allowing Wine to Breathe

by Anne H. Flythe

On his return, her held breath exhaled,
his presence needed to complete their symmetry.
Radiating a kitten's blue-eyed innocence, he sprawled,
slid deeper into his chair, thighs widespread.
She didn't ask him where he'd been or what he'd done,
nor whom he chose to see.
His womanizing irrelevant, heart sure,
she had no fear of his casual lechery.

Confident, to celebrate, a glass of wine or two;
the only toast to open minds, experience, life on their terms.
As she bent to fill his glass, she recognized
the beard burns on his neck, caught the scent
      of unfamiliar aftershave.
It was a quick roll of thunder after a lightning bolt.
She stood, cupped her mouth to disguise the sound she made.

Still carrying his empty glass, she turned away,
her lips as thin and tight as an old scar.
As silence swelled to fill the space between them,
she toyed with her bracelet, telling each gold charm
      like a rosary.
Beside them on the coffee table an open bottle of Merlot;
tacit, wine left too long open turns to vinegar.

Saudade

by Anne H. Flythe

Cradling him in her arms,
pressed hard against his back,
her lips against his nape,
she took in great gusting breaths
memorizing his scent,
spooned to his long self
in futile lamination.
Despite her urgent warmth,
the soles of his bony feet
grew cold as stone upon her shins.
She begged blankets, quilts,
more heat, something more,
until within her desperate embrace
a sudden fluttering
as life soared from here to there
leaving a great stillness,
the presence of absence.

Brimstone

by Norma E. Redfern

Nights are ominous
My dreams shine fiercely
Clear as clustered stars
Burning across the sky
After dusk I wander the beach
Watching the reflection
Of stars and moon that dance
A subtle glow across ocean's flow
I stand waist-deep in summer surf
Merge mind with water's breathing

The tide beckons me to the deep
Easy to dream of a long sleep
I am not the man I was
Wasted body, my time grows near
A history too late to change
Now I know he comes for me
I see him in my dreams, fire and death

If only I could kiss your lips
Caress you in my arms again
Morning brings only a haze
My vision is nearly gone
I'm incapable of feeling
I often dream of the past with you
The devil scratches at my door

An Undeliverable Condolence
by Anne H. Flythe

After Maria's death he shallowed up,
Internalized his loss, encapsulated
Maria and all that might have been,
Stored the ache somewhere
Between his liver and his heart,
Closed up shop and moved away.

Nothing stirred the deeper waters of his being,
He skimmed across surface tension
Like a water strider,
His passage barely dimpling the sky mirror.
For a time his seasons went unchanged
Then he remembered how to breathe again.

A *tabula rasa*, he reinvested in a cool pale woman
Who could never comprehend
The man he used to be.
She gave him two winsome children and her love,
But no one burned bright or hot enough
To warm him.
He slept with his back to her at night
Curled around the treasure in his vitals.

The Nightstand

by John M. Wills

Stepping inside, he closed the door and locked it. The end of the day had seemed like it would never arrive. The worst part had been the luncheon. How could anyone refer to it as a celebration of life when someone you've loved your entire life is gone? Moreover, whose idea was it for a grieving spouse to host a gathering at the worst time of his life?

His wife of over forty years was dead. It had begun as just another ordinary day—she had backed out of their driveway, waved, and set off for work. He was confident, as always, that he would see her that evening at the dinner table where they would discuss their day with each other. But in an instant, the routine of their lives had ended; a truck changing lanes had forced her car off the highway and into a tree.

He knew when he got the call that it wasn't just a simple fender-bender. No, the police officer was tight-lipped; he wouldn't give any details other than to say, "We need you to come to the hospital right now." As he drove, he wondered if it was a broken bone, or maybe she was unconscious. *That's it . . . they need me to provide insurance information.* A couple of years earlier she had been involved in an accident when a driver behind her ran into her car at a stoplight. She was shaken, but unhurt. Her car had suffered the worst of it, a few thousand dollars worth of damage.

Nevertheless, they weren't getting any younger; broken bones took more time to heal. He wondered how long she might have to take off from work. At least he would be home to help her recover. Being retired gave him the freedom to either go to work or not. When he inquired about his wife at the ER, he knew immediately something terrible had happened. He was led to a room down the hall, and moments later, a chaplain broke the news that she had died.

He couldn't remember how long he had stayed with her body, but a kind, compassionate nurse finally persuaded him to let her go. It didn't seem possible the accident could have killed her. She had some visible injuries to her face, but none of them seemed like they should have been fatal. Holding her hand while whispering to her, he couldn't accept the reality that she wasn't really there. *Wake up, honey, please . . .* When he finally left, he felt guilty, thinking he'd abandoned her, that she would be lonely there without him. After all, they had rarely spent any time apart. They had been each other's constant companion since their engagement so very long ago.

The next several days had been memorable in that he had no clue how he got through them. He knew he had made the burial arrangements, but that task was more mechanical than anything else. Ten years earlier, he had gone through the same exercise when their only child had been killed in the war. After his death, neither one of them thought their lives could ever be joyful again. But the more they turned to each other for strength, the more the stabbing pain in their souls became a less painful ache. They commiserated that at least they still had each other. And even though there would never be any grandbabies running around, they were thankful that, at least for awhile, they had been able to enjoy a child who had given them wonderful memories and had died a hero.

The house was dark; he had no intention of turning on any lights, for it was no longer a home. He had no desire, nor any need, to see anything. He trudged up the stairs to their bedroom. Walking into the closet, he stumbled over her slippers. It had been their little joke. He'd always told her she needed to set them aside so he wouldn't trip over them; she'd always replied it was her way of knowing where he was. He didn't move them then; he didn't move them now.

He undressed and crawled into bed. Their nightly ritual had been to watch the news before they fell asleep. Tonight, there would be no newscast; nothing in the world held any meaning. Turning onto his side, he grabbed her pillow, inhaling her scent and lovingly pulling it gently to his body. He held it as if he were holding her, and at that moment the enormity of it all stuck him like a metal mallet, shattering his controlled façade into a million pieces. His body rocked in pain, anger, resentment and remorse. As wave after wave of tears and gut-wrenching sobs contorted his supine form, he cried out—"Why?"—over and over again.

Then the memories flashed non-stop, flickering like an old movie reel. Their younger years, the difficult times, the baby, the school years, sending him off to war, and having him come home—in a box. The hurt they endured . . . together. The partnership, the two of them, her and him, always victorious, a pair, a couple . . . lovers, friends, two becoming one to overcome. Now all that once was, was no more.

He'd always fancied himself the stronger of the two. Truth be known, it was she who was the secret ingredient that allowed their dreams to come true. It was she who possessed the power to enable them to endure the adversity and challenges. He had the physical power—after all he was a man—but it had little impact compared to her emotional strength. Without her by his side, he had as much chance of surviving as a sandcastle on the beach as the surf engulfs it.

No future, no past, only darkness. He dozed, but awoke shortly with a start, as he rolled onto her side only to find it full of nothing. His tears began anew, the despair—crushing, suffocating and relentless. A sliver of moonlight sliced a slit through the bedroom drapes, like a spotlight seeking an actor on a Broadway stage. He turned to the nightstand and saw the highlighted object—an almost full bottle of sleeping pills.

The Urn
by Madalin E. Jackson

The dark wooden door with etched beveled glass opened into a large entry hall. The sweet musty hint of lavender wafted through the air joined by an aroma of old fabric, dusty lace, and long forgotten family dinners. Lit by a dim vintage chandelier, walking into the house was a step back in time.

Mary Elizabeth closed the door gently and walked to the marble-topped cherry table where she gently set the white box along with her black leather purse. She turned and gazed into the aging gilded mirror and gently removed her felt hat. With her long elegant fingers, she fluffed her graying blond hair, sighed, and walked into the living room.

It was her mother's room, from the highly polished table to the dainty porcelain figurines. Now it belonged to her.

The funeral had been long and dreary. It was a memorial, not just to a life, but to a life style faded and tired like so many of her mother's friends. With her mother's death, an era came to an end. Years ago the rest of the family had left to pursue their own lives leaving her to look after mother. She alone had stayed and kept her mother company, cooked, cleaned, and supported her through life's little trials and tribulations. Now it was over and the vast brick house was hers along with its artifacts and memories.

Mary Elizabeth slowly returned to the hall and picked up the white box. Everyone tried to get her to bring some of the flowers home, too. She had encouraged other members of the family to take as many flowers as they liked. Bringing home the box was quite enough.

She carefully untied the heavy cord around the box and removed the lid. Spreading back the packing paper, she gazed down at the cream colored urn etched with gold. Slowly she lifted it out of the box. Light kaleidoscoped from the chandelier to the mirror to the urn and into her eyes. What was she to do now?

The door chimes called Mary to the front door. After placing the urn back in the box, she opened the door and greeted her sister and brother-in-law. They came through the door carrying trays of food balanced precariously atop boxes of pastries. It was time to celebrate.

"Mary, mom's friends have sent more than we will ever eat. I'll carry this to the kitchen. Howard can get the rest from the car." Mary smiled and hugged her sister Kit as she chatted away and they made their way down the hall.

"I'll put these on the table and go for the rest," called Howard as the two made their way to the kitchen. He set two trays down, one on top of the other, and headed back out the door.

In the kitchen Kit placed the tray and box on the table and began taking off her coat. "Honestly, Mary, how do mom's friends think we will ever devour all this? Just look. There are sandwiches on the tray, cookies in the box, and heaven knows what is on the trays Howard set on the table."

"You'll be surprised" said Mary. "There will be neighbors in and out of here, if not for the food, out of curiosity!"

"The beasts! How can they be so morbid, She was old and she died."

"Oh, they want to see the house and find out what we're going to do with it now. Rumors have been flying since mom became ill last month. I'll deal with it."

"Mary, what are you going to do now?" Kit bit into a crumbling cookie as she talked and began arranging them on a plate.

"Rest, Kit, rest."

"Do you want us to help clear out some of mom's things? You know clothes, shoes, toiletries. You can't want to stay here day after day looking at that stuff!"

"It can wait. I closed the door to her room and it can stay closed until I'm ready. You're welcome to go in there, but I'm not ready yet."

"I'm not sure there is anything in there I want. She pretty much gave me and Jim what we wanted."

"Jim and me," corrected Mimi.

"Yea, right, brother Jim and me. So, what's next?"

"Hey girls, here's the rest of the food from the car. I'll get the ones from the hall, too. Who's going to eat this stuff?" Howard plopped the food on the table, grabbed a cookie, and headed back to the hall.

"I'd say with Howard around, it won't take long," snorted Kit.

Laughing, Mary Elizabeth replied, "Let's put some of the food on the dining room table and refrigerate the rest. I'll get a cloth for the table."

With the ritual begun, the women, with a little help from Howard, arranged a buffet on the table. Finally, they went into the living room. Howard lit the gas fireplace while Mimi opened a bottle of wine. Kit kicked off her shoes and mused "Where the hell is Jim? He should be here by now."

"He said something about stopping for gas," Howard added as he took a large sip of wine and the door chimes sounded again. "Maybe that's him now."

Mary Elizabeth went to the door and let in Jim with his new girl friend. Right behind him trooped in several neighbors. Looking over her brother's shoulders, she could see several cars pulling into the long driveway. The food would be gone by six.

Mary, Kit, and Jim, with a little help from Howard, kept the glasses filled and entertained all the friends who meant well and overstayed their welcome. Finally, about six thirty with darkness pushing away the dim light of day, the last of the guests left. Jim took his girlfriend home and returned just as Mimi and Kit put the last of the food in the refrigerator. "Ok, let's look at it. We've put it off long enough. Where's the urn?" asked Jim.

"It's sitting rather unceremoniously on the hall table," answered Mary.

"I'll get it," replied Jim.

In the living room, Jim removed the urn from the box and set it on the coffee table. They looked at the twelve inch high vase with its gold trimmed lid. "That's it? That's mom?" asked Kit.

"Well, she's not in there yet!" said Mary. "That's just the urn I picked out. What do you think?"

"I think there isn't room for all of her. Don't they say there is more than just ashes. You know, bones, and stuff. I heard not everything is turned to ashes," spoke Jim.

"Oh, don't be gross, Jim. Whatever goes in there I'm sure will be just right. At least it was what mom wanted. 'No one is going to walk around my grave,' she had said. So, do we just walk around this urn?" said Kit.

"I suggest we put it someplace where we can't walk around it. I don't want mom coming back and haunting this place because we are all walking around her like a merry-go-round!"

"Oh, Jim, be serious," said Mary Elizabeth, "Mom just didn't want to be in the ground. I suggest we place it on the hall table for now. When the ashes are added, we can decide what to do."

"Sounds like a good plan," said Kit. "Howard, what are your thoughts?"

"We could add it to the kitty litter...."

Kit threw her husband a dirty look and Jim threw a pillow barely missing the urn.

"That's it guys," said Mary as she swept up the urn and returned it to the hall.

"Anyone for Mahjong?" asked Kit.

* * * * * * *

Several days later, the funeral home called to inform Mary Elizabeth that she and her siblings could come and retrieve their mother's remains. Kit, Mimi, Jim, and a less than enthusiastic Howard arrived at the funeral home Friday afternoon. Mary Elizabeth handed the box with the urn to the proprietor dressed in his somber suit. The four of them sat rather uncomfortably in the French provincial chairs and waited. Soon Mr. Blackwood, the owner of the funeral home, returned with the box.

"Please accept our apologies for taking several days to complete your mother's internment. We think you will find everything in order. Do you have a special request for placement of the urn in any of our mausoleums? We have some rather special niches available."

Mary Elizabeth spoke up first. "No, mother made a specific request that no special arrangements be made other than not being buried in the ground."

"Yes, she had contacted us about prearrangements for her internment and requested the urn and cremation," replied Mr. Blackwood. "She did not, however, reveal any special requests she had for the urn."

"That's just fine, Mr. Blackwood," added Kit. "We have discussed where to place the urn and how best to give mother her final resting place."

"I am happy to hear that. Is there anything else Blackwood and Sons can do for you now?"

"I don't think so. Do we owe you any balance for the funeral? Jim is handling the estate finances and as the trustee can write you a check," Mary said as she looked at Jim.

"I believe we have everything finalized for you. Here is the final receipt and as you can see there is a zero balance." Mr. Blackwood handed the receipt to Jim.

"Thank you, Mr. Blackwood. Anything else?" Jim turned to look at his siblings.

Everyone seemed to be satisfied with the outcome. Mary Elizabeth picked up the box and Mr. Blackwood ushered the quartet out the door and to their cars.

Back at the imposing brick house the group sat around the coffee table and continued the discussion of what to do with mother's urn. The women moved about the living room, dining room, and entrance hall trying a variety of locations. Bookshelves, tables, and even the television set were tested, but none seemed appropriate.

"What about placing the urn on mother's dresser in her bedroom?" asked Kit. "We certainly won't be walking around her there."

"Yes, with the door closed no one will even know she's in there," added Jim.

"We could pretend she is still here, just in her room watching TV," Howard said. "You could even leave the TV on, Mary."

"Honestly, Howard, can't you ever be serious about anything?" asked Kit.

"I am serious! Mary could put in a never ending video of one her favorite movies!"

"That's enough," said Mary. "I'll take care of it. If you don't have any further suggestions, I'll place it on the hall table for now."

The urn was placed on the round cherry table and the group returned to their wine and games. Sometime after midnight, everyone decided it was time to call it a day. Howard, Kit, and Jim left. Mary closed the door and locked it.

She walked into the living room and refilled her wine glass. Slowly she walked back into the entry hall and around the table. She raised her glass in a toast. "Well, mom, all I can say is, it's about time."

* * * * * *

With Kit and the men back at their homes and jobs, Mary Elizabeth proceeded with her plans. The large van arrived early Monday morning several weeks after the funeral. Watching the

Riverside Writers

men carefully load her mother's things into the truck, she contemplated again the placement of the urn. Her siblings hadn't contacted her since the day they retrieved it, so she felt free to do as she wished.

When the truck was loaded, Mary Elizabeth had the men follow her to the storage facility. She had rented the largest unit available. Within a couple of hours, all of her mother's treasures had been carefully stowed in the unit and the door closed. She attached a lock with her mother's birth date as the combination. The truck left and soon she headed back home.

Upstairs in the room she had occupied since her childhood, she finished packing her own things. Clothes, shoes, jewelry, and a few other personal items were packed in her newly purchased luggage. She methodically placed the items in the trunk of her sedan. Inside the house again, she looked around the entrance hall then walked once more through the downstairs rooms. The musty lavender smell still lingered, but with time, it should dissipate. She gathered up her coat and purse. Jingling her keys in her hand, she walked through the door, turned around and locked it securely.

Her last view of the inside of the house was the urn, already gathering dust, in its final resting place. On the table beside the urn was a carefully worded note to Kit and Jim. "Please don't walk around the table. Mary."

The Save Pile
by Margaret Rose

Recently I spent some time examining the contents of a box in the treasure trove that I call my basement. This particular box contained items that had belonged to my mother at the time of her death six years ago. It was time to start the difficult task of considering what was worth saving in that box and what could be given away or tossed. I began by opening a small purse that she kept in her night stand during those last years at the nursing home. There were the obligatory feminine accoutrements—a finger nail file, a small package of Kleenex, and a tube of bright red lipstick that my mom kept handy for last minute touch-ups; a woven cloth change purse containing a few coins and one-dollar bills; and a 2004 pocket calendar which bore the barely legible, feeble scratchings of her once meticulous but now tired, 91-year-old handwriting, noting doctor's appointments, family birthdays and visits from friends. When I spotted the list of frequently used phone numbers, I realized how much I still miss those regular Sunday night phone calls.

Lastly, I pulled out her leather wallet, slightly worn but immaculately organized. I was taken aback by a sudden but gentle wave of nostalgic anticipation. Quite unexpectedly, I felt my mother's presence, as if she were in the room with me. How many times had her slender hands carefully opened this very ordinary but at the same time very intimate repository of documents and pictures? Living her last months in a nursing home, my mom no longer needed ready access to cash but, there in the first slot of the center of her wallet, was her faithful friend, her MasterCard. Mom insisted on keeping the credit card which allowed her to continue to make purchases from mail-order businesses— bedroom slippers from J. C. Penney; a blouse from Coldwater Creek; a comfortable pair of lounging slacks from Land's End. While just about everything else in the way of personal responsibilities and privileges had been stripped from her, she was still strong enough and possessed the mental acuity to pick up the phone to place an order for a piece of classic women's apparel from one of her favorite catalogues. To my mom, her money was her independence. She was never extravagant but it gave her much pleasure to know that she had the means to buy gifts for her grandchildren, her children, her husband or herself.

I began to finger through the neatly-ordered plastic pocketed inserts in the center of the wallet. Predictably, she had her social security card, her driver's license, her insurance cards, and her blood type identification card. Next were the membership cards for organizations that represented what she had spent her life working for--Maryland Teacher's Retirement, DAR and the Republican Women's Club. Mom was most proud of that DAR (Daughters of the American Revolution) membership which represented the family heritage of love for and service to the nation.

Then there were the photos. I recognized the posed portrait of my mom and dad, probably taken for the church directory soon after their sixtieth wedding anniversary. A larger print of the same picture had hung in the stairwell in my parents' home. The second picture was an old black and white photo (circa 1940) of my Aunt Mary, my mom's beloved older sister and partner in genealogy research. In this picture, my aunt was smartly dressed for work, at the beginning of what was to become a forty-year career as a middle school geography teacher. She was the first of what would become a long line of teachers in the family. The final five pockets contained, in the order of their births, the elementary school and graduation pictures of Mom's five grandchildren, five jewels in the crown of the finest and proudest moments of her life. Just when I was about to close the wallet, a small card fell out of the section designed to hold dollar bills. It was a small card on which was printed the 23rd Psalm, a symbol of her faith and a source of comfort for her that she kept within easy reach to be read over and over on days when life seemed hard for her. How appropriate that these verses were read at her funeral.

To the casual observer, this wallet may not have seemed in any way remarkable. But to the daughter, it was totally Mom. This wallet was definitely to be placed in the "to save" pile.

As I put the wallet back into the box, it occurred to me how much this simple possession told about my mother. I wondered about my own life and my possessions. When I am gone, what single object will most sum up my life, my accomplishments and my happiest moments? Will I leave behind for my children a clear statement of who I was and what I stood for? Thoughts to ponder and possible guidelines for my own personal process of de-cluttering and simplifying my life.

Blue Collar Shadorma

by Michelle O'Hearn

Suspended
Seven stories high
Equipment
A failure
He tumbles to the ground – Crack!
God bless Laborers

Overtime

by James F. Gaines

"………………….No less than all

The younger
rises when the
old doth fall
King Lear

I asked if I could put this off,
Still in the mechanical bed
Where I never thought to lie.
The cardiologist never cracked a smile
Or blinked an eye:
"Not long enough for you to brush your teeth!"
No time outs.
Wheeling down the corridor, face in mask,
I barely remembered them counting down
Anesthetic numbers fading into clotting thoughts
Then they cut

The blood eagle on my chest,
Stretched my scarlet ribs to fly,
Rolled up my lungs like rubber gloves,
Simply because they were in the way,
Dug out two arteries
From naked forearm and deep hidden thorax
And a vein that ran from ankle to knee,
Stitching together four new solutions,
For my stubborn, bloated heart.
Miraculously I came back
Aching into life,
Gagging for a fresh unaided breath.

But always the shadow of a memory--
I dimly heard the whistle blow,
Felt the scuffed leather dropping from my hand,
Hung my head,
And took more than one sad step
Towards an unforgiving sideline.
Suddenly I am here.
A referee with shaggy brows
Stares me square in the face,
"First and ten!"

Pain

by Norma E. Redfern

The ache steals in during the night
Festering until first light
I wake afraid to get out of bed
Not knowing what further anguish
Will haunt my sunlit hours

If only this pain were punishment
Then I could duck away and hide
But the stab pokes again and again
Slicing at my body when I move

Excruciating throb with each step
Once tall, my back curves
I'm a stooped old woman now
I've fallen victim to old age
Before my time
Only able to creep as I walk

Lying in bed or in my chair
Brings relief to my body, no pain
My mind wanders, as I close my eyes
Will I ever be able to walk
with no pain?

My spine grinding, bone on bone
I try to fix dinner, unable to stand
Or even walk far; pain never leaves me
Agony spreads crossways
Buttocks aching with every step

Now crippling pain with movement
Scalpel incision, extirpation of pain
But will agony stop, allow me to walk
Or will it render me
more incapacitated than before?

Poe
by Madalin E. Jackson

A conundrum in life,
An enigma in death,
Wailing from feminine loss,
And paternal lovelessness.
Arrogant in prose,
Poetically deep and cinematic,
Searching
Deep within himself
For anything but despair.
A bleak alley,
A dismal damp night,
Darkness and death.
Poe - Nevermore

Panic at Milepost 42
by J. Allen Hill

Where has it been
This swift train?
Bolting through the landscape,
Melting down the miles.

So much country has passed by.
So much is left to do.

Here and there I've touched a hand,
Blown a kiss. Heard a prayer,
Walked a mile on the thorny path,
Laid down beside the brook.
A secret or two I've tucked away,
Wrapped in velvet all the hopes,
Scrubbed away despair,
Pressed petals full of dreams.

The time it took – a whisper.
The mark it left – a breath.

Stop! You catapulting monster!
Your wheels a clacking
Windows blurring
Whizzing through the night.
Oh damn you, Stop!
Give me time to sup and savor
This bacchanalian feast,
To satiate desire
Before we reach the station.

The Crocheting Class
by Laura R. Merryman

Last night, I felt close to you
For the first time in years.
I was in a crocheting class (yes, with the hens)
At the rec center, and almost,
As though it was instinct,
I could remember how to start a
Slipknot and chain a row of
Downy yarn.
It was as though the....muscles....remembered.

And then it came back to me,
An afternoon at the splintery picnic table,
When you and Papaw came to visit
Which you rarely did because the
Trip from the mountains was hard,
And your leg, left shortened by Polio,
Made traveling difficult, along with
      Papaw's motion sickness.
But you were there then, and your
Spotted hands twisted and caught
The flamed-touched yarn like a blur;
Metal bobbing in and out among loops of variegated yarn,
An artisan by necessity,
a craftsman when chores were done.
Sharing something of your life, your wisdom,
      with your granddaughter?

You tried to show me how to
Make an extra loop, twist and turn
Down a new line,
But I was too young and impatient
To know that the first steps were
The hardest, that once you hit
The third layer, you could duck under

Things, take two steps and then two steps more.
I was only on the first row.
At eight, what could I know of diligence?
And patience, and a practiced life so that
Movement becomes memory
Patterns become ingrained,
And in the end, you have a flamboyant tapestry
    that keeps away cold.
I tried a few loops, chained a row, and feigned dumb
(Due to my impatience)

It was not time for me to turn corners,
    endure the difficult stitches,
So that later the easy ones would come when I
    was too old and too tired,
And crocheting would be cheaper than therapy.

So I'm sitting there, at the rec center (yes, with the hens)
And every woman is at least 40,
You can tell by the road maps on our hands
And the gray spinning from our roots,
And each woman has a tale of a relative who
Conjured afghans, or booties, or doilies,
from movement and motion.
And there is yearning in the voices.
If only we had our grandmothers here,
With us now, as we try to extend our
Lives in chains and loops

I Miss You, My Friend
by Patricia A. Moton

Sadness surrounds my soul at the first hint of the dawn,
As I awaken, bleary eyed, and find that you are gone.
My eyes once filled with morning joy
And opened wide in anticipation,
Knowing you, my friend, were with me,
And would be for the duration.

I should have been more watchful,
Should have seen the subtle signs of change.
But, instead, I forged on happily,
Never expecting to be estranged
So suddenly from one so dear—
Who caused my cheeks to puff with pride.
What caused this onslaught, this change of heart,
This dip in my roller coaster ride?

The lids of my eyes now droop,
And from the corner there flows a tear
Tracking its way down a crevasse in my face,
A face now filled with fear.
As I gently wipe the tear
From the downturned corner of my mouth,
I long for your kiss on my now thin lips,
And they turn into a pout.

Were there a way to undo what I did,
I would. I miss you being a part of me.
When we were together, my soul soared with the birds. There was
love, laughter. I was free.
But now the evening cloaks me in darkness
As the sky begins to dim,
And with my final, desperate breath I wail—
I need you my friend, COLLAGEN!!!

The World of Children

The Butterfly Song
by Elaine J. Gooding

Butterfly, Butterfly, where are you going?
You are so pretty, please take me with you.
Momma says it's time for me to go "night-night,"
But I want to fly with you.

Close your eyes, my sleepyhead,
Dream sweet dreams tonight.
Fly on the back of the beautiful butterfly,
Dream 'til morning's light.

I smell sweet flowers, oh, look at the colors,
Purple and orange and yellow and blue.
Butterfly, Momma says it's time for "night-night,"
But I want to fly with you.

Close your eyes, my sleepyhead,
Dream sweet dreams tonight.
Fly on the back of the beautiful butterfly,
Dream 'til morning's light.

Pane Glass Window

by Stanley B. Trice

"I'm telling you straight out, Dad. I'm coming home because me and Bobby are having a baby. I know this isn't what you want to hear, but it's what I want and it's what'll make me happy." Debbie's thrusting voice pushed through the cables and wiring to the phone he held.

"What are you going to do? How are you going to college with a baby?" Zachary's mind did not function well when he was overwhelmed with surprise. He had just stepped into the house after riding an hour on a commuter train. He got little sleep on the train and now he stood with his coat half off and his briefcase laying part way between him and the door.

"I think it's best I came home until Bobby graduates next May. But, aren't you excited?" Debbie's voice ascends, spurned on by youthful energy. "This is so new for me and Bobby. I'm excited. I can't believe it's really happening. Don't you think it's exciting?"

"I thought you were taking summer courses so you could finish school early and hike the Appalachian Trail next year." Zachary envisioned his daughter's dreams in diapers. He wondered if a son would have been so quick to make life altering decisions.

"There will be time for that later. I can't very well be trouncing around in the mountains with an infant. Besides, Bobby and I are married, remember?" Debbie sounded irritated.

"I remember." They called him at three in the morning the day they got married. He thought his daughter was drunk, but she was only high on her endless roller coaster life. "When are you coming home?"

"Day after tomorrow. I've cleaned out my course schedule and refunded my books. I know this wasn't planned, but I'll go back to college, I promise."

How will you ever go back with a baby, Zachary thinks. He realized his hand hurt from clenching the phone receiver too tightly. With his other hand, Zachary rubbed the graying hairs on his chest with an open palm. He thought about the breast cancer that consumed his wife two years ago. Nowadays, he faced too many challenges alone.

"I'll have your room fixed up and cleaned. I've kept that set of dolls you got when you were ten."

"I didn't know you still had them. They could be worth money."

"Don't worry about money. We'll do fine."

"Bobby will get a job right after he graduates. He already has some serious prospects. Then I'll go back to school and one day we can all hike the Appalachian trail."

I'm already too old, Zachary believes. After their voices end the conversation, he found himself preparing for his daughter's return home. First, he unlocked the door to a room with furniture and a bed unchanged since the two women in his life left.

Eight days later she drove up in a twelve year old Ford compact with the nameplate missing and the type forgotten. She has had her previous long brown hair trimmed razor like up the sides and back of her head leaving bristled stubs. Longer remnants were softly curled on top to fall gracefully across her forehead. Zachary saw a woman wearing a loose pink blouse that hung over her unbuttoned jeans. He had pulled up behind her after driving the short distance from the train station.

"I didn't realize you were so far along," Zachary said while pulling colorful bright satchels and brown paper bags from the trunk. He maneuvered his thin frame away from a broken tail light to avoid the sharp edges. His legs felt like he was standing on a moving train car as it thumped along the railroad tracks.

"It's hard to think I'm only three months and showing. Was Mom this big with me?"

"I don't remember." Pregnancies were alien to him and remembering his wife was getting more distant. He brushed his fingers through thinning hair and heard the hoot-hoot of a train whistle in the distance as it pulled away from a station.

The next day Debbie transitioned to a new lifestyle as Zachary left for work. He rode his usual train car and sat in a vinyl seat on his way to work. The baseboard heater at his feet pillowed waves of heat up his body until the hot air blew away each time the train stopped and exit doors opened. Soon the heat would not be needed to chase away chilled air.

Zachary worked in an office with mismanagement, turmoil, and gossip that he avoided as best he could. He left his work place without accomplishing anything constructive or completing any useful purpose. On his train ride home, he placed the imprint of his body into his favorite front row seat with plenty of leg room to stretch out and no back of the seat in front to stop him. Yet, by the time he drifted off to sleep, the train slowed toward his stop. As he drove home, Zachary wondered what his daughter did that day.

"I sold my car. Bobby and I can use the money to help you out some. I don't want to be freeloading," Debbie was enthusiastic while spooning up dinner as soon as Zachary walked in the doorway. He used to wait awhile and adjust to an empty home before eating.

"You didn't have to sell your car. I've got enough money. And, daughters don't freeload on fathers. Besides, you'll need something to drive after the baby is born."

"Bobby still has his car at school and I don't need a car while I'm home. Anyway, I didn't get much money, but that doesn't matter. It's progress. Now, eat dinner."

Looking down at the swirls of reddened pasta, Zachary thought things were fleeing past him in a rush. His daughter adjusted too quickly, he thought. "I guess we need to get the upstairs ready for the baby," Zachary said.

"But, that's what I've been doing all day. I called some of my friends and they're rounding up a lot of baby things. Some of them have kids already, you know. I'll probably need to borrow the car on Saturday because Sarah wants me at her house. I think they're giving me a baby shower."

"Sure."

On TV that evening they watched a program on sterilization. During the vasectomy each vas deferens was snipped unceremoniously by a faceless, masked doctor. Later, during a tubal, a woman's fallopian tubes were clamped in dry, medical fashion. Another show had a construction site where two people contracted out to build a house to enclose their soon-to-be family. The woman's pink blouse hung over her protruding stomach as she explained the complicated tile pattern that would be on her kitchen floor. Zachary thought he could be dizzy in the morning if he looked for coffee and saw swirling lines at his feet.

The days sped quickly down arrows of time. Zachary left home each day always surprised by Debbie's changes. When he came back home after bouncing around on a commuter train,

Zachary walked through the door way at night and found the furniture rearranged, fabric draped over the windows in some fashion, or the kitchen dishes put where they were not normally kept. At least the train schedule stayed reliable and the same.

Zachary did not know anyone enough to talk to them on his train ride, yet at least they were there in case he did. Instead of conversations, he worried about what he would be doing a year after the baby was born. He wondered if, when the baby became an adult, would the person ride the same commuter train he did and sit in his same seat when he was gone.

On Halloween, Zachary found himself sitting with Bobby's parents in a hospital lounge waiting for announcement of the birth. Bobby was with Debbie somewhere amid the branching corridors that meandered like tree limbs through the monolithic hospital. While waiting, Zachary read a family magazine about a male child born in a truck on the way to the hospital. A stretch of interstate would represent the child's origin into this world.

Looking outside, Zachary watched the illuminating moon hold back the darkness. The moonlight let him watch a falling leaf touch the window's glass on its downward, haphazard course from the branch to the ground. Zachary wondered about the uncontrolled life courses he was carried on and how the child born on the interstate and a falling leaf can lose their origin so easily. He wondered what course he was on.

"It's going to be a well provided child," spoke Bobby's father. He was tall, muscular, and a few years younger with broad shoulders and a square jaw. In this man, paternal instincts were in motion. Zachary wondered which grandfather the child would favor.

Bobby's mother sat quietly crocheting a wool afghan for the baby. The colors were too subtle and pastel for Zachary to understand. Having her around was uncomfortable for him and Zachary wished he were nowhere.

When the baby girl Alysson was announced, Zachary lost himself in the expected excitement. In the next few days, responsibilities were paired with future roles and traditional foundations assigned to the new and old parents.

Throughout these days Zachary saw the new parents growing realization and fear. He heard the run-or-stay decision in their discussions even as they realized there was only one decision. Meanwhile, Bobby's parents looked at immortality and continuity to their species and blood line. Their decisions had been made.

On a sunny day a week and a half after the birth, Zachary listened for Alysson's cry as he looked outside a smudged window pane of the house. Debbie was saying goodbye to Bobby. Bobby's parents had left two days ago and now their son was leaving responsibility behind, also.

Each day for over three weeks, Zachary saw Debbie struggle with the new born as if it was an alien just landed from another planet. Finally, one morning at 3 a.m., she entered his bedroom.

"Can you get up with Alysson? You don't have work tomorrow and you can sleep as long as you like in the morning." Debbie pleaded while standing in the doorway cradling Alysson in tired arms. "I've been up with her twice already tonight. I don't know how Mom did it. All Alysson wants is her bottle."

Struggling to reach an awakened state, Zachary sat up in bed as the baby was placed in his arms. As Debbie left responsibility with Zachary, he woke to the warm bottle in his hand and Alysson suckling down the pale white liquid. After she finished, he laid the child across his shoulder and tuned into a Washington Dulles airport frequency on the multi-band radio he had since childhood.

Zachary listened to the pilots and control tower banter back and forth maintaining control of the airways. He thought of who the people were on those planes, where they were going, where they had been, and if they ever thought someone else listened to them at three in the morning. Zachary looked out his bedroom window and watched the constellation Orion rise in the sky. The baby burped. He liked to think that sometimes before the confusion of the day begins there was order, routine, and predictability.

Winter arrived by creeping into the weather patterns and forecasts on TV and radio. Cold weather doldrums enveloped Zachary's consciousness and he believed his internal clock was slowing down too soon.

"Bobby may go to graduate school here in town," Debbie told her father unexpectedly as he walked in late from work one night. His dependable commuter train had been held up by a fast moving Amtrak followed by a freight train. For Debbie, it had been another day of feeding, bowel eruptions, and cleaning.

Christmas decorations littered the living room floor to await organization around relocated furniture. "We'll pay rent to live in the basement. And, don't worry. There'll come a time when we're all out of your way."

"You're not in my way and you and your family can stay as long as you need to." Zachary said while thinking about guilt.

"Bobby will be home for Christmas break after finals next week. Can you watch Alysson sometime so we can go off by ourselves?"

"Sure. Do you think you and Bobby will live here in town after graduate school?"

"Probably not. We want to move somewhere different. Don't you think the couch can be put up against that wall and can't that chair go in the storage shed outside?" Debbie said as she cradled Alysson on her protruding hip. Zachary maneuvered around the dull and frayed ornaments and worn furniture.

"Your mother upholstered that chair and I don't want it outside where it can get moldy." Zachary said decidedly. "I'll put it upstairs in my bedroom."

"Mom did a lot of things around here, but she's gone and I've got a family to be concerned with now."

"You're too much like your mother, throwing away the past because it's not needed anymore."

"Here, take Alysson. I can move the couch."

"Do you have to be so independent about everything?"

"I want this Christmas stuff up. I've been fooling around with it all day and I don't like being around so much memorabilia. Bobby, Alysson, and I will build our own memories one day."

"I hoped you would want some of these things for yourself."

Debbie thrust the couch upward a few inches before dropping it with a thud two steps away. "Yes, I'll take things if that's what you want. There, the couch can stay here. I can't move it any further. Now, let's go buy the tree before supper and get this over with. Why don't you just get an artificial tree when they go on sale after the holidays? That's what I'm going to do."

Zachary hated plastic trees. He remembered his mother having a silver, artificial tree when he was growing up while other families living in warmer houses had real ones.

During the Christmas holidays, Debbie spent time with Bobby to soothe her fears about separation. Zachary and Alysson became used to getting up at three in the morning and seeing what the world looked like at that time. Each morning, Zachary comforted his granddaughter during the coldest time of this twenty-four hour cycle people lived in.

They listened to the conversations of pilots and controllers try to maneuver planes through heavy traffic. While listening, Zachary told Alysson about his train rides and how the people aged over the years. Like himself.

After the hectic holiday commotion, Zachary pulled an already awake Alysson from her crib. The hurry of the holidays had gone and Bobby had returned to finish his last semester.

Alysson was not drinking her bottle and Zachary realized something was wrong. Unable to soothe the whimpering child who began to squirm uncomfortably, he carried her to Debbie's bedside. "I think she has a fever," Zachary said.

Debbie was quickly alert and she checked Alysson's forehead with the back of her hand, then her wrist. "I can't feel anything. There was too much excitement for her over the holidays. I hate it that people were going in and out. I still can't feel where she's warm. Are you sure?"

"Here," Zachary said bending down. He places his cheek to the infant's cheek. "You can tell like that."

Debbie immediately complied. "Yes, she is warm. Oh, my god. What'll we do?" Debbie stood up holding her baby close to her breasts. Her stance was the posture of action waiting for direction.

"Let's give her something cool to drink and call the doctor."

Debbie was already on the move toward the living room. Her long night dress flowed after her releasing a ghost like image as she passed through the shadowed rooms. She focused on reaching a phone in the living room. Zachary followed behind, taller than his daughter.

"I'll talk to the doctor. She's my baby. I don't know how I could have let this happen. What's the number? Never mind, it's in memory. What number did you make it?"

"One. You didn't do anything to make her sick."

"Shhh! It's ringing."

Debbie spoke hurriedly into the phone as she rocked Alysson in her arms. Zachary went to find the thermometer in the bathroom cabinet.

"All, right," Debbie commanded while marching back to her bedroom. "I think I know what to do." Zachary followed behind with a drink and the thermometer.

They complied with the doctor's wishes, they sat silently and tensely in Alysson's room waiting for results. The darkness and the situation held a silence between them. Slowly, Alysson's whimpers became rhythmic breathing. Eventually, the sun's orange glow peered through the pane glass windows and thin curtains to thrust away the night's darkness. Alysson slept peacefully in Debbie's lap absent of any flush look. In the child's quiet room, the crisis seemed over.

"Mom died so young. I don't want Alysson to lose me. I want to be there when she has children. Suppose I die and Alysson forgets who I am? What if I'm not there to help her take care of her sick child like this? Where is Bobby when I need him?" The remnants of her long hair went unstyled and drooped haphazardly across her head to touch the bristled ends on the sides.

A flash of high school memory brought to Zachary's mind the face of a boy who was Zachary's protector from childhood challenges. He saw the face brighten once into a smile, then he read the name on the Vietnam Memorial. He thought his brother would be there for him, but life bent in a different direction.

"There are too many turns of life to think about them all. You haven't forgotten your mother, I won't forget you and Alysson won't forget us. That's immortality."

"I don't know if I can handle all this. I mean, there's too much to worry about. Suppose I forget something or do the wrong thing or just not know what to do?"

"Your mother wouldn't like you talking like that. Remember when she got you those mirror sunglasses and you thought you looked great?"

"Yeah, people couldn't see where I was looking and Mom didn't like that. I think she regretted buying them."

"I always told you where you were looking and you got angry and finally wouldn't wear them. But, it was your mother who told me where you looked."

"I never knew that. So, you two teamed up on me. But, both of you were always a team. I want to be a team. I want to be a family and there's so much I don't know. I'm glad Alysson is better. Thanks for your help."

"You'll learn what to do."

"I want to fix up the basement for Bobby and me to live in after he graduates. You'll have to help."

"We can carpet the garage and put in heat. It'll give you more room." A more permanent place, Zachary thought.

The day Bobby came home after graduation, he and Zachary worked on halving the home. The basement evolved and Zachary welcomed the change because it meant completion and acceptance of his daughter's new identity.

"The toilet has hung up again," Debbie shouted from upstairs.

"I replaced all the inside guts, but it still hangs up," Zachary told Bobby.

"The toilet is old," the Bobby said.

"That has nothing to do with the inside."

"If the outside is old, then any new parts inside will never work right. You can't put something new on the inside with the outside still old."

Bobby embarrassed Zachary sometimes.

The next day, Debbie had a party for Bobby's graduation. Almost everyone there was a friend from college days. The abounding youthful energy belied the tremor in each one that reality would soon mean looking for a job. Zachary watched this generation feed off each other searching for comfort and support. Too soon, changes in their lives would consume their energy.

On the fringes of this youthfulness, Debbie contentedly held Alysson in her lap while talking to her friends about responsibility. Bobby's dark blue graduation cap sat in her lap, too. Zachary watched his granddaughter try to put Bobby's tassel in her mouth. The scenery made Zachary move outside to the porch to get away from young strangers populating his house.

The fresh air filled his face like an oxygen mask filled an asthmatic lung. Zachary opened his eyes wide letting the air bringing tears to his sight. He turned to look through a pane glass window and saw Debbie washing her baby's bottle at the kitchen sink. The image was fractured by wooden strips which sectioned off the glass. In the right corner of the view, a vase of flowers sprouted blue, thin stems of plant life that reached upward.

Baby in a Box: Jesus and Two Marys
by Larry Turner

Unable to conceal him any longer, she got a rush basket for him, made it watertight with pitch and tar, laid him in it, and placed it among the reeds by the bank. Exodus 2:3

Recently I realized that among all the stories about the baby Jesus, there is none about his rescue by being put in a box and placed in the water. Moses, Romulus and Remus, Mordred, even Superman: Each has such a story, but not Jesus. As my own gift to the holy babe this Christmas, I offer this one to add to the many others, each with its own explanation of how it came about he was raised in Nazareth, yet born in Bethlehem.

Cradling her son in her arms, Mary was among the first to see the man approach Bethlehem. Some noticed that his expensive clothing was soaked in sweat. Others recognized him as a Bethlehem native and observed he had gained weight while serving in Herod's court in Jerusalem. Why was such an important man running in the afternoon heat? He entered the village and halted. Twice he opened his mouth to speak, then stopped to breathe. Finally he called to the gathering crowd, "Friends, we are in danger here."

The gathering crowd murmured in surprise. He caught his breath, then spoke in his normal voice. "About a month ago, three men came riding into Jerusalem from the East. They said they were looking for a child who was born King of the Jews. Folks soon told them there was no newborn king in Jerusalem, and they had better leave as quickly as they had come. The last thing Herod should hear about was a rival king."

The messenger did not know the further adventures of those three wise men. They never found the king they sought. They never again saw the star they had followed. Soon they began arguing with one another and split up. But I will tell you this right now: No one who follows God's plan, as they had, will be disappointed at journey's end.

The visitor continued, "Not much happens in Jerusalem that doesn't come to King Herod's attention, and soon he learned of the strangers seeking an infant king. He called in the scribes and demanded an explanation. In the scroll of the prophets the scribes found that Micah had predicted the expected king was to be born in Bethlehem.

"Herod flew into a rage and said that unless you people of Bethlehem give up this king to him, he will kill all your children. His troops will be here in the morning to seize the baby and take him to Herod."

His listeners turned to one another in dismay. No one knew anything about a king, but they did know they had to do something, and soon. One of the village elders spoke. "It is better that one should die for all. But who?"

A swell of voices rose, then a man whom Mary recognized shouted, "If someone has to be sacrificed, let it be that bastard son of the unwed mother." The crowd turned their eyes to Mary. Many murmured agreement.

Mary felt as though a sword had pierced her heart. But what could she do? Not even her own family had spoken up for her son. She disappeared into her room with the baby. Eventually her terror dissipated and, fortified by prayer, she began to make plans. There were many stories in the holy scriptures of how God had saved children in peril. She could hide her baby somewhere outside the village. Hadn't God's prophet said, "The nursing child shall play over the hole of the asp, and the weaned child shall put its hand on the adder's den"? No, that was to be in the days when the Messiah came. Then she remembered the baby Moses, and how his mother had saved him. Mary prepared a wooden box, waterproofed it as best she could, and hid it. Long after everyone else had gone to sleep, she slipped out of the village with her child and the box. She would place him in one of the streams that flowed to the Dead Sea during that season. Unless—in some way—something would occur to allow her to remain together with her son.

Not long after Mary had gone, another man entered Bethlehem, the brother of the earlier visitor and, like him, serving in Herod's court. He pounded on doors and roused everyone. "Herod is angrier than ever and has changed his plans. Now he is not satisfied with one baby, but is going to kill all the boys in the village two years old or younger. You must flee and save your children."

Somehow or other, those eleven other children survived; one couple of means even took their entire family and moved to faraway Egypt. In any case, when Herod's troops arrived in the morning, the children were gone. Their leader knew better than to admit failure to Herod, so he went back, pointed to his sword and reported, "Not one boy under the age of two remains alive in the village."

Meanwhile, around dawn the sorrowful Mary came upon a band of men. Could these provide a way she could keep her son? No, they were shepherds, about to move to the mountain pastures for the season. That night they had killed and eaten a lamb. Mary told them what she was about to do. One shepherd looked disdainfully at the box and said, "In that box? You might just as well place him in a manger and throw that in the stream."

Another was more helpful. He wrapped Mary's child in the lambskin and sealed the box with fat from the lamb. None of the shepherds thought she should put the box in the nearby stream. Although it was running, its course twisted, the water was shallow, and the box was likely to run aground. Several shepherds offered to accompany her to the sea, where she could set the box afloat. One shepherd, trying to encourage her, remarked that the Essenes in Qumran might find the boy and raise him in their community. Although some say that is indeed what happened, we shall see that a better fate awaited Mary's son.

Mary waded into the sea and lowered the box to the water. She released it and then returned to the shore. As she watched the box drift off in the sea, Mary fell down in tears, knowing she would never see her son again. Never. She tried to pray, but her heart was too heavy.

Young Matthew was sitting on the shore of the Dead Sea, where the Jordan flowed into it. He often came here to escape; his mother was sure to find chores for him if he stayed home. He could sit for hours watching the fresh water of the Jordan spread out over the salty water of the sea. Today he saw a wooden box swirling with the eddies. Around and around it circled, and then he saw something he had never seen before. An unseasonable south wind sprang up. As if deliberately, it pushed the box into the Jordan and upstream while Matthew watched in wonder. How could something rise from the Dead Sea?

Grace radiated from that box as the baby sailed up the river: a daughter reconciling with her mother, food appearing for starving children, a young worker suddenly healed of his wound.

Another Mary, middle-aged and barren, walked along the shore of another sea, the Sea of Galilee. Her husband, the carpenter Joseph, noticed her drooping shoulders, her dead footsteps. Her blank face looked as if all joy, all hope had been sucked out of her. He sighed. He had hoped that accompanying him on this trip to Capernaum from their home in Nazareth might divert Mary from the constant sadness that had shrouded her for months, ever since her cousin Elizabeth, almost sixty, had announced that she was pregnant. Many years before, Mary had walled off the part of herself meant to hold a mother's love, a mother's care. Inevitability had led to acceptance; acceptance had led to forgetting. Now Elizabeth's news had broken down that wall. Elizabeth was older than Mary. Why had God placed an infant in Elizabeth's womb? Why not hers?

As they walked, she imagined holding an infant to her breast, and then imagined a baby playing, running in her home. She could almost hear a child's cry. Suddenly she realized a real baby was crying nearby. The sound was coming from where the water lapped the shore. Looking down, she saw a box drifting ashore close to where they were standing. With a quickness in her step that had been absent for months, she hurried toward the water with Joseph following. She waded into the sea, grasped the box, picked it up and returned to the shore. She opened it. Her hands reached in and touched something soft. Mary pulled it out. There was a baby, wrapped in a lambskin.

Her arms trembling, she clasped the young boy. He looked up at her as she rocked him gently to and fro. "Jesus," she whispered. "His name shall be Jesus, for he will save me from my life of despair." Her eyes filled with tears as she prayed, "The Lord has looked with favor on his servant, lowly as she is. The mighty God has done great things for me."

The Substance of Youth
by David Mitchell

It's heard at night in bedtime tales
Told on bunk bed ships with bed sheet sails
That sail along fantastic streams
And come to port inside your dreams

It's commonplace in tree house castles
Where puckish lords rule impish vassals
And overtly theatrical barefoot knights
Can save the damsel by play swordfights

It's a beverage served in little teacups
To teddy bear guests and cute wag-tail pups
By little girls in frilly white dresses
In training to become future princesses

It can be found inside old attic chests
And inside the pockets of grandfather vests
It's available for free yet more precious than gold
But gets harder to see once you grow old

The Birds and the Bees
by Larry Turner

"I have a real surprise for you after breakfast, Jonathon. Aunt Catherine and Uncle Jeff have gone to Chicago for a wedding. Scamp and the cats will be okay alone overnight, but Aunt Catherine brought their new ducklings over for us to watch."

Breakfast seemed to take forever. When it was finally over, Jonathon ran to the garage. The car had been moved outside to make way for ducklings—as well as for a wire pen, straw, food and water bowls, and two heat lamps. He stood and stared at the dozen fluffy ducklings for nearly an hour, then dragged his rocking chair from the house to the garage and rocked and watched them some more until his mother called him in for lunch.

"Mommy, I've got a question. I've seen how ducklings get out of the eggs on TV, but how do they get in?"

Choosing her words carefully, his mother answered. "A mother duck lays the eggs. Most of them are just ordinary eggs, the kind we eat for breakfast. But some are special eggs, and baby ducks grow in them while the mother duck sits on them to keep them warm. Then later for more warmth Aunt Catherine puts them under a lamp."

"What makes those eggs special?"

"The father duck pollinates them."

"The father duck pollinates just the ones that are special?"

"Kind of. They are special because the father duck pollinates them."

Back in the garage, he sat in his rocker, watching the ducklings, and thinking about what his mother had said. He knew that for fruit to grow on the fruit trees and for squash and melons to grow in the garden, the bees had to pollinate the plants. He tried to picture the father duck hovering above the eggs to pollinate them, but he couldn't imagine it.

But it was easy to imagine the mother duck sitting on the eggs to keep them warm. When his mother came to check on him, he shared his thought. "So the mother is more important than the father."

She thought of the long days her husband spent on the road, often arriving home long after Jonathon had gone to bed. "Yes, sometimes that's so."

"When I grow up," he said, "I'm going to be a mother."

Best Friends Forever

by Donna H. Turner

"I don't know, Mrs. Daniel. We were digging for worms. That's why I had the hoe in my hand. I was using it to dig with. While I dug, Teddy was picking them up and putting the worms inside our soup can. That's when it happened. It's not my fault. Tell them, Mama, it's not my fault. Teddy is my best friend. I wouldn't hurt him on purpose." Everyone looked at Billy without saying a word. "Teddy, you tell them, it wasn't my fault. Wake up, Teddy. You know I wouldn't hurt you on purpose." Billy's voice was shaking and rising in pitch.

Alice Pendergrass bent down and put her arms around Billy. "It's all right, baby, Mama's here. We know you didn't do it on purpose. Muriel and John, I'm so sorry this happened. I know you need to get Teddy to the hospital, but please let us know what we can do to help."

With all the Daniels in his Chevy, Mr. Reddington set out for the emergency room. Everyone else was left standing where they were. No one said a word. As the group watched the car move off, people started drifting away to go about their business. Soon there was no one left except Alice and Billy. She held him in her arms and rocked him back and forth, trying to comfort him.

"Mama, will the cops fry me?"

"What? Where did you ever hear talk like that?"

"That's what Mr. Johns told us when he came to talk to our class. He said that is what they did to kids who get in trouble. I'm in big trouble, aren't I?"

"Sweetheart, that is not going to happen. I think Mr. Johns was trying to scare you. Who is Mr. Johns anyway?"

"He's in charge of detention after school. Only the bad kids go to him. I don't want to be there. He might send someone like me to the electric chair." At this point Billy began sobbing uncontrollably. "Mama, am I really that bad? Don't let him take me, please. I'll be good, I promise. Is Teddy going to be okay? We were just pretending the hoe was a sword. We were both playing and taking turns. On my third try, Teddy didn't get out of the way soon enough and that's how he was hit. Why was there so much blood, Mama?"

"Sweetheart, I know. It's a scary thing to see all the blood coming from Teddy's cheek."

"I'd like to go home, Mama. I want a glass of chocolate milk and maybe a cookie from yesterday. If Teddy comes home from the hospital, maybe we can take cookies for him. He always liked your cookies."

"That's a splendid idea. I'll call Mrs. Daniel and make arrangements. Billy, I know you didn't hurt Teddy on purpose. The Daniels and Teddy know it as well. But you do have to be careful with tools of any kind. Let's go home, son, there are goodies just for the eating."

"Yeah, I'm ready, Mama."

The Daniels arrived at the Pleasant Community Hospital emergency room. Dr. Oslo, one of the emergency room doctors, cleaned the cut to see how deep and wide it was. It turned out to be a fairly small cut on his cheek. The doctor placed ice on it to stop the bleeding.

"You are lucky, son. You are the very first person to have stitches today. Once we do that, you can go home."

"Will it hurt? Will it take long?" As Teddy touched his cheek, a little blood came off onto his hand. "Will the stitches stop it from bleeding?"

"My, you certainly have a lot of questions. Stitches are just like your mother's embroidery thread. They help hold the skin together until it heals. No, it doesn't hurt very much. Do you know the X and O game? It's something like that. First, though, I'll spray the injured skin so you won't feel it. Besides that, I'll tell your mom you can eat as much ice cream as you want. It will help your cheek feel better. What do you think of that?"

"Yum, I love ice cream. As much as I want?"

"You bet. You'll be fine no matter how much you eat. It will help the cheek feel cold, and that makes it feel better. Before we begin, I'm going to tell you what I'm doing so you'll know. First comes the spray." The doctor sprayed Teddy's hand. "See, that didn't hurt, did it?" Teddy looked at the doctor warily. "You won't feel it anymore on your cheek than you did on your hand. I told you it would feel cold. Now, I'm all done with the spray.

"The next thing we'll do is put in a couple of stitches. You might need a little more cold spray first." As he spoke, he sprayed the cut again. "Now we're ready to stitch. See, I take a little of the thread, and before you know it, we'll be finished. It will only be uncomfortable for a minute or so."

Large tears started to fall as Teddy said, "It does hurt a little."

"I know it's uncomfortable, but it's not terrible. Anyway, I'm finished. That wasn't so bad. Here's a chance to see what you look like." He held up a mirror for Teddy to see his cheek. "Now the only thing left to do is to put a clean band aid on it, and you're good to go home." The doctor opened the curtain around Teddy as his parents came in to see what had been done.

"Teddy was so strong and brave, I told him it would help to eat as much ice cream as he wants."

Mrs. Daniel helped Teddy off the table. "So it's as much ice cream as you want?"

"Yep, Mom, and you know what, I didn't cry at all. Well, almost. I have stitches under the band aid, and they're like little X's. Let's go to Billy's house and show him my stitches."

"Maybe not today, but certainly tomorrow," Dr. Oslo said. "Why don't you go home today and see your friend tomorrow"

"That's a good idea. On the way home we can stop and buy your ice cream. If you feel like it, you can watch your favorite program. Why don't you go see Daddy while I talk to the doctor."

"Okay, Mom. Bye, Doctor. If I ever need stitches again, I hope you can do them."

Back home again, the phone rang. Mrs. Daniel called Alice and Billy to visit Teddy the next day. Alice was relieved to know that Teddy would be fine. She accepted the invitation and offered to bring chocolate chip cookies. Alice and Billy spent the afternoon making cookies.

Next day they drove to Teddy's house, and while Muriel and Alice talked over coffee in the kitchen, Billy and Teddy played in the family room.

The first thing Teddy did was to show Billy his stitches—and give a blow by blow description of what the doctor had done.

"Wow, didn't it hurt?"

"No. I didn't even cry; at least not very much."

"I didn't mean to hurt you, I'm really sorry it happened."

"I know you didn't do it on purpose, Billy, but when I saw all the blood I got scared."

"I did, too. I thought you were gonna die and the police would come and take me to the electric chair. Besides that, you're my very best friend. I would never want to hurt you."

"My mom told me all that, and I promised I wouldn't use the hoe for a sword anymore."

"Boy, me either. We can still be best friends can't we? I mean forever. Let's do our magic handshake to make sure it comes true. Clap two times, touch your nose and think about chocolate chip cookies. Let's go get some real cookies. My Mom and I made them yesterday just for you."

"Great idea, Billy. Hey Mom, can we have some of those chocolate chip cookies now?'

Closer to Scratch

by R. L Russis

People don't appreciate our ease of means today,
of being able to flip a switch or turn round a dial
to get the heat to start or bring cold water to boil
for coffee or tea, without the use of wood or coal.
But, it wasn't so long ago for me, even if it seems
like a lifetime to you, hot water could only come
from off the stove and only after the wood or coal
had caught and built a flame, a cheery, cherry glow.
You kids only know from stories, but me, I know
firsthand how that was, how some chores never did
seem to end, how just when finished it was once more
time to begin them again. And Ma kept me busy
feeding the woodstove at one end, the woodpile
at the other, those chores filling my days the full year
long, and not only for winter's luxury of warmth
against the cold, but for every meal Ma ever made,
and always made from scratch.

Memorare

by Elaine J. Gooding

Once upon a time, I was a little Catholic girl. Now you might ask, "What's with the 'once upon a time' introduction? That's for fairy tales." Well, to my way of thinking, at least in the beginning, it was kind of a fairy tale: very distinct good and evil, and definite consequences. That was before Vatican II began mucking up the waters. At least I didn't add. "... long, long ago." Fifty years isn't that long ago. Is it?

My mother, being a good Irish Catholic, and my father, being an Italian Catholic, determined to send me to Catholic school. My big sister was already in the second grade at St. Agnes Elementary School.

Everyone knows private schools have uniforms. Popular for girls was the white blouse and jumper, usually plaid and pleated. Ours was a green, gray and white plaid, with a goofy soufflé-type hat. (If you forgot to wear your hat on Fridays, Mass day, you had to wear a handkerchief bobby-pinned to your head.) An easily lost item of the uniform was the clip-on ribbon bow tie. It would get buried and crinkled in my top dresser drawer. Anklet socks, following fashion dictates, eventually became knee socks, with elastic that wore out quickly with washing, and had to be held up with rubber bands. Shoes were the only item that weren't passed down. Every year, Mom would take us to Dannon's Shoe Store, where Mr. Dannon would fit us with sturdy, new Buster Brown oxfords. By eighth grade these had morphed into the classic black-and-white saddle shoes.

Now picture me. My too-cool second grade sister, drags me by the hand, and without so much as a backward glance, catapults my little freckled-face curly head through the door of Room 1-A.

Sister Marie Amatius yelled, "Name? Fourth row, seventh seat!"

I had met my first drill sergeant. Looking back, I realize why this woman had to establish order quickly, in a classroom packed with 50 munchkins who hadn't sat in one place longer than a half-hour Lassie show on TV. No lie. Fifty.

"Sister..."
"Raise your hand."
"But, Sister..."
"Raise your hand!"
"Is it lunchtime?"
"Sit down."
"I have to go to the bathroom."
"Sit down!"

Sister Marie Amatius was tall. To a six-year-old, any adult looks tall, but the black and white habit—nuns didn't wear uniforms—accentuated her height. The black veil was raised up in front about four inches by a stiff white cardboard thing (I don't know what the real name for it was) that started just above the eyebrows. Rosary beads the size of acorns hung from the black belt, and probably could have been used as a bicycle lock. St. Agnes School was staffed by Dominican nuns, and a handful of lay teachers. In high school, where I encountered the addition of Immaculate Heart of Mary nuns in navy blue and black, I learned that Sisters came in penguin and blue jay varieties. Dominican nuns, long, long ago, also wore a white cap that tightly covered all the head and neck area except the face from the eyebrows to the chin.

"Sister, do you have ears?"
"Raise your hand."

About three months into the school year, Theresa Pendleton transferred to our school. Her desk was jammed in the back corner of 1-A, almost in the coat closet and halfway out the door. By that time, Sister Marie Amatius had already tied twin cherubs to their desks. Attention deficit hyperactivity disorder hadn't been identified as yet, and Joey and Angela McCullough were constantly up at her desk garnering more attention from the class than Sister was. It was a matter of survival of the species—teacher over students.

Various classroom duties for students were: line leader, classroom monitor, window opener, and eraser cleaner. The first is rather self-explanatory and a prized role. The second duty, classroom monitor, was coveted even more. When Sister left the room, which a teacher could be fired for today, the room monitor stood guard. The best part of the job was that you got to report anyone who talked or got out of his seat. Getting sent to the Principal's office was a crime, the news of which quickly spread through the school during recess.

The window opener had a job worthy of a circus acrobat. One wall of the second-floor room was all windows, above the radiator. Unlocking and opening or closing these windows was done with the aid of a long pole with a hook on the end. Watching a first grader wield that pole would have struck fear in the heart of any mother, had she but known.

Finally, at the end of the day, the eraser cleaner had to hang out the window and bang the erasers together. It's a wonder we never lost anybody. Occasionally, though, an eraser would get dropped, warranting a mad dash by the culprit to retrieve it and get back in time without missing the school bus.

St. Agnes students, as alluded to earlier, walked down the street to church every Friday morning for confession and Mass. Since a first grader had to be properly prepared for First Confession and First Communion, Sister Marie Amatius had a lot to accomplish with us. We had to learn quick and accurate responses to the clicker. Each teacher had a clicker, which was concealed somewhere on her person (I don't think I ever actually saw one). One click, genuflect. Two clicks, sit. I guess the training was somewhat akin to dog training, without the treats.

Catholics usually genuflect—go down on one knee—prior to entering the pew. If every child in the school did that, we'd still be there genuflecting. Instead, the whole class would file into the pews, remain standing until we heard the click, genuflect together, and then sit after two clicks. It was probably three clicks to stand up again when the priest came in, and then . . . who could keep track after that? Sit down, stand up, kneel (heel?). Without that clicker, a first grader could really get lost, what with the priest speaking in Latin, and all.

Most everyone knows that wooden rulers in school had three uses. The first, and least important, was for measuring. The second, and very important, was to aid in drawing straight lines for neat columns and underlining. Many were the papers I had to redo on account of neatness, or more precisely, the lack there of. The third, and most important use, was for discipline. Some rulers were actually thin enough that they'd break when applied to the knuckles by an avenging nun. Plastic rulers must have been designed by a kinder, gentler, former Catholic school student. But

Riverside Writers 121

woe is the poor student whose parent spent the extra money to provide a ruler that would last forever--the metal one. And this was no measly simple metal ruler, but a three-sided, triangular one. I'm sure it was designed by Sister Attila the Hun!

In second grade, we had Mrs. McKenna. She was a sweet lady who made it her aim to help us recover from the trauma of first grade. God bless Mrs. McKenna. Third grade—a lay teacher again! But, Mrs. Kelly wasn't a sweetheart. She was tough, which actually turned out to be a good thing. Otherwise, our class might have suffered group early-onset heart failure on reaching fourth grade: Sister Anthony Marie.

Could she ever yell. At recess, kids from other classes would say they heard her down the hall in their rooms, through two closed doors! When Sister yelled, I think the force, combined with the restrictive head gear, put pressure in her carotid artery and her face turned beet red. Perhaps she felt she had to yell so much because she was small in stature? I suppose we gave her ample other reasons for her tirades.

One of them, I'm sorry to say, was ethnic. Pretty much the same fifty kids were together that had begun in my first grade class: McDonough, McElroy, O'Brien, O'Toole— a lot of Irish, and a fair amount of Italians. I was a mutt—half Irish, half Italian. On the subject of names, let me digress.

Amongst Catholics back then, it was common practice to name your child after a saint. Our class had at least four Johns, two James, Andrew, Timothy, and so on. For girls there were Marys, Maries, Mary Anne, Mary Jo, Mary Ellen, Catherines, Christines, Angela and Elizabeth. Who names their kid "Elaine," I want to know?! Not a very common name. Greek, in fact. Tell me my mother wasn't a rebel underneath all her Catholic propriety!

Okay, back in fourth grade, we had a racial problem. An African-American was introduced into St. Agnes Elementary, in our class. Her name was Macquelline Hampton. Probably she was a nice girl underneath, but she didn't stand a chance with that name. I could no longer complain about mine, that's for sure. Macquelline was tall, large-boned, strong, and mean. She shoved me out of line into the street one day on the way to church, for no reason that I can remember. I do remember having fingernail scratches on my wrists from her. She scared the living daylights out of me. Maybe, in a different time, we could have been friends.

I had been the butt of teasing for how skinny I was, and because my pretty curls had begun to get a frizzy look. Macquelline was teased because she was alien to our all-white world, and it made her a bully.

One day, during recess, one of the boys sneaked back into the classroom and placed a box on Macquelline's seat. Inside the box was a frog. When we returned to the room, Macquelline opened the box and screamed bloody murder. After her mother came and raised a ruckus in the Principal's office . . . well you know the old saying, "sh__ rolls downhill?" Sister Anthony let loose on us.

Fifth grade. Mrs. Bingle. Confirmation was the highlight of the year. We studied about the Holy Ghost and Pentecost, and knelt in front of the bishop so he could slap our cheeks. I don't mean to sound irreverent. At the time, it was a very special event in my life.

Sixth grade, we finally were blessed with Sister St. Augustus as a teacher. I had spent some younger recesses with other little kids gathered under her cloak like chicks, smelling the freshly ironed scent of her habit, and clinging to her wide black, leather belt. If I learned anything from that woman, it was love. Sister was every bit as tall as first grade's Sister Marie Amatius, but built wider, with shoulders like a football player. She had the large, warm eyes of a St. Bernard dog, and the heart of one to match. A gentle giant. Desks and chairs were welded together in one piece, back then, and Sister would sometimes lift a child up, desk and chair, too, just to make us laugh! She was hardly ever without a smile. I would yearn for those carefree days years later, when I caught a glimpse of her unawares, in a place of depression. Perhaps it was Vatican II that put her there, I wonder now, in retrospect.

Change can be a scary thing. Knowing that, and wanting to ease the transition to high school for us, administrators at St. Agnes Elementary School required that seventh and eighth graders change classes. Grab your stack of books, binders, and other paraphernalia, and move to the room across the hall, or next door. It was a good idea, but that wasn't the only change. The school had grown, and we now had four classes of seventh graders, and four of eighth graders. Someone wasn't satisfied with having us move between four rooms. The class rosters were shuffled, so that we were no longer with the same 50 kids we'd grown up with from first grade! Talk about shock! When we graduated eighth grade in 1967, and received our diplomas, the diploma books had cute little pictures of 50 kids we hardly even knew.

The baby-boomer generation had swelled our grade school and caused four new Catholic high schools to be built on Long Island. Deciding I was tired of being known as my older sister's baby sister, I did a rash thing, and opted out of St. Agnes High School. I went instead to one of the new diocesan high schools, Maria Regina D.H.S.

Wow! Two kinds of nuns. Wow! A long-haired hippie teacher in the music department and another in an English class about Mass Media (not the church Mass). This school was all about liberal arts and liberal thinking. They still had a religion class, so it couldn't be all bad. But wait! Sister says the miracles of Jesus were easily explained by natural phenomenon. What? I'm not feeling so well. You mean they weren't miracles? And I believed it? By the way, those sins you were worried about growing up, they're not really sins. And here come the changes of Vatican II.

Vatican II was a meeting in Rome among 2500 bishops, cardinals and the pope, mainly for the purpose of bringing the Catholic Church out of the Stone Ages. It took place from 1962 to 1965, while I was in grade school. Two years went into planning it, and it was two years after it closed before it began to change what Catholics had taken for granted for years. While its influence was worldwide, I can only speak to how it affected my life.

I take two years of Latin, and I'm finally starting to understand the priest, and they switch to English! The altar is turned around so I don't have to look at the priest's back the whole time, but I have to participate and respond, in English. Where's the mystique, and the incense that makes your stomach queasy on a hot day? And all the nuns' pretty saints' names are changed to their real names. And their habits are shortened and you can see their hair now! The Latin nun, who looked like a Scandinavian movie star, left the convent and married the football coach. For real! I kid you not. "I feel the earth move under my feet..." and "the times, they are a-changin'."

After high school, I was lost almost 25 years. Went to college. Went home. Went to college. Went home. Joined the

Marines. Got married. Had children. Went to college. Retired from the military. Taught school. Questioned. Cried. Searched. Prayed. Cried. Tried. Failed.

And one day, Jesus showed me. He called me and I answered. And the hole in my heart that was shaped like Him was filled. By Him. And I found answers. In the Bible. And I'm not a little Catholic girl. I'm a Christian. And my story ends ... happily, ever after.

The Oasis

by Tracy Deitz

Laughing children stampede into turquoise sea
of suburbia, splashing as soon as the whistle
beckons a welcome,
armed with hot pink floaties,
a sun-kissed girl
buoys her smile
white sleek seals
surface goofy goggles
one, two, three impromptu ballet
leap over ledge chlorinated lagoon
pruney soles wave from upturned feet
channel marking underwater handstand
parent sentinels draped on hibiscus towels
littles porpoising below "Marco Polo"
honor the Venetian merchant
who traveled Asia for 24 years—
his name traversing
North America centuries later

Lifeguard sphinx burnished back
black shades inscrutable gaze
twirls key ring round and round
freckled Doc Holliday spurs flippers
loads ammo into mighty bazooka
Wyatt Earp missing front tooth sneaks up alley
barrage fired only casualty an adult sunning
watch where you squirt O.K. Corral gang giggles
so does my skin newly christened in
summer's sauna teased by a cool breeze.

A Gift of Grace
by Donna H. Turner

As a young girl of eleven, I began volunteering at our church two or three times a week. I didn't do anything spectacular—mostly folding bulletins, putting on stamps and sorting weekly newsletters. I worked alongside a seventy-year-old woman named Grace Frauens. While we worked, we talked about our lives: Grace about her lifetime of teaching nursing; me about my eleven-year life.

One afternoon, Grace invited me to lunch at her home the following Saturday. I accepted, and arrived at noon. Her tiny apartment said welcome, from the fresh flowers in a vase to the white ironed linen cloth over her hope chest as a makeshift table. Matching china held the food she had prepared. To this day I still remember the red tomato filled with chicken salad on a green lettuce leaf. The plate was accented with ripe cantaloupe and blueberries. I had never seen anything as beautiful.

This lovely elegance contrasted with the PB&J sandwich I normally had for lunch every day. It never occurred to me to use a plate or sit down at the table to eat lunch. Most days I ate my sandwich on the way back to school so I could go into the library early and read books of fairy tales.

I realized sometime later that this lunch was the first time I had ever been formally invited to anything. Grace saw me, a kid from a low-rent housing development with a chaotic home life, as a person with possibilities. Further, she helped me see myself as a person with possibilities. What a gift of grace!

Fishing with My Dad

by Norma E. Redfern

The year I started fifth grade, my mother and I moved to Fort Richardson, Alaska, with my dad, a warrant officer in the army. There I saw two things for the first time: snow and the Aurora Borealis. Snow was wonderful, fluffy and soft like clouds, white and clean. On clear winter nights, I could look up and see the Aurora Borealis shimmering like satin ribbons and dancing across the sky in cascading colors of blue, red, green and purple. It's a sight I will never forget.

When the weather was warm enough, Daddy and I spent weekends camping and fishing on the Kenai River. One spring weekend, while we went fishing, we ran out of the trout eggs we were using for bait. I pulled the stringer of fish out of the water and selected a nice fat rainbow trout. I took her off the stringer, slit open her belly and stripped out the eggs. Now it was time to put the stringer of fish back in the river. But the stringer was so heavy with fish—each trout had to be at least twenty-seven inches long—that the whole thing slipped through my fingers. Six fish, gone! The water was freezing cold. Patches of ice lined both banks. Still, I had no choice. I jumped in, clothes and all, found the stringer of fish, and brought them back to shore. Daddy didn't know whether to laugh or yell, so he carried me to the car, got me out of those wet clothes, and wrapped me in an old army blanket.

Another of our trips didn't go as well. It was one of the few times in my life I was left speechless.

On a Friday evening in summer we went fishing. In an Alaska summer it stays light well into the night. We set up our campsite along the Kenai River. The river was about forty feet across at that point and, though not rapids, moved at a good steady flow. Anxious to be fishing, we rose early on Saturday. After Daddy made breakfast, he stowed the extra food in a specially designed pack and tied it high in a tree so as not to attract animals.

We had to hike a short way to an eddy where fish rested and lay low in the water to feed. We fished for some time, and landed several rainbow and Dolly Varden trout. By then our bait was running low, so Daddy sent me back to camp after the fish eggs we used. I found the jar and was skipping back down the path to where my daddy waited.

That was when I heard something I couldn't quite place. Birds flew out of trees, and the woods grew silent. A crashing sound came from my right. I stood stock-still and listened, just as Daddy had always told me to do when we were in the wilderness and heard strange noises. Looking around and listening hard, I decided something was coming toward me.

Just at that moment a large brown bear emerged from the woods. I stood my ground. The bear stood up and glared at me. He looked at me; I looked at him. I swear he was huge, at least six feet tall. His fur was the color of a piece of butterscotch candy, but matted in places. He smelled terrible, like wet dog on a hot day. We stood about four feet apart.

It was a warm day, but I shivered as an ice cold chill covered my body, as if I were caught in a snowstorm and unable to find my way. Fear crept through to my bones, overwhelming me with the urge to flee, but my feet were frozen in place. It seemed hours we stood there, neither one of us moving. Then the bear turned, ambled into the water and swam to the other side. I stood there for a while, too petrified to move. When I did, I ran as fast as I could to where my dad was still fishing.

All my life, I've been a talker, but now in front of my dad, nothing–and I mean not one sound–would come out of my mouth. I was so scared, I must have scared him. He kept asking, "what's the matter?" but I couldn't make a sound. That's when it happened: I peed in my pants. I started to shake so hard and cry so loudly that Daddy took me back to the car and packed up camp. Once we were on the road home, I was able to tell him about the bear—and that I didn't want to go fishing again, at least not on the Kenai River.

These and many other memories came rushing back to me in October 2002 when I got the news my father had had a car accident driving home from Wilmington. My sons and I took turns going to the hospital and staying with my mother. Early in December I went down for the last time. He was no longer able to breathe for himself; a machine forced air into his lungs in a vain effort to keep him alive.

I'm so grateful I was with him when he died, able to hold his hand as he took his last breath. I hope he could feel how I felt;

it meant the world to me to be with him. When he could no longer breathe, I rose from my chair, kissed his forehead and called for the nurse.

Daddy's passing left a big dark hole in my world that nothing, not even children of my own, could ever fill. I sought comfort in my memories: Daddy's kindness, integrity, and devotion to his family. He always held my hand when we went places together, even after I was married. I found solace in the countless hugs and other expressions of his love for me. There is no greater joy than knowing you are truly loved.

At Twelve
by R. L Russis

The well handle that at first I couldn't well-reach,
then couldn't pull down, then having pulled down,
couldn't push back up to pump the water, to force
a flow from deep below to fill our garden's pails,
that same pump, at twelve, I was able to stroke
with new-found ease and I found it a simple thing
to swing the head of the axe around, to bring it
down and through the blocks of wood last year
I could only saw to size and pile for Pop to split.
My spring's sprint in growth came just in time
for winter's chores – that sudden two inch spurt
giving me extra height and adding girth about my
shoulders, building a weight, a mass of muscle
leaving me strong and lending me able to do
much more than possible mere months before.
And Pa and I, in the little window of time before
or after supper, would whittle away at that pile
of logs and cut and split and stack the needed
cords to keep our little house and family warm
against the winter's cold, those coming storms.

Favored Sayings—and Sage Advice

by R. L Russis

"Overcome by events," I imagined you saying,
"too little time, too many chores." I heard it
as if you were here, leaning over my shoulder,
still offering me advice for how or why… of
what to do – or not – and ending with, "Now,
make your choice and live with it." You never
told me what to do, instead pointing out how
there were options, sometimes, if one looked
close enough; and how, sometimes, even with
options, there was only a single choice a man
could make, and you always let me make it.
You taught me how to see what lay beneath
a thing, made me mindful to give scrutiny
to the obvious, as well as to complex things,
to take nothing for granted, but freely assume
obligations I knew to be mine and to always
shoulder the fault, while sharing the credit.
They were good words, sound lessons, and
fair rules to live by – and I have, Pa, I have.

Yo, Paper Boy

by Mr. Kelly Patterson

Hello, I'm your paper boy.
Morning paper…, fat and thick.
I'll pitch it on your front porch,
Or anywhere you like.

I'm not like the other kids,
Living life in style.
When two in the morning comes around,
I am pitching papers in the quarters.

Fifteen dollars is the best money I have made.
My paper route frequently feeds us.
I collect on Saturday and go to church on Sunday.
Early Monday morning, it starts over again.

Eleven years old. I'm head of the house
When Dad is gone.
Dad fights for the American Way.
He fights with Mom.

Sometime Mom takes my paper route money.
She needs something. I don't say a word.
What the heck, I have plenty of time.
A boy delivering newspapers.

Do the job well or not all!
Ragged white boy on a bicycle.
Warning of danger from the quarters.
Nothing new, I deliver anyway.

My old Hawthorn bike has three wire baskets,
Sunday papers make it hard to pedal.
I know where the mean dog's live.
Little guy…big business. I handle cash.

Best Paper Boy in New Orleans!
Nice award but no extra cash.
Add it up,
Daily Paper, ten cents; Sunday, thirty. "Ninety cents please!"

A hundred and fifty customers. My cut is thirteen-fifty.
A new tire on the back once in a while and
Sometime a new chain are my expenses.
I pedal two hundred miles a week.

My boss gives me an extra Sunday paper for Mom.
I sell it at the pool room.
Leon's Store…, he lives above it. I deliver up there too.
Leon pays me with a pack of Pall Mall cigarettes.

Frenchy's Bar sits on the street corner.
He say, "Boy, let me teach you something 'bout retail."
After he reads it, I get his Sunday paper back.
It's half price to Mrs. Ida Johnson. She's poor as me.

But I do Ok.
In a year or two I'll buy a scooter and double my customers.
I'm always tired, but you get use to it. I know hard work and
I know people. People is what it's about. It's all about people.

On Stephanie's 16th Birthday

by Laura R. Merryman

If these words live,
Then you live.
It's as simple as that.
Shakespeare's verse has no monopoly
On immortality.

And yet, my winter child
In a hundred years,
Nobody will care
That your eyes were blue,
Your body young and lithe;
Your mind quick to so many things;
Your life so new.

Nobody will care then.

But in this moment,
I celebrate the essence
That is you.

The first time I heard you
Mewing on my chest,
Chubby toes with knobby heels,
Your daddy driving a circuit
So you could fall asleep,
A stitched up knee,
A winning soccer goal,
First love, first heartbreak;
So many synchronicities bring you here.

You, 16, like a sonnet.
Me, like Whitman,
Singing the joy of this instant.

Our Animal Companions

Thwarted

by Tracy Deitz

All is not idyllic
in the backyard—
frenzied shrieking
indicates something's awry.

Outside the window
I see my husky mix
contemplating a baby bird
huddled on the ground.

Despite the odds,
eighty pounds to an ounce or so,
the fledgling opens its beak
imitating a fierce lion.

From above, the parent robins
scream their protests
to distract, buying a second or more.
I thump on the window and yell too.

Then run pell-mell down two flights of stairs
arriving at the crime scene breathless
I tell the dog, "No!"
She acts indignant.

I drag her away by the scruff.
She looks up as if to say,
"I'm only doing my job
getting rid of this intruder."

Leashed to me by the picnic table,
she eyes the fluff hopping about
trying to get its bearings
as the adults chirp encouragement.

Soon the drama subsides
when the little one gets
enough strength to flutter
above the fence.

I give the dog ice cubes
to chomp on,
my peace offering
for spoiling her fun.

After Fieldwork

by R. L Russis

In the days just after we'd cut the hay or tilled a field open
and planted our seed, we often saw the hawks slow-gliding,
wingtips barely moving, circling the thermals and whatever
hid beneath those narrowing spirals that always grew nearer
to ground and tighter in focus the longer those birds soared,
then ending in a sudden dive with an uplifted mouse or vole
or rabbit and sometimes even an unlucky cat that found itself
unexpectedly hunted and on the other, the underside of claw.

To Me It Was Magic
by R. L Russis

The first time I tried I grabbed two teats on a side.
Pa laughed while the cow shuffled her feet and mooed.
"Not like that," he said, "like this," as he took hold
of a teat on each side of her bag. "Grasp one towards
her horn and one towards her tail. Work both sides
at the same time. First pull the left, then pull the right,
but not too tight; go gentle, a light squeeze is all you
need to bring a stream of milk." Like yesterday to me,
his words, this sight, taking me back to ten, to when
he first taught me the magic for milking the cows.
How well I remember that tinny sound, the noisy way
those first few squirts struck bottom on empty pails
and how those same squirts became a gradual swish
and then a full-throated slurp, as their streams rose up,
as they climbed to the brims of our three-gallon pails.

Lady, King, Queenie, Max…

by R. L Russis

They were all just farm dogs, mixed-breeds mostly,
that became 'the boy's dog,' a guard dog, and, if
one was lucky, a damned-good hunting dog

and if one was unlucky, an egg-sucking dog.
And a dog that would suck an egg was one
that would eat a chicken, or so Pa said.

And those we raised for ourselves, Ma selling
their eggs and us eating their meat most Sundays.
And Pa seldom allowed for any second chances,
and none of the dogs ever got past their first.

No, he'd call them out behind the barn, tell them,
"Sit" and "Stay," beside a hole already dug –
and stay they did.

And after time wildflowers or grass would grow
and cover the once barren, brown patches
of their otherwise, unmarked graves.

For Ollie

by Laura R. Merryman

Along the abandoned trails we walk,
My shoes crunching against the loose gravel
The pads of his poodle paws silent.

There is joy and purpose in his lanky step,
The gait and artistry of a Cirque Du Soleil performer.
He keeps pace with me as I sing,
"Mares Eat Oats" inside my head.

I enjoy the moment, but not in the way he does.
He tastes it.

And then I begin to wonder,
Wonder how a fellow human being
Could have kept him in a chicken coop
For *two years*.

A little stud dog, matted all over,
Your tiny form bathed in your own filth.
My gorge rises when I think about it.
The protruding ribs,
The tiny form that cowered in fear,
When anyone lifted a hand to pet you.
-A shade, a shadow,
Not even certain you knew how to be a dog!

We cross the mile marker, and I ask,
"You wanna go back?"
There is knowing in his gaze,
And I get the feeling that his wooly form
Would gladly ford 10 miles more.

So we continue anew.
My feet crunching, his silent,
Step, after step, after step
And I look down at him as though
      he is the most wonderful dog in the world,
And he looks back at me with worship in his eyes.

And I am embarrassed to be human.

My Boy Rex

by Mr. Kelly Patterson

The puppy palace at the mall
where fancy dogs are found,
could not compare to what I saw
while browsing at the pound.

I'd passed him by when, "Hey, look here!"
brown eyes divulged his soul,
"tie a red rag round my neck
and I won't look so old."

"Fetch paper, slippers, firewood too,
I'm good for all of that,
won't soil the rug, nip the kids,
or even chase the cat."

I turned to leave when he seemed to say –
in English like before,
"Don't fence the yard, I'll never leave,
sleep just outside your door."

Upright he stood with wagging tail,
said "I am yours to take,"
as I walked by to hail the man,
his paw reached out to shake.

"My bones are brave, I don't eat much,
and I never show no fear,
please free me from these hostile binds,
'cause today's my last day here."

Bomhyr's Leash and Tycy's Collar

by Larry Turner

An expansion on "How Culhwch Won Olwen,"
from *The White Book of Rhydderch*, more often called
The Mabinogion, a collection of Welsh tales
first written in the thirteenth century.

The next morning Culhwch set out for the fortress of Chief Giant Ysbaddaden seeking the giant's daughter Olwen as his bride. Accompanying him were Kei and the other five heroes Arthur had sent. Also accompanying him was Brawd Dauddeg Pedwar (*Son 24*), the shepherd's son, who had spent much of his life in a blanket chest, hidden from Ysbaddaden, who had killed Brawd's 23 brothers. Not an auspicious background for one setting out on such a quest, but Brawd's mother was the daughter of Arthur's cousin, and Brawd knew himself ready to face the challenges to come.

Brawd heard Ysbaddaden pronounce forty difficult tasks Culhwch must accomplish to win Olwen, and he heard Culhwch reply to each, "It will be easy for me to do that, though you do not believe me." These forty tasks appear in *The White Book of Rhydderch,* and I need not list them here.

These challenges would test the mettle of the six heroes. Some would require the might and craft of Arthur himself. But might not Brawd accomplish one or two of the tasks?

He could not seek the silver comb and shears, the only ones in the world that could groom Ysbaddaden's hair for his daughter's wedding. The comb and shears were hidden between the ears of Twrch Trwyth, the evil king who had been turned into a boar. Catching Twrch Trwyth would be accomplished only by the bravest heroes and most skilled huntsmen—and even among them there would be great loss of life. He could not get the hunting dog Drudwyn, son of Greid, son of Eri, the only dog in the world that could hunt Twrch Trwyth.

But perhaps he could obtain the leash of the black dog known as Bomhyr Hundred Claws and the collar of the fawn-

146 Rappahannock Review

colored dog known as Tycy Hundred Paws. These were the only leash and collar in the world that would hold Drudwyn. After all, while others were out rescuing maidens and freeing kings from captivity, Brawd had stayed home playing with dogs.

Fearing the mockery of others, he did not tell them what he was doing, but set out alone searching for Bohmyr and Tycy.

Brawd had walked half a day when he realized he had no idea where to find the two dogs, or even whether they were in Cornwall or Wales, Ireland or Brittany. Then he heard the desperate bleating of a flock of sheep. He followed the sound and came upon the flock. One ewe was bleating as if her heart would break. He asked her why and she answered, "A great tree has fallen upon our leader, the ram Odan Haf Coeden (*Under a Summer Sky*), and if someone does not lift it off him, he will die."

Brawd thought: Is this an opportunity to prove my valor as a hero, or is it a temptation sent to distract me from my quest? But the sheep's bleats became louder and sadder than before, so he said, "I do not know if I can help, but what I can do, I will do."

He went over to the tree, put first his arms and then his shoulder under it, and lifted the entire tree off the ground. The ram, Odan Haf Coeden, emerged unharmed, shook himself and thanked Brawd. "If ever you need my help or that of the flock, take this tuft of wool from my coat and hang it high in the tallest tree, and we will come to you."

Brawd continued walking in the late afternoon until he heard a wail of deep distress. Stepping out onto the moor, he saw a maiden in tears, watching two men running away. He asked her the reason for her sorrow, and she answered, "Those two men you see just stole a purse of gold from me. My father is the breeder of fine dogs. He has bred a mastiff that can stand on his back legs and reach the bell in the church tower. He has bred a greyhound that can travel faster than rumor. He has bred a bloodhound that can track the scent of the clouds across the sky. I had just delivered two dogs to the prince, and was returning with the purse he paid."

Brawd thought: Is this an opportunity to prove my valor as a hero, or is it a temptation sent to distract me from my quest? But the maiden sobbed so piteously and she was so beautiful with the eyes of a spaniel, that he said, "I do not know if I can help, but what I can do, I will do."

By now, the two men were a mile away, but Brawd picked up a stone the size of his head and threw it at the fleeing figures. It struck one in the head and he fell down dead.

The maiden looked at him with a sad smile. "You did well to kill Doesganddoddim (*He doesn't have it*). He was the father of Maeganddo (*He has it*), and taught his son to be more evil than himself. But Maeganddo has the purse and he is fleeing still." Then she began wailing again.

Brawd thought: Is this an opportunity to prove my valor as a hero, or is it a temptation sent to distract me from my quest? But she was in such distress and was so beautiful, with the silky hair of an Afghan hound, that he said, "I do not know if I can help, but what I can do, I will do."

Until Brawd arrived, Maeganddo was the most fleet of foot of all the men of the land, and now he was three miles away. But Brawd caught up with him within a minute, then bound him and regained the purse, leaving him to hobble about with his ankles tied together.

When he returned to the maiden, she thanked him and extended her hand; it was as dainty as a whippet's paw. She told him her name, Hoffi Cim (*Likes Dogs*), and invited him to stay the night in her father's house.

The next morning Brawd Dauddeg Pedwar told Hoffi Cim of his quest. She said, "You have chosen two difficult tasks. To take Tycy's collar, you must catch her, and she can dig deeper than any badger. Bomhyr dwells in the midst of a forest of sleeping flesh-eaters: cannibals, wolves and birds of prey. If you touch his leash, Bomhyr will bark and awaken all the flesh-eaters. You will not return alive."

She continued, "Nonetheless, you can get the collar and leash. It will be easy for you, though you do not believe me.

"You will need the aid of the Nightingale of Misery. Take the terrier Ayesha to find the nightingale. But beware. The Nightingale of Misery sings with such beauty that all gather to hear her, but with such sadness that they spend the entire night in tears and sobs. If you listen to her, you too will exhaust yourself in crying."

Brawd took small pieces of wool from Odan Haf Coeden and stuffed them in his ears. He rolled up Ayesha's ears and tied them. Then he set Ayesha free and followed her. In the late afternoon they came to a place where the ground was so sodden they could hardly proceed, and they sat down to rest. As it grew dark, the Nightingale of Misery flew to a branch overhead and began to sing. All the creatures of the forest came to hear her sing. Natural enemies sitting side by side, they began to cry. Their tears nearly flooded the clearing where they sat.

In the morning, when the singing had ceased and the animals departed, Brawd took the wool out of his ears and asked the nightingale, "Why do you sing with such sadness?"

She answered, "I have no offspring. Every year I build a nest and lay eggs. Every year the eggs hatch, but within three days the cat Gabriel comes and eats my fledglings."

"That is indeed a source of sadness. How can I find this cat Gabriel?"

"Every night he comes along with the other creatures to hear my singing. You will recognize him by his white body and his seal-colored face, ears, feet and tail."

Throughout that night, Brawd and Ayesha watched Gabriel. In the morning, the singing ceased and Gabriel stood and stretched. With a bound, Ayesha took off after him and chased him all the way to Cath Tref, the village of the cats. With Gabriel out of the way, Ayesha returned home to Hoffi Cim as Brawd had instructed her. That night the nightingale must have sung a different song, for all the animals who gathered to hear her fell asleep and slept the whole night long.

The Nightingale of Peace, as she was now named, accompanied Brawd to the place where Tycy lived. They recognized the ground by all the holes Tycy had dug. In the evening, Brawd replaced the wool in his ears and the nightingale sang. Tycy came up out of her deep hole and listened to the song, then fell asleep. Brawd easily removed her collar, and at dawn they set off for the forest where Bomhyr lived. They watched all day; then as it grew dark, the nightingale began to sing. As soon as Bomhyr fell asleep, Brawd went over and removed his leash, but Bomhyr awoke and began to bark. The cannibals, wolves, and birds of prey also awoke and approached Brawd. Brawd uprooted a rowan tree, broke it off at the roots, then tied the roots to the end of Bomhyr's leash and began swinging them around in circles to keep the creatures at bay. The nightingale sang more lustily still, and soon first Bomhyr, and then the flesh-eaters began to blink, yawn, and finally fall asleep.

The Nightingale of Peace and Brawd left the forest the next morning carrying the collar and leash. The carnivores remained asleep. Bomhyr wagged his tail, but did not bark.

It was sundown as Brawd and the nightingale approached Hoffi Cim's house. She ran out to greet Brawd, and the nightingale was so delighted to see the lovers reunited that she sang the most beautiful song of her life. The song made Brawd and Hoffi Cim immediately fall asleep on the ground. When Brawd awoke the next morning, the Nightingale of Peace had returned to her home, and Hoffi Cim still lay asleep where she had fallen.

Soon the time arrived for Brawd to take leave of Hoffi Cim, and return to Arthur's court with Tycy's collar and Bomhyr's leash. He promised to come back soon and take Hoffi Cim for his wife.

"Then go quickly and return quickly, for I will have no man but you for my husband. When you come back, you will learn what tasks my own father requires of you before he will let us marry." Before he had a chance to reply, she smiled and added, "It will be easy for you, though you do not believe me."

Brawd looked into her eyes, so like a spaniel's. "I am prepared for whatever your father or King Arthur requires of me. He tucked Odan Haf Coeden's wool back in his belt, and set out for Arthur's court.

Genghis and the .55 Magnum
by Rod Vanderhoof

On a bright Saturday in early spring, a very dapper John Huntington Hardwood inspected himself in the full-length hallway mirror. He hummed as he admired his maroon and gold ascot, navy blue blazer with family crest, grey flannel trousers, and black, English leather shoes. *I am indeed elegant and debonair,* he thought, *and so handsome.* He adjusted his boating cap to a jaunty tilt. He was now ready for the annual powerboat show at the Richmond Arena.

When Hardwood stepped toward the front door, his wife shouted, "Be careful, John, predatory salesmen are everywhere at those boat shows." She worried about her husband, particularly where money was concerned. He was an impulsive spender.

The Richmond Show exhibited scores of powerboats, from luxurious yachts to car top bass boats. There were pontoon boats, boats with V-hulls, tri-hulls, flat bottoms; single and twin engine; inboard, outboard, or inboard-outboard; jet or propeller; gasoline or diesel. All were proudly displayed on blocks or trailers with sharp-eyed salesmen at the ready.

An hour or so after arriving, Hardwood spotted a flashy, V-hull speedboat, one that would ride atop the water. *This boat can fly*, he thought. *Look at the sleek lines.*

A salesman with a pencil thin mustache, a bow tie and too much aftershave, spotted Hardwood. Grinning like a mackerel shark in a feeding frenzy, he stepped forward. "Hi, I'm Slick Wilson...and you are?"

"John Huntington Hardwood."

"Isn't this boat beautiful, Mr. Hardwood? It has an innovative polyethylene hull. It's state of the art."

"State of the art?"

"Right, the polyethylene hull prevents algae. Without the accumulation of algae, the hull cuts through the water at an amazing speed, no drag to speak of, and the inboard engine takes you from zero to fifty in mere seconds, great for water skiing and thrills."

Hardwood walked around the boat inspecting every square inch. "This boat is indeed beautiful," he announced, as he climbed in and examined the instrument panel. Grasping the wheel, he closed his eyes and envisioned himself navigating heavy seas: *Suddenly, he was being slammed by one of those storms that whip across Lake Jefferson. He squinted, steely-eyed into the powerful onslaught, bouncing his craft skillfully from wave to wave, constantly adjusting for engine torque using the tab adjuster on the side of the throttle to get the speed and steering just right.*

"Ooh, yeah!" he shouted, causing people several displays away to turn and see what pompous prig was making the ruckus. Wilson noticed, too, and smiled.

"Do you want to take delivery of this fantastic boat today, Mr. Hardwood, before someone else snaps it up, or would next week be better?"

"Well, it is a terrific boat and I'd like to be on the lake this afternoon...." He paused, but only for a moment. "Yes, I'll take it right now."

"Oh, one more thing," Wilson added, "You need to fasten the registration numbers on the hull, up near the bow. If you don't, the game warden will give you a hassle."

"So why don't you put the numbers on for me?"

"The guy who does that is out."

Hardwood hesitated. *How hard can it be to put numbers on the hull? I'll do it myself.*

He gave Wilson a check when the paperwork was complete. The boat and trailer were fastened to the trailer hitch on Hardwood's Cadillac Escalade and he was off. He whistled and bellowed a song as he drove down the highway. He could barely wait to be on Lake Jefferson and try this beauty.

At his lake house, Hardwood changed into an elegant, Burberry all-weather jacket and trousers, white deck shoes, and a baseball-style cap bearing the Lake Jefferson Cruise Club logo. Next, he tended to the registration numbers.

He placed the numbers on the hull, but they held for only a moment before dropping off. He tried twice more with the same result. He didn't know you must first use the flame of a small blowtorch to heat the polyethylene surface; then, and only then, will the numbers stick. But nobody told him. Being naturally cautious, he knew he shouldn't go out on the lake without visible numbers; on the other hand, it was early in the season and no other boats were out. Surely, it wouldn't matter.

Hardwood's first task was to break in the new engine at slow to moderate speeds, with only short bursts at full throttle. After twenty hours of break-in, the engine could be revved to full, sustained power for as long as Hardwood chose.

He summoned his faithful dog, a mischievous pit bull named Genghis, and went out on the lake. Genghis hung over the bow, his nose in the air, breathing the delectable scents of deer, rotting compost, putrid carcasses of dead fish and other enticing odors. For Genghis, this smelled of dog heaven, but for Hardwood, it smelled of boredom.

Hardwood didn't realize how tedious these hours could be. He drove around for an hour or so, mostly in big circles: first clockwise, then counter-clockwise, and then back again. He did figure eights for awhile then circled once again. Then inspiration struck: *I'll head across the lake. It is several miles but I can cruise in a straight line.*

The county boundary ran right down the middle of Lake Jefferson, so when he arrived at the other side, he'd left Malvern County and entered Chocataw County. He was now in the legal jurisdiction of the infamous lady judge, "Lock'em Up" Llewellyn.

To say Judge Elsie May Llewellyn had a vicious streak was an understatement. She found one man guilty of loitering in front of the county court house and gave him six months at hard labor, which included mopping out the jail each morning, mowing the judge's lawn three times a week and washing the Sheriff's patrol cars every day.

Hardwood's powerful craft was bounding porpoise-like over small whitecaps just as a fast-moving boat zoomed up from behind, siren blaring and blue lights flashing. A uniformed officer stood at the helm in all his law enforcement glory. *He wants help in tracking some criminal,* thought Hardwood. *I'll cut my engine.*

As the lawman pulled alongside, Hardwood observed that the boat was painted a prominent yellow with bold, black letters along the side that announced, "State Game Warden." The nametag over the officer's shirt pocket read, "Rufus Kranepool." A plainclothes sidekick in blue denims, a plaid shirt and a Baltimore Orioles baseball cap worn backwards, dropped boat bumpers over the side and helped the game warden secure the two boats together with grappling hooks.

The game warden was a giant who could have played defensive lineman for the Redskins. He had a buzz cut and carrot-red hair, with an ample beer belly that threatened to hide his too-tight, cartridge belt. If he'd flown the Jolly Roger and gritted a dagger in clenched teeth, he could not have been more menacing.

Leaving his engine idling, the warden boarded Hardwood's new craft. He squared his hat and made a big show of adjusting his sidearm, a huge silver revolver that was pearl handled and engraved with intricate patterns. Hardwood had never seen such an imposing weapon.

"You seem fascinated with my gun," Kranepool said. "It's a Colt .55 magnum, custom-made to my specifications. It's very expensive. The bullets are armor-piercing and can go right through an engine block."

"Amazing."

"Let's get down to business. I need some identification." Becoming impatient with the delay, Hardwood thrust his driver's license at the officer, who noticed the rudeness.

"So, Mr. John Huntington Hardwood," he snapped, "where's your boat registration number? It's supposed to be visible on the hull. That's the law."

"The numbers fell off. Since no one was on the lake, I didn't think it mattered."

"Without numbers on the hull, I can only conclude that you haven't paid your taxes," he said. "The law *is* important. Can you imagine the chaos we'd have without the rule of law?"

"Yes, but the numbers wouldn't stick, and I just bought the boat this morning."

"Where's the sales slip?"

"In my lake house, over there," Hardwood pointed.

"That's what all you rich city guys say."

"If we cruise over, I'll run in and get it."

"I'm not going there, not for an unscrupulous scofflaw," said Kranepool, his voice edgy. "I'm placing you under arrest!"

"Go ahead and arrest me if you dare, but the governor is an old friend of mine. I'll have your badge on a platter, you backwoods bumpkin." *He doesn't need to know I've never met the governor*, thought Hardwood.

"That settles it, you bag of Lake Jefferson muck," Kranepool said. "I've heard all that before. Turn around and put your hands on the windshield." Frisking Hardwood for weapons but finding nothing, he said, "I'm taking you in."

"How dare you arrest me, you six-gun, back-country buffoon, I've never broken the law in my life."

"That's what they all say, Jerkwood," snapped Kranepool. "Okay, put one arm through the steering wheel and put your wrists together." The officer snapped on the handcuffs and removed the ignition key from the dashboard. "I'll fasten a line to your bow cleat and tow you to the boat landing. We can't have *criminals* like you on the loose."

"I am *not* a criminal, you Paleolithic boob."

"You violated the penal code, you half-fried catfish. That *makes* you a criminal."

Genghis was riled by the shouting and was skittering from side to side, yapping and snarling.

As Officer Kranepool tried to climb back into the police boat, his feet became entangled with Genghis. Becoming furious, Kranepool kicked him.

Genghis retaliated by jumping into the lawman's boat, going straight for the officer's leg and locking on with his jaws. Kranepool screamed and tried to pull the pit bull off, but Genghis just bit down harder.

In desperate pain, the officer drew his gun and fired. He missed Genghis and, instead, hit his own foot, blowing off his big toe. The bullet went through Kranepool's shoe and through the hull. Water began to gush into the police cruiser. The shot frightened Genghis who let go and chased Kranepool's sidekick, who dove overboard.

"Come here, Genghis!" Hardwood shouted, but the pit bull paid no attention.

Kranepool fired another shot but missed the dog and blew a gaping hole in the police boat's engine compartment, causing the engine to clatter to a stop. Gray smoke oozed out. Kranepool fired a third shot but nailed his gas tank, dead center. Gasoline gushed from both the front and back of the tank onto the floor and into the engine compartment. Gas fumes permeated the air.

Kranepool hollered to the shackled Hardwood, "Jump, fish ball, before she blows!"

"I can't, you slobbering eel," Hardwood yelled back, "I'm cuffed to the steering wheel."

Kranepool dove over the side and Genghis followed in hot pursuit, barking and growling the whole time.

Although fastened to the steering wheel, Hardwood stretched forward with his leg and kicked off the front grappling hook with his foot. He did the same to the hook at the back and he began drifting away from the police boat. He hunkered down on the floor below the instrument panel and the driver's seat, just as the explosion rocked his watercraft with a force that left him unconscious.

The blast rattled windows in homes along the shores of Lake Jefferson and could be heard, like a sonic boom, for miles. Rafts of ducks and Canada geese scattered airborne. Workers at a distant marina scanned the sky for thunderclouds and impending rain squalls, but were mystified when they saw nothing.

When Hardwood awakened, the mushroom cloud was still rising. The police boat was destroyed by the resulting inferno and, except for a few floating pieces, had completed its journey to the bottom. Game Warden Rufus Kranepool and his sidekick were splashing in the lake and screaming for help. Since Kranepool still had the ignition key, Hardwood could do nothing.

Along the shore, a home owner heard the explosion and saw the rising smoke. He launched his boat and rescued the game warden and sidekick.

Meanwhile, Genghis was back in his own boat sitting next to Hardwood. Using his forepaws, Genghis had climbed onto the swim platform at the stern and made an additional jump that landed him in the boat. He shook the cold water from his fur, spraying it all over Hardwood. Genghis was wagging his tail and having a wonderful time.

"Bad dog!" Hardwood scolded. Genghis put his tail between his legs and whimpered, but Hardwood smiled: *the game warden got exactly what he deserved.*

Once aboard the rescue craft, the warden and sidekick fastened a line to Hardwood's bow. Kranepool had a State Game Commission pickup truck and now-empty boat trailer at the boat landing. Hardwood's boat was winched onto the trailer while the rescuer returned home.

Officer Kranepool's sidekick drove them to the Chocataw county seat and left Kranepool at the Emergency Room for treatment of the gunshot wound and dog bite. Genghis was deposited at the animal shelter, and Hardwood's speedboat was impounded.

Hardwood was taken to the county jail and booked for verbally abusing a law officer, stealing a boat and operating an unregistered water vehicle. He was fingerprinted, photographed and thrown in the slammer.

A few hours later, a bedraggled Rufus Kranepool arrived at the county jail and limped over to Hardwood's cell. He was teary-eyed. "My gun is buried in deep mud at the bottom of Lake Jefferson. I'll never see it again."

"Oh pity." *But you had it coming,* thought Hardwood.

"All of this is your fault, Klutzwood. I lost my magnificent Colt .55 magnum, your dog bit me, and my big toe is gone. Not only that, my police boat is blown into small pieces of scrap. I'll drown in paperwork for six months trying to explain all this to the State Game Commission." Kranepool turned to go, but stopped and came back.

"Lock'em Up Llewellyn will take care of you early next week. I'll be there, too, as the prime witness. You'll be cleaning johns and mopping floors in the jailhouse for a long time. I'll enjoy every minute of your misery."

On Monday at eight a.m. sharp, Hardwood was frog-marched into the courtroom past his wife who was a spectator. She handed him the sales slip for the boat.

Hardwood was surprised to see that Judge Elsie May Llewellyn was not only a woman, but a very attractive one. Her hair was long and dark and her lipstick, bright red. She wore a black, dignified judge's robe. "Mr. Hardwood, how do you plead?"

"Not guilty."

"Officer Kranepool, please describe what happened." Kranepool presented his version of events with the proud confidence of a lawman accustomed to winning his cases.

"And what do *you* say, Mr. Hardwood?"

"Here's my sales receipt, your honor." Hardwood handed it to the judge. She examined it.

"Officer Kranepool, this receipt shows that Mr. Hardwood owns the boat and that he paid the required taxes. Why did you arrest him?"

"I didn't believe him and, well, he acted guilty and called me a 'slobbering eel.'"

"What say you, Mr. Hardwood?"

"Officer Kranepool called me a 'half-fried catfish.'"

"You two should be ashamed," she said. "If you were schoolboys, I'd wash your mouths with soap." The two men stared at the floor.

"The case against Mr. Hardwood is dismissed due to lack of evidence. Bailiff, release him."

"Officer Kranepool, according to your own testimony, you kicked a poor little dog named Genghis. Then, you repeatedly tried to shoot him. As chairwoman of the Chocataw County Society for the Prevention of Cruelty to Animals, I abhor your behavior. You are a disgrace to state and county law enforcement."

"A disgrace?" he asked in disbelief.

"I hereby place you under arrest," she said, scowling. "Bailiff, book this man for extreme cruelty to animals and place him in a cell. I'll sentence *him* tomorrow."

As the bailiff escorted Kranepool from the courtroom, Hardwood heard the judge mutter, "Besides, the shrubs around the courthouse need pruning!"

True justice prevails, thought Hardwood. *Is this a great country or what?*

One Fish, Two Fish
by Kathie Walker

Somebody Dad knew was selling goldfish. He bought some, of course. Then he dumped them into our pond. The goldfish took over the pond. The goldfish became lots of goldfish. No more big-mouth bass. No more sunnies. If you fished, you got a goldfish. Maybe two. And those suckers got really really big, eating all the other fish. I'd have nightmares—dreams of big goldfish crawling out of the pond, like the first primordial life forms that had inched their way onto dry land, fish crawling up the hill towards the house and into the den where I slept. They'd take over the house and turn it into a huge goldfish bowl, and I'd wake up when it started to fill with water. After I used the bathroom I knew it had been just another dream, except one night in October when there was a full moon. I looked out my bedroom window towards the pond, and I swore that I saw the glistening backs of a thousand goldfish as they crawled up the hill towards the house. My Mom said it was newly fallen leaves in the wind. What she didn't see was after she had left to go back to bed, the fish all turned around and crawled back into the pond. In the morning all that were left were oak and maple leaves floating on the surface of the murky water, and no sign of what had happened in the night under the moon. But I always thought that maybe Dad had seen what I saw that night, because he never, ever brought home goldfish again.

Whiplash Takes a Ride

by Elaine J. Gooding

Once upon a time there were three cockroaches. This particular cockroach family, names of Sherman, Wilhelmina, and their teenage son, Whiplash (it was really Junior, but he hated that name), were well-known for being great dancers. Everyday they'd sing and dance: "La cucaracha, la cucaracha, we love to dance the whole day long." Of course, they were careful not to dance around the humans.

Whiplash had higher aspirations than dancing. He was bolder than his parents, him being a typical teen and all. He liked to spy on the human Kid. The Kid had this gadget called a fingerboard. It was a miniature skateboard that he would push and flip on the kitchen counter, driving his poor mother crazy. Another trick the Kid did with the fingerboard used a big mixing bowl to simulate the half-pipe ramps the kids in the street skated on with regular boards. Down and up, fast as can be. Whiplash was fascinated. He knew he had to ride that thing just once.

Small as the fingerboard was, it was still a little big for Whiplash. He figured he had the advantage not only of strong legs from years of dancing, but he had six of them besides. Using his teen intuition, the Whip knew better than to let Sherman and Wilhelmina in on his plan. They certainly would have tried to stop him, don't you think?

He picked a night when the humans were gathered round the box in the family room. The kitchen was dark, but a bit of moonlight shown through the window over the sink illuminating the corner of the counter where the Kid had stored the fingerboard. Breathing hard, Whiplash skittered across the cold floor, up the cabinet door, and onto the counter of champions. He was trembling with excitement.

Grabbing the board and praying to whomever cockroaches pray to when about to make cockroach history, he jumped on. Using his right legs, he pushed as fast as he could and barely was able to skirt the sink and avoid the edge of the counter. Heading towards the dark end of the counter, he spotted the shape of the bowl the Kid always used for tricks.

Just then, the human mom stood up saying, "I can't believe I forgot to put the jello in the fridge to finish hardening."

Horrors! Whiplash, stomping on the back end of the fingerboard had already launched himself airborne. Phwap! Glug.

"Eek! My green jello!"

And that's why there are only two cockroaches left in the story. Rest in Peace, Whiplash.

A Mice Christmas
by J. Allen Hill

This is the story of three little sisters named
Blossom and Winkie and Bim.
The three small girls have cherry red noses
and tummies quite fashionably trim.

The sisters live on Mulberry Street
in the Dingleby family's house,
They live there in secret, in a nest in the wall,
for the sisters' last name is Mouse.

The humans who live in the white clapboard house
are a lovely family of five:
A father, a mother, young Sammie and Sue,
and an orange tabby cat named Clive.

Humans don't like a mouse in the house.
Mice nibble on the veggies and bread,
Leave crumbs in the kitchen and damage the walls.
Folks generally view them with dread.

The sisters eat veggies when it's all they can get,
but their preference is cheeses and sweets
which mother had warned them are bad for their health.
They agreed – and gave up meats.

One day, Blossom, using whisker antenna,
was listening to local mouse radio
And heard of the visit of a jolly old elf,
dressed in red, who laughs, *Ho Ho Hodio.*

Suddenly the Dingleby house turned chaotic.
Soon Winkie reported with glee,
*You'll never ever guess what I saw,
in the parlor, by the fireplace. A tree!*

They sat beneath the wondrous tree,
its branches aglow and aglitter.
It smelled of snow, pine nuts, and forest
and set their three noses atwitter.

Bim, Winkie and Blossom were born in the wall
and had never been in the forest.
Their mother once sang of it, calling it verdant,
but deadly for all but the hardiest.

No matter they didn't understand those words.
They just wanted to go there.
A little frightened, they crawled into bed
and dreamed of the courage to dare.

Soon the Dingleby house rang merrily,
with the sound of music and bells.
Tinsel was hung, packages wrapped,
the house filled with wonderful smells

Of cinnamon, mint, spiced walnuts and chocolate,
the almonds in marzipan.
The sisters feasted on macaroons, bon-bons
and taffy, fudge plain and pecan,

Nibbled on sugar nuts, tasted the rum cake,
swam laps in the strawberry punch.
But when they tried to go back through the wall,
they didn't fit. Too much lunch!

Blossom's tummy had grown round as a ball,
Winkie was round all over. Bim was fat.
The door they had carefully nibbled in the wall
was too small – and here came the cat!

They tried to run, but could only wobble.
Clive, the cat, was close behind them.
He nipped Winkie's tail, trapped Bim with a paw!
Then a very loud voice said, AHEM!

As the sisters were lifted high in the air
Clive, the cat ran away. But what now?
A red suited fellow lifted them high –
frightened by the frown on his brow.

His cheeks were rosy, his eyes twinkling and kind,
And his round belly shook with glee
as he laughed, *Ho Ho Hodio. Merry Christmas,
Little Miss Mouse sisters three.*

*Christmas is magic and that is why,
you may ask for anything you like.*
Anything? *Anything.* What should it be?
Roller skates? Ballet shoes? A bike?

Of course not. Blossom can't skate.
Winkie doesn't dance. Bim has never ridden a bike.
They asked to visit the trees of the forest,
to live there, to know what it is like.

*You have asked for something too dangerous.
Mother warned you. Wish again,* wise Santa said.
No! three tiny voices demanded. If mother had been there, they'd
have been sent straight to bed.

You shall have it, said Santa, and quick as a wink,
they were nestled in a warm hollow tree,
On a pine needle bed, lined with fur; sun was rising,
snow was falling. Oh happy three.

Bim was excited and ran out to frolic,
Winkie to roll in the snow. Blossom was shy
And waited behind, watching her sisters play.
A dark shadow dropped out of the sky.

Winkie suddenly flew into the air,
in the claws of a swift owl on the wing.
She screeched in fear, Bim ran like the wind,
Blossom could do nothing but cling

To her sister. The two of them shivered and wept
for Winkie, whose fate they dare not guess.
They were sorry they ate too much, sorry they wanted
too much, and promised to give up excess.

If they could have Winkie back, if they could be slim again, and
live in the hole in the wall,
They would be good mice, eat only veggies –
well tofu if they could get it – but that is all.

Then suddenly, faintly on the cold night air,
they heard, *Ho Ho Hodio, Mother Owl.*
Take this cheeseburger home to your babies.
Drop the little mouse – she tastes foul.

Then the three sisters found themselves in a cage, in a box 'neath
the tree in the house.
Sammie tore open the package and excitedly shouted,
Santa knew I wanted a mouse.

Sue cried, *Santa forgot me. I wanted a mouse too.*
It's not fair, you have three.
We will share, said Sammie. And don't you suppose
that this gift under the tree

Was specially designed by Santa himself
for five – maybe six – little folks in this house?
Fun for Sammie and Sue, and safety from Clive,
for three small gray sisters named Mouse.

Merry Christmas.

Seasons of Nature

Manic Implications of a February Thaw

by Anne H. Flythe

To the north winter stirred, drew cold white blankets higher.
Beneath a lowering red sun, ruddy mountain faces
shifted subtly beneath beards of pine.
Here the air was warm and mild.
A gentle wind clothed my bare arms with silken sleeves.
Disoriented peepers sang a silver filigree
in premature salute to spring.
March has no monopoly on madness;
the dementia of a February hare is valid too.
I dreamed I munched on moon cheese, drank night wine,
a sparkling black vintage, effervescent with stars,
to wash it down.
Clocks ran backward, their lying hands and faces
telling true time only four times a day,
their hourly chimes a cacophony of lies.
I morphed into a silent Arlington paved with losses
marked by stones. Immobilized by pain,
I could no longer expand, disperse my atoms,
until a distant dog raving on its chain broke the spell,
precipitating me into a perilous dimension,
trying to catch the light of time past and gone,
reaching for the pitiless ago of yestertime.

Spring Rain
by Norma E. Redfern

The rain feels soft, soaking the skin

Dripping, and spattering on our tin roof
Drenching as it falls to the lush green grass
Saturating dark jade foliaged on the ground
Warm rising mist like sleeping fog

Scents fill the night air as rhythms fall
Fast, hard, relentlessly severe and persistent
Driving rivets seeping and tortuous
Cascading down in search of tributaries
Flowing in time to the sea

Footprints in the Grass
by Michelle O'Hearn

One day I was skipping through a field enjoying nature.
At each step I noticed an odd color in the green palette I
    travelled
Sometimes there was one large mass
Other times, several bits of color splayed out in mock design.
This bothered me because I noticed that no other hands
    inspected the display.
So I said to the nature about me, "What is this mess you
    leave for me?"
And nature gave no reply, reminding me that the times I see
    this trash,
It is only my set of footprints in the grass.
So I pick it up.

Rebirth

by Norma E. Redfern

Settled in my chair,
I gaze out the window
on a cool damp spring day.

Fringed along the woods,
Daffodils, yellow petals stand tall.
Seek the sun as they grow.

Redbud's branches bend,
filled with dark rose pink,
the tiny buds that spread.

I wait for dogwood flowers
enclosed, tight and green
not yet opened to the heat.

The breeze warms and blows.
As yellow forsythia's flowers
Die and fall to the ground.

Apple green leaves fill branches.
Trees flowering in profusion,
shade of pink against blue skies.

I sit chair-bound, unable
to walk, my pain grows
as I watch the flowers bloom.

Slow Food

by Anne H. Flythe

A spiral of buzzards
glide the thermals
circling kites untethered,
flight feather splayed
wing tips fingering the updrafts,
Chopin, the music pianissimo,
inaudible here among the grasses.
Vision irrelevant,
flying hounds, they track
the dark sweet stench
of death across the sun-bleached sky
until they teeter down
silent as black ash
to blanket rotting flesh.
Ugly naked heads wattled blue and red,
plunging deep into the carcass.
diners tearing at their meat;
squawks, hoarse comment,
no convivial discourse
no postprandial brandy.

Our Valley
by R. L Russis

Our valley was an island made remote by its trees, by
the thousands of trees that stood and watched, staring
down like sentries, unblinking through the seasons.
They were mostly maples, but here and there stood oaks—white
and black and red, all this on a side—and on the other,
on the western side, grew a thick mix of evergreen, a blend
of balsam and fir that mingled with tall stands of spruce
and hemlock, a blue-green wave that climbed up to meet
with and cross over that crest of ridge or found themselves
stopped by its glacial ledge, its jagged, prehistoric spine.
And there, those melding colors of green and gray and blue
from the trees, the rocks and the sky lent my small world
a most ambiguous hue which made for an uncertain and
stormy shade when those clouds dropped low, fell below
successive treetop-tips and that purplish haze obscured
our island from view and closed the door to our domain.

Dog Days, Snake Days

by R. L Russis

Late summer, August on Grampa's farm,
and not even the cats bothered to stray
and the dogs seldom ever left their shade,
even the air sat still, like a hen on eggs.
The only break from the torrid heat, from
that torpid air, was sleep, if anyone could,
and the older folks did, but all of us kids
spent the worst of those heat-filled hours
in laughing delight with splashing leaps
from off the rope that hung on the oak
and swung out and over the deepest pool
of the creek, those leaps ending in a goose-
bump plunge. But in getting there and back
we had to take extra care, watch close,
at this time of year for the grass was high
and the snakes were thick. They'd be out
in force in the high-heat of the day, those
loose balls of snakes, basking on stones,
where the whole of the den had come out
to catch some rays and each length of snake
writhed and slithered, turned and twisted,
trying to keep the sun. And on those long
walks back up to the house sometimes
someone would yell, "Snake! Snake!"
and sometimes there was… and
sometimes we boys just grinned.

A Personal Equinox
by Anne H. Flythe

I'm familiar with autumn;
I live there amid the drying leaves.
The staccato static of cicadas' incessant din
bleaches August with white sound,
the clicks of seconds passing.

November will crystallize on naked twigs,
fill the ruts cut deep by rain last spring
with iron, glass and cold.
The weight of winter
slows the turning of the days.

Desire can no longer sting me
into change or optimism;
no matter when or what I do,
Autumn's sun will keep its rendezvous
among the standing stones.

Land Bridges

by Dan Walker

Bar Island isn't an island at low tide.
It's stapled to the mainland then by a strip
of mud-slick granite thick with mussels, mooncrabs,
and colicky seagulls.
So, for a couple of hours in human history,
there's a land bridge.
But if you lose track of time out there watching the harbor,
you're trapped, and you won't get back for a long time.

Here's what you do:
You look at that sea where there used to be land
and you try to remember the way it was
when your ancestral self and his mate walked
        across bare ground there,
and you make up stories (to impress the kids)
about what it was like when all that water rushed in.
You evolve. You make up new stories,
invent new tools, new gods.
You look at your mate now and remember the legends.

She notes that you are both now stuck
        and will miss the crab-cake special.
"This," she adds, "was your idea."

You say:
"Yes, my love.
And if you are worthy, when the time is right,
I will wave my wand and raise new land from the sea."
She observes that you are a very strange person.

You say:
"And your children will walk forth
with new tongues and faces, new dreams and knowledge.
See that…?"

You point to a cloud bank on the horizon.
"That's an eight thousand-foot-thick ice sheet on the way."
She suggests that your strangeness may amount to a public
>hazard.

You smile.
For you know that hazard is a narrow bridge
and when the ice returns only the strange will cross it.
She says:
"*Your* children will wonder what in the world happened to their
>parents."

You smile again.
For that wonder is the grandest bridge of all.

Black Spruce

(for Emily)
by Dan Walker

She likes a boggy acre,
And also other things.
Like, for instance—Fire and Death—
And revolution songs.

The others spread their arms aloft—
With geometric Care—
And toss their young out year by year,
Prolific—as a Fair.

A ragged Saint, she jabs her Stake
Up thirty feet, no higher,
Then holds her cones in withered Hands
For years—and dreams of fire—

A Flame so hot—if all goes well—
Her Progeny burst through
So that—when marsh and glade return
A Wood may rise— anew—

To nurse its Young in Secrecy—
In water, moss, and mire—
Whose Eyes can only open—if
Their Mother dies by Fire.

Fall

by Norma E. Redfern

Days grow shorter
Nights much longer
Air turns crisp
Apples ready to pick
Making pies and freezing
Fields are full of pumpkins
Waiting for Halloween
Red, orange, rust and yellow
Leaves swirling around
Frolicking breezes spread
Leaves on the ground
The sky will turn
Heavy with snowflakes
Chasing away fall
Ready for winter

Three Haiku

by Norma E. Redfern

Dogwood red berries
Now eaten by birds in flight
Gone till next year fall

White, and pure, it falls
Diamonds covering the ground
Sunlight without heat

Love tasting my soul
Luscious like a sweet ripe pear
Moist succulent rush

Twelve Haiku

by Elaine J. Gooding

Thunder rumbles now
Tomorrow will be better
Then daylight will smile

                Moss like a blanket
                Carpets quiet forest floor
                Soft and cushy rug

Groundhog sits alert
Like a prairie dog guarding
Against an attack

                Dark green cool forest
                Breezes flitting to and fro
                Like a butterfly

Simple dewdrops shine
Reflecting joyful sun rays
Into my heart's hole

                Hummingbirds hover
                Sipping nectar oh so sweet
                Flying backwards fast

Dismal drizzle day
Stolen childhood lost in fog
Little girl wants love

                    One remaining leaf
                    Wilting, waiting, wanting rest
                    Hangs on forever

Hush my child and sleep
Mother's voice gently singing
All is well tonight

                    Yucky, mostly gross
                    Are slugs upon my sidewalk
                    Do not go barefoot

Teenaged boys are loud
Invading my private space
Lord give me patience

                    My trust you betrayed
                    Special gifts for marriage robbed
                    Leaving emptiness

Marks

by Dan Walker

Out of school again and even out
of grading to do, I decide
to go out through the snow for the mail and papers.
The snow is deep. How deep is it?
I'm a southerner. I don't have the metaphors for this.

Maybe all the moonlight since Gettysburg
has fallen, settled ... Never mind.
You see where that's going.
Try this: So deep the driveway through the woods
is a wormhole to an alternate poetry.

Now I'm a trapper snow-shoeing to the fort for supplies,
a sergeant of special-ops hunting the Hindu Kush...
And just as it's getting interesting, I see marks in the snow—
real marks, so I have to make this clear—
three lines in parallel, two sets of them side by side,

just wide enough for a pair of wings,
or a pair of trademarks, the swoosh
turned up in the first set, down in the next—
Nike triple-endorsed, then un-endorsed?—
and in between these a small confusion of snow

where something happened.
And there are no tracks away,
so whatever it was came down from the sky
and happened
and went back up.

And I see now that this goes on all the time,
whether or not there is school,
that it asks no grade from me,
asks nothing of me really,
except, finally, to shut up,

and go away,
and give it a few million light-years.

Meditation on Winter's Solstice
by R. L Russis

Those great, shaggy beasts*, not overly bright but not
overly stupid either, when it came to dealing with this cold
or even summer's heat, insufferable in August, and their
hunting dense shade beneath those spreading oaks, the same
that gave no cover now, no relief with that lack of heavy
      leaf—
their groping branches giving only shadows—sparse barrier
to keening winds careening past bare, protesting arms.
All in a perspective, I thought as I watched and shivered,
and the natural cycle. Yes, let the frost come and the fall
of leaves rain down and let the snow and sleet come too,
and in its turn, the thaw, those rivulets of spring. Yes,
each in its turn, but now was the time for profuse snow
and pervasive cold, now was the time for enduring the slow,
patient working of time and its relentless turning of the
seasons. And so they did, as they stoically stood, hock-
deep in a wintry mix of freezing mud and slush, backed
against snow-covered stones, white walls of rock that
discouraged the wind, blunting the force of the cold that
came in sporadic gusts, as they stared silent and intent,
concentrating on who knew what aside from the present
cold, the prevailing winds, and this interminable interval
until the inevitable arrival of spring… and their concerted
focus Zen-like, patiently waiting, wanting warmer, gentler
breezes and softened blue skies to replace this sideways
sleet, the slowly building piles of snow and these darkened
skies that threatened, promising of yet more to come before
that longed-for arrival of a still much-distant spring.

*Scottish Highland cattle

Whiteout

by Elizabeth Talbot

The Friday evening before Christmas week, my family and I were bracing for the mother of all snowstorms, or that's what the local media promised. Scoffers on many internet sites dismissed the hype as an example of media hysteria which would induce millions in the Mid-Atlantic region to clean off the supermarket shelves. When the schools canceled all basketball games and sports practice. I suspected at the time that coaches and school officials were trying to get a head start on Christmas.

The system was speeding northeast from the Gulf of Mexico. As usual, we had enjoyed a temperate fall and I believed that we would merely experience another heavy soaking. The landscaper had even administered one last haircut to the lawn the week before.

Mary Ann and Kristen, my teenage daughters, insisted on eating out that Friday night. The flakes had started to fall, light and sugary. There was an inch or two by the time we arrived at the restaurant. Mary Ann had brought along her new laptop so she could take advantage of the Wi-Fi. As my family huddled over it, I suggested that this was a good time to take advantage of a nearby Wal-Mart since we had only three rolls of toilet paper left.

Tom, my husband, scoffed at me. He had grown up near Lake Erie and Lake Ontario in Niagara Falls where the "lake effect" snows smother the area from November through April. The snow, with a few exceptions, does not disrupt daily life in upstate New York. Like many transplanted Northerners, he held the opinion that residents of the Mid-Atlantic turned into complete ninnies at the mention of any winter precipitation.

I announced that I was going to the Wal-Mart anyway and that he would thank me later after waking up at 3:00 in the morning to find himself in dire need of a fresh roll.

The supply had receded, although I found enough toilet tissue to get us through a weekend. Apparently, the hordes had left work early and already paid a visit. By the time I left the store, the snow had established a foothold and began transforming the

Riverside Writers   185

landscape. Some cars were game enough to try the road, although I did not see the snowbirds from Canada and the Northeast clogging the route to I-95, as they usually did on weekends. They were hibernating in parking lots, motels, or wherever they could find shelter from the incoming storm.

Mary Ann had placed some lighted mini-trees, no more than a foot high, outside the front doorstep the weekend before. Then she had set up a two foot high reindeer decoration. We could still see the lights as we prepared for bed.

The snow fell, fell some more, and then some. When we woke up the next morning, the mini trees had disappeared. A soft glow underneath the snow suggested where they still stood. The deer stood up to its belly in snow.

Like a bowl, the deck in the back had filled with snow. The dog, who usually used the deck to reach the backyard, was baffled at the snow which now reached over her ears. I showed her another way to reach the backyard through the basement, which had not been completely blocked off by drifts.

For a while, the heavy snowfall interfered with the satellite reception. I feared the TV would become useless, like it did shortly before Hurricane Isabel killed the power. The signal managed to penetrate the snow laden clouds, and the set continued to blare. The local stations were giddy with hysteria over the storm. Was this one of the biggest storms in the area's history? You betcha. A surveillance camera showed how the eight lane Beltway had shrunk to a single track in a field of white.

The snow fell through the day. For most people, it was a day of no responsibility, a well deserved break from adulthood. Christmas shopping, indoor sports tournaments, rehearsals for Christmas services had vanished from the calendar. Catholics would not even be obligated to attend Mass. No one ventured out except for a few four-wheel drives which silently rolled by.

The local newspaper decided to demonstrate its relevance by featuring an online blog about the road conditions. The reporter posted a few entries before she got in the spirit of the day and the blog faded to white. The blog was not necessary. Anyone could see that road travel was well nigh impossible.

On the surface, newly fallen snow appears to be harmless, pure, innocent, like a Pieter Bruegel painting. That's when the snow is most deceptive, even dangerous. Over 80 years ago, a similar snowstorm had lured Washingtonians, who had been stranded indoors for days, into a movie theater for an afternoon matinee. They did not know at the time, but the heavy snowfall had weakened the structure of the theater's roof, causing it to collapse. Dozens were killed in what became known as the Knickerbocker Theater tragedy.

Tom and I become restless after spending an entire day in confinement. We decided to hike to our local Wal-Mart, which was a quarter mile from the house. I put on my reliable waterproof Adidas hiking boots while he slipped on some rubberized black loafers. I chided him for wearing such inadequate footwear. The deep tread etched in the soles of my boots would enable me to remain upright on any surface, or so I believed.

We followed the track created by the vehicles in the snow. The tires had packed the snow into solid ice. But this did not impede my husband's progress in the least. He shot out ahead. I caught up with him when we cut through the woods past the swimming pool. There the snow was powdery although physically challenging to wade through. We crossed a four lane highway which had reverted to its original state, a path in the woods.

When I saw the Wal-Mart, I was reminded of a scene from the movie "The Day After" when the inhabitants of Lawrence, Kansas, decided to hit the supermarkets as a nuclear attack became imminent. They quickly cleaned out the meat department, grabbing the steaks as quickly as the butcher could carve them. Maybe they wanted one last barbecue before the end of the world.

The meat department was cleaned out, except for some frozen turkeys, and who knew how long it would take for one to thaw out. Frozen fish abounded. I suppose Americans will prefer red meat over fish, especially during times of crisis. I surmised plenty of bacon and egg breakfasts would be taking place this weekend and these would be washed down by mimosas, since very few cartons of orange juice and eggs were left. The Wonder bread had disappeared while the store-brand bread still lined the shelves.

A shopper groused about the lack of freshly ground burger. I was tempted to tell him that soy burger, which was available in the frozen foods section, would be a perfectly good substitute, but kept the secret to myself. Who knew when the resupply trucks would reach the store?

Tom and I looked for gloves and hats which had already been cleaned out. A clerk suggested checking back in a few days since they might discover an unopened box in the back. Unused to this Soviet-style Wal-Mart, we decided to take what we had collected and check out.

The carts, which were usually lined up next to the main entrance, were missing, the clerks having decided that they weren't worth pursuing in the snowdrifts. The empty area now presented another way to the outside. For some reason, my husband detoured from the main entrance, and used this passageway, ducking under a heavy half-open door. I was about to ask where he was going but he had disappeared into the falling snow.

I followed. I remember a girl and her dog who had taken advantage of the relatively snow free passage to sit against the wall. There were puddles of water standing on the smooth cement. Suddenly, I slipped, hitting the half opened door, with my mouth taking the blow. Then I fell backwards, with both feet in the air. The young girl looked on with horror.

At once I realized why. I licked the metallic taste of blood off my lips.

The blood was spurting out. I was sure of that. I called out, but Tom was already too far ahead.

Grabbing my bags, I struggled to get back on my feet and ducked under the door. Why hadn't he slipped since he was wearing those crazy loafers?

The bleeding was not stopping. I grabbed some snow and held it against my lips. I threw it away after it had been soaked with blood and grabbed a fresh handful. Between carrying the bags and holding snow to my lips, I managed to catch up with him.

"Oh, where were you?"

" Fell n' bust'd lip," I managed to say. I couldn't tell if the cut or numbness from cold was interfering with my speech.

Ever the lawyer, Tom asked, "Did anyone see it? We could sue the store."

"Culdn't win. Were'nt suppose be there firs' place," I mumbled back.

We made it back without any additional slip and falls. One glance in the mirror confirmed a hideous cut right on my lower lip. Stitches at a local hospital? Only if our non-four wheel drive could make it beyond the driveway, which was not likely. And right before Christmas, when I was scheduled to distribute Communion.

Rappahannock Review

Any unsightly stitches would be put on prominent display for the crowds. My best hope would be that the communicants would be so preoccupied that they wouldn't notice my mangled lips.

The next morning, I could still feel the cut, but it was growing smaller. My lip cells must have gone into overdrive to repair the damage as I slept. My lips were completely healed by Christmas Eve. That was the closest thing to a Christmas miracle I had ever experienced.

On the Ground

And Us Almost Done
by R. L Russis

I recalled Pa's anxious glancing and the horses'
impatient waiting, ears pricked-up, pointing
east toward that building storm and the noise
of their in-place shuffling coupling with the
dry creaking of leather, dull rattling of chain
hardly muffling the darker sounds of gaining
wind, of growing storm. And so we forced
the pace along, as Pa tried to hurry us done,
ahead of this advancing storm that could wet
and mold the hay laying waste our best efforts
should we not beat the weather back to barn;
but that fast-moving storm caught us midway
across the field with its wet cracks of thunder,
its quick slaps of rain that came pelting down
amidst lightning strikes that flashed strobe-like
chasing us home to a dry and welcoming barn
with us just four, long rows short from done.

There Is a Sweetness In Country Life
by Laura Merryman

There is a sweetness to country life
That liberates one from
The got to look likes
And have to seem likes.

And one does what one must,
Or when the musts rest complete,
What one wills.

So it was with the bonfire today:
Garbage and leaves
Old logs and twigs
Burning in homage to a forgotten god.

Ten inches of snow,
Wreathing the spastic flames
And smoke clinging low
To the glimmering grounds.

I lay and loafed
Like an otter in the sun.
My dogs tossing powder with their noses,
Bounding through the blinding drifts.
They leave for their miniature Iditarods,
Returning only to lick the goo
From a charred marshmallow stick.

Forgotten laundry cringes on the line,
And clay pots host huge poufs of icy meringue.
They look rather elegant in this concoction.

I wear no make-up;
My clothes don't match,
And my family about me
Waddles like overstuffed pigeons.

We clear paths between the pyre and patio,
And there is a lightness of heart
That comes with being snowed in.

Mirth in sledding in laundry baskets.
Contentment watching ash blow.
Fullness with homemade chili.
A sweetness in country life.

A Question of Horse-Power

by R. L Russis

I shifted the tractor into low
and it lurched, almost stalled,
but after some time and much-
repeated effort slowly crept
forward, crawling up and out,
inching itself higher to escape
that wallow of mud the rains
had spawned in that sunken spot
of this shallow field where had
gathered all the wet, as if for
Sunday Meeting and a crowd-
rousing, roof-raising sermon.
I thought, as it first slipped
through gears, then slipped in slop,
spewing water and mud, that
I'd be forced to fetch a team
of draft to haul us out, but then
the treads suddenly gripped,
clawed deep enough to find
a trace of solid ground, a base
of rock or gravel sufficiently
sound to support our weight
and permit our climbing out.
And the 'almost not' of our
getting out is the reason why
I still kept about that Morgan
team – slow, but steady, whose
work is true and even more
sure and whose only real fault
is the rarely-thrown shoe.

Between the First and Second Milking
by R. L Russis

Emily had reminded me when she said,
"Cow plops follow cow paths."
No small truth to that and no surprise,
it's what cows do… that and chew cud.
Her turn of phrase made me recall an earlier time,
when I, too, had walked behind the cows,
had followed those same dust-cradled lanes
that led to shade or water and both to and from
their stalls in the barn, to when I had closely
followed the sound of the lead cow's bell,
as it echoed through the seasons, in all but winter,
for in winter they were kept in the barn
or contained to the south-side yard.
But, for the rest of that time I was assigned
to follow and keep track, to see they got
where they were going and that they made
their way back in time for the evening milking.
Then I, too, would turn down a stool
and take a pail and milk my way along
that long row of swollen, low-slung udders.

Her words had taken me back across those
long-ago pastures – to when a tow-headed lad
had called, "Home, bos. Barn, bos.", while
their long tails swished at flies and lazily
swatted their sides, as they'd shaken their heads
and ears and as those brown eyes rolled around
and back to follow the circling drone of horseflies
that either knew no difference between or thought
the flavor of Morgan horse or Jersey cow or even
of freckle-faced boy all tasted near enough alike
to make a meal, to steal a quick bite and fly on,
gone buzzing beyond our hearing and our sight,
but leaving us all with those painful reminders
of reddened welts that stung, of those bites
we collected each time I chased the cows out
to pasture or herded them back to barn. But that
was just the nature of things then, the way things
were for me and the cows and that daily chore
we shared that wasn't much of a chore at all,
aside from fending off the flies.

Watch! Watch!

by R. L Russis

Pa repeated his warning, "Watch the blade!
Watch the blade!" It was something I'd hear
often, one form or another, with him saying,
"Watch the blade, the chain, the teeth, the gears."
And all those things pointed or deadly-sharp,
able to: cut, chop, puncture, drag you down
or draw you in… And he always had a story
of someone he knew or had heard of in turn
who had lost a finger to carelessness or haste,
or maybe had a hand taken off at the wrist
by some old thresher or combine under repair
with the spark yet connected, still left live,
the gears ready to turn and waiting some
thoughtless act to torque and turn, release
a charge to whir and blindly slice the grass
or air or flesh and bone and each the same
to the functioning of the machine's working
with mindless indifference. And as I leaned
in for a closer look I heard him warn again,
"Watch! Watch out!" as Pa jerked me out
of its way and the combine's blades churned
where my hand had rested, and would have lain.

Visiting Home after Long Absence

(Old Ways and Means)
by R. L Russis

That stone smokehouse stood as a tribute
to old ways and means, as a reminder
and record of our family's past, of times
and troubles overcome, of our ties to the land
and a way of life that has mostly passed us by.

So stood the pump that no longer worked
to draw water for the house. And the out-
house was gone too; well, not gone, but no
longer in use, a mere piece of rustic décor.

And the rain barrels were gone as well,
those oaken kegs that had sat at the corners
of the house, catching the runoff rains
for the washing of clothes or for watering
the garden and flowers my Gram had grown
on the steeper, upward side of the house.

I can still see her in my mind, on her knees,
weeding down-row or dippering a drink
to the plants, coaxing them through the heat
to harvest, and always done with a song
or a quiet humming—and the plants and
weeds waving, as if in time to her tune.

Collateral Damage
by Elizabeth Talbot

I rattled off my old address to the driver
who gave me an uncomprehending look.
How foolish of me.
The Panamanians have probably renamed the streets.
But then he took pity on me.
Of course, that's where the Americans used to live.

The banyan tree still rules the back yard
plotting to take over the grass.
Should I ring the doorbell
Request permission to review the scenes of my youth?

But there is no need to,
With them already embedded in my mind.
My father leaving for his job
at Canal Administration Headquarters
just as the yellow school bus arrived,
Daily, like in the states.

Always taking us home at the same time.
with the exception of one Friday evening,
when after a football game
the driver took a wrong turn
and as the jungle swallowed us up,
he kept muttering to himself, "Madre de Dios!"
wondering how he would feed ten mouths without his job.

Left in the care of Señora Martinez
who presented me with a glass of cold milk
from that white sepulcher of a Frigidaire
that steadily hummed away,
who drilled me in the conjugation of Spanish verbs
as she starched and ironed the tablecloths
just like the ones at the Officers' Club.

Until my mother returned, just in time,
from the Women's Auxiliary
to fix my father's first martini.

A routine set forever, it appeared,
until that peanut farmer from Georgia
decided to give back everything
the Canal, the Administration building, the Club
the football fields, and finally the backyard
with the banyan tree.

My father retired to New Jersey
vaguely remembering his grandfather had lived there
before he was recruited to dig the big ditch.
But it wasn't the heart attack that finished him
rather, it was the strangeness of a foreign land.

Afraid to pronounce it myself
I present the cab driver with an address
written by a palsied hand
and entrusted to a flimsy airmail envelope.

Struggling to stand on a prosthetic leg
Señora Martinez embraces me.
Served now by the nieces and nephews
she managed to put through school.

Too polite to discuss how before one Christmas
during the Invasion of Panama
her tenement got in the way
of the Air Force's efforts to extricate Noriega.

She did not dwell on the endless wait for rescue
or the plight of having a leg amputated
on top of the indignities of old age.

She remembers we were nice enough children
unlike some of those brats
the other domestics complained about.
My parents were nice too.
But after all these years, she still wonders
why my mother never told her "Thank you."

Loved by All

by Elizabeth Talbot

Cliff tried to reach the main highway before the storm broke but the narrow country lanes of the Virginia piedmont hardly let him make any time. Then there was the cow that stupidly wandered into the middle of the road. The sky turned inky black, and the next minute he felt trapped in a car wash beside a bowling alley. At least the lightning had the courtesy to flash as a huge tree trunk crashed into the road ahead of him. Well, that changed his plans for the evening.

He looked back and could not see any extra margin in the road which would allow him to turn around. He also realized that the road had taken him into a low area, and storm runoff from the mountains to the west might come rushing through any minute in its race to the Chesapeake. A flash flood was a real possibility.

As he tried to think about what to do next, the windshield wipers flailed, rendering them useless. Glancing backwards, Cliff switched into reverse, and backing up, alternately tapped the accelerator and brakes. Fortunately, the back windshield wiper continued to thump back and forth. But the brake and backup lights failed to illuminate the darkness. Cliff hoped that the tires would maintain contact with the pavement. No branches crashed through the back windshield, so he assumed he remained on the road.

Patience, he cautioned himself. Cliff was not used to driving with his head turned backwards and so he had to straighten his neck once in a while. The storm had smothered any remaining daylight and now he was in darkness. Cliff, accustomed to the artificial light that flooded suburbia, was disoriented by the total darkness. It was like traveling in a cave. He was almost overwhelmed by claustrophobia.

Lightning flashed again and thunder rattled his car. But the flash revealed he was backing into what appeared to be some kind of commercial establishment, a one story wooden building covered by hand lettered signs promising groceries, dry goods, hardware and tires, interspersed with brightly colored round signs for soft drinks he did not recognize. An antique store, maybe? Then another flash followed, allowing Cliff to make out more details. Rocking chairs waited on a wooden porch while the water from the roof gushed into a wooden barrel on the side of the building. Perhaps this was the place he had looked for so long.

Cliff had attained the rank of instructor at the local university and then his career had plateaued. The tenured positions that guaranteed a lifetime of financial security, minimal teaching loads, and leisure for academic pursuits were always just beyond his grasp, if they still existed. Recognizing the need to "publish or perish," he racked his brains until he came up with a topic of the role of the country store in the economic and cultural development of rural Virginia. Using the jargon that only other academics could understand, he put together a proposal and obtained a grant from the Virginia Council of the Humanities.

His wife, who was originally thrilled, was dismayed when he spent every spare hour in search of an actual country store. At first, Cliff made a show of unity by taking along the family in search of the "real Virginia." But he soon realized this was not enough to hold their attention. He glanced back and found his son engrossed in a new game on his Nintendo DS while his daughter stared at the video playing overhead. Finally his wife started to hint about returning in time to walk the dog.

Cliff began making these journeys on his own, crisscrossing the countryside between the major highways. But he was disappointed. He could see a few signs that a building, occupied or abandoned, may have been the kind of place he had in mind. A covered apron where drivers once filled up their tanks had been converted into a carport for a modest residence. Or faded lettering on a weathered board announced "Groceries." In Stafford County, he even discovered some narrow necked gas pumps in front of a boarded up building that had rocking chairs left on the porch. Sadly, a snarling pit bull prevented him from making any additional inquiries at the modest frame home located behind the store.

Cliff realized that Virginians now obtained their gas from "marts" with the prefix "fast" or "quick" attached to them, staffed by newcomers who barely spoke English and acknowledged their customers with the briefest of nods. Or purchased their goods from big box retailers staffed by minimum-wage drones in nondescript blue smocks. He wondered if he was pursuing a phantasm.

This trip, which had ended with the tree crashing just inches in front of his vehicle, had begun badly. This time his wife had blocked the door with her body.

"Don't go!"

"You know the Humanities Council is expecting something out of this."

"You've spent more in gas than what the entire grant was worth!"

"But I need to write the article," Cliff explained, as he had many times before, "To get tenure, I have to write articles!"

"Articles nobody reads!" The tension rose in his wife's voice. "Forget tenure, go to business school before it's too late!"

"Well, if you would socialize with the faculty wives, uh, spouses, once in a while."

"God damn you!" she screamed. It was like a thunderclap, then the downpour. "If I wasn't working full time we'd be underwater right now! I'm not living this way for the rest of my life."

Unable to explain himself any further, Cliff maneuvered around her and headed straight for the car. Fortunately his keys were stuffed in one pocket of his corduroy jacket, his digital camera in the other, and his wallet bulged out of his jeans pocket. He liked the drives; they gave him a chance to sort his thoughts without interruption.

He began tinkering about a new class to teach. He usually taught one of those "Philosophy" of some popular TV show or movie. When he began teaching, he had started with "Philosophy of 'Star Trek'" and then moved on to "Philosophy of 'Star Wars'" and then "Philosophy of 'The Simpsons.'" Lately, he sensed that the students were losing interest, so he speculated about replacing "The Simpsons" with "South Park" or "Jersey Shore."

His class was popular because it was one of those "easy" grades that would improve any student's grade point average. The grade point average, in turn, helped determine who would be admitted to graduate school, the perfect escape for any able student during a prolonged and painful recession. And after graduate school, then what? Jobs for which a high school diploma would have been sufficient in the past.

More than once, Cliff had felt like throwing down his notes and shouting, "This is all a lie. In case you haven't noticed, we are now experiencing the worst job market since the Great

Depression! Why put yourself in all this debt? There aren't going to be any jobs when you get out."

Then Cliff reminded himself that he did not have tenure yet and he should keep his fat mouth shut and go along with the program.

Cliff tried to call his wife but his cell phone did not respond. He must have been in a dead zone. He remembered the wrench buried in the cubbyhole and briefly toyed with fixing the wipers himself, but discarded the idea since he did not want to be drenched in the process. If the store was still open, Cliff would run inside, get a soda, and wait for the thunderstorm to pass. He dashed through the standing water and pushed the screen door open.

The store was bathed in the soft glow of candlelight provided by candles placed on any available shelf space, which was hard to find because of the cartons and boxes crammed on the shelves. An older man in a rumpled cotton shirt and off-white slacks waited behind the counter. "Good evening," he greeted Cliff, "Nasty weather we're having tonight."

"Indeed," replied Cliff, "And my windshield wipers chose this time to quit working."

The old man turned around and retrieved a soda from a refrigerator behind, as though he had already read Cliff's mind and knew what he wanted. "Electric's out but these will stay cold for a while. You from the city?"

Cliff nodded and accepted the bottle. It was made of glass. He had not drunken Coke from a glass bottle for a long time. Already he could see a film forming over the glass from contact with the warm, muggy air. The bottle was that cold.

Two elderly men, dressed in flannel shirts and overalls, sat hunched over what first appeared to be chess. Cliff, an amateur player himself, took a step or two closer to see what move they were contemplating. However, he was disappointed to find they only played checkers. He could not figure out why the men would be so engrossed in such a game.

"They're like sunning turtles," explained the old man, "don't see 'em moving for hours."

"It's suppertime, dear." A woman appeared in the back doorway. She was stout as older women are prone to be, a white apron tied against her ample bosom, her hair streaked with grey and twisted into in a tight knot. She noticed the man in the damp corduroy jacket. "My, look what the cat brought in! Why don't you take off that wet thing and have supper with us?"

Cliff demurred. "Nonsense," she exclaimed. "There's no trouble setting an extra plate. We have plenty to share."

He followed the couple into what appeared to be a dining room with an unpretentious wooden table and chairs. A kerosene lantern sputtered on the table. She snatched his jacket and placed it on an empty chair, and then swept over to the china hutch to grab a plate and silverware.

"We like catching up on the outside world," explained the old man as he unfolded a napkin over his lap. "What brings you here?"

When Cliff explained that he was engaged in a research project at the local college, the old man asked, "The University at Charlottesville?"

"Mary Washington at Fredericksburg."

"That women's college," exclaimed the old man, "Did you hear that, Elsie? How is it teachin' all those women?"

Cliff was about to explain that the college had been coed for years, but he was interrupted by Elsie, "Pshaw, dear, women now go to college like everyone else." She went around spooning peaches out of a Ball jar into empty bowls.

"You sell a lot of things here," remarked Cliff. "With the times the way they are, how is your business doing?"

"It's rough, with all those folks bein' thrown out of work" Then he gave his wife an all knowing smile. "But we've got it all figured out, haven't we dear?"

"We've extended credit to everyone," she said, "Told 'em they could pay it back later."

"That's generous of you," remarked Cliff, "But aren't you worried about not being repaid?"

"Not at all," replied the old man, "we know all these people, gave their kids candy, and then gave the grandkids candy too. They've been right kind to us." He winked at his wife, "Shall I tell the young man how we met?"

"He was a Fuller brush salesman when he showed up at my mother's doorstep one day. He caught a glimpse of me while he was selling my mother a brush."

The old man beamed. "She was a prettiest thing I had ever seen so I kept coming back with some new gadget or another. Finally, her mother looked me right in the eye and declared

'You're not here to sell me an extra brush. It's my daughter you want to see.' She durn well was tellin' the truth, right dear?"

"And then after we got married . . ."

"I wanted to go sellin' my brushes but Elsie wanted to settle down so we bought this store, see. If it hadn't been for her, I would have been another salesman with fallen arches." Elsie patted the old man's hand.

Cliff noticed that the couple appeared to take great pleasure in each other's company. When had he last shown any affection toward his wife?

"Times are tough everywhere," said the old man, "but as long as we have each other, we'll survive. Because tough times won't last forever."

His wife nodded in hearty agreement.

After the meal, Cliff rose. "Maybe I should leave now."

"Not in this weather," Elsie insisted. "We always keep a spare bed for salesmen." She nodded in the direction of another dimly lit room. "You're welcome to stay." The patter of rainfall had become less insistent on the roof, but the thunder continued to growl in the distance. Cliff did not want to be caught in another torrential rain with his ailing windshield wipers.

Once in the bedroom, Cliff took out his cell phone to call his wife but discovered that the battery had died. He considered asking the couple about using their phone, but they had already turned in for the night. Lifting up the blanket, he found the sheets were stretched so tight he could bounce a quarter. Finally, he blew out the solitary candle on the night stand. The only light remaining was the phosphorescent glow from an old fashioned wind-up clock on the stand, not unlike the one on the bed stand when he stayed with his grandparents.

How much the couple reminded him of them. In August, his mother would take him and his siblings to his grandparents in the country. His grandfather would load the children in the back of his Chevy pickup and they would head for the country store to pick up sodas. But his grandfather did not make the trip simply to pick up sodas. The storekeeper was a font of information about the goings on in the neighborhood, and with neighbors and friends dropping in, it was a chance to catch up between Sundays. Listening to the patter on the roof, he then realized why he had become so enamored of the topic of general stores. They reminded him of a time in his life when he was free from writing theses and competing for scarce positions, when he was liked for who he was, when he saw other people, for once, behave in community.

When he awoke, he laid a while before he realized where he was and the circumstances that had brought him here. He pulled on his pants and peeked into the dining room. The couple had not gotten up yet.

Cliff vaguely thought of a cup of coffee but remembered he had to make it back in time to teach his class. If his wife hadn't already contacted the highway patrol, she would worry about his failure to return. He could charge the cell phone in the car.

No use troubling these people any further. They had been generous enough. He took a couple of twenties out of his wallet and left them on the night stand.

The sun had just peeked over the horizon and rays were lighting up the store in a way the candles the night before never could. The checker players had left, although the checkers remained on the squares as if the game would resume at any moment. Cliff could now read the lettering on some of the boxes. Shoes made in Massachusetts. How long had it been since shoes were made there and not somewhere in China? Perhaps America had begun manufacturing shoes again.

Cliff whipped out his camera and took picture after picture. His article could use some pictures. Maybe he would have the opportunity to come back and conduct an additional interview with the couple.

He drove back to the main highway and decided that his schedule would allow him enough time to have his windshield wipers fixed at a garage while he had breakfast at a diner across the street. A real waitress, not a student pretending to be one, came out and took his order and soon Cliff was digging into a stack of pancakes and a steaming mound of scrambled eggs.

"That was quite a storm last night." the waitress remarked as she refreshed his coffee. Cliff could tell she had done this all her life. Her uniform, from her hair net to her white canvas shoes, was spotless, neatly pressed.

"I was caught right in it," said Cliff. "A tree crashed in front of me and then my windshield wipers quit. Fortunately, a nice couple who ran a general store took me in for the night."

"Really, where at?"

"Along Route 633," said Cliff.

"Don't know of anything along that road anymore." She spotted a spill, and whipping out a rag, proceeded to wipe it up. "A store was there when I was a kid. The nicest couple ran it. They used to give out candy to all the kids."

She tossed the rag into a tub of dirty dishes. "My grandparents told me they gave out a lot of credit during the Depression. In fact, that was how a lot of people survived.
What you could grow in the garden, hunt in the woods, and for everything else, there was the credit at the general store. Burned down twenty or thirty years ago. A candle had been left burning after the electric had been knocked out during a storm."

Cliff was so startled that he almost dropped his coffee. "And what happened to the couple?"

"Their charred bodies were later found in the rubble," she said, "Everyone was saddened since they had helped so many, especially during the Depression. No one knew if they had any family so everyone pitched in for a funeral and a stone. 'Loved By All' their customers had carved on it."

Cliff gulped down the last bite of eggs and asked for the check as soon as possible. Scarcely bothering to look before crossing the road, he narrowly missed being flattened by an eighteen wheeler. An emergency had come up, he explained to the mechanic, and he had to leave right away. Cliff settled the bill and took off in search of the road where he had met the couple. His students would have to wait for graduate school.

Barely paying attention to the curves which the road now threw him, Cliff craned his neck out of the window for any glimpse of where he had been the night before. Here or there, a trees or a shed would look familiar, but no store.

Cliff stopped in the middle of the road and took out his camera.

"That place has to be real," he exclaimed. "I took pictures!"

He hit the review button. Nothing came up.

Cliff wanted to blame the battery, but nothing indicated that his camera was less than fully charged. Cliff tossed the camera in the passenger seat and resumed his rush to find the store. He drove into the same depression where the storm had reached its peak. In plain sight, the tree, which had barely missed his car the night before, still lay in the road. He slammed on the brakes and got out of the car, as if to reassure himself that it was real.

"It's the same," Cliff muttered to himself. But he still wasn't sure if he had experienced what happened afterwards. The muggy heat, the cold glass, they felt real enough at the time. He had even eaten there!

After reentering the car, Cliff alternately tapped the accelerator and the brakes as he had done the night before. He resisted the temptation to hurry. But no garish signs, no wooden frame building appeared.

Cliff noticed a little clearing at the roadside where he could park. He got out of the car to continue his search on foot, peering into bushes, pulling apart branches for a better view.

The barrel, brimming with water the night before, lay on its side, unconnected to any gutter. Cliff took another breath, refocusing his concentration. Although the kudzu did a good job of covering up whatever had stood in the first place, he recognized the foundations of a building. He gingerly stepped into a ruin of sorts, being careful not to allow the vines to trip him. The rubble crumbled beneath his steps.

To his left, Cliff saw a rusting hulk on its side, like a shipwreck. The refrigerator from the night before? He couldn't tell. There was no sign of any other furniture. Cliff decided to take a few steps in what he hoped would be the direction of the spare bedroom.

There he found the night stand, badly singed, but still standing, the alarm clock melted over the edge, like a Salvador Dali painting. And the two twenties, as crisp and new as he had left them earlier that morning.

The Fifty-Cent Tour
by David Mitchell

Good afternoon ladies and gentlemen. Welcome aboard the Magic Trolley for the I-Can't-Tell-What's-Real-and-What-Isn't Tour. Before we begin I must tell you some important safety instructions. In case of emergency, please direct your attention to the threat level indicator located above my head. This will tell you what level of anxiety you should be experiencing. Should the threat level be orange you will find an emergency kit located below your seat. Inside you will find plastic sheeting and a roll of duct tape.

Now that that's out of the way, we may begin.

We are entering a dream world
A things-aren't-what-they-seem world
A world where fact and fantasy collide
A crazy world where black is white
Where war is peace and wrong is right
Just stick with me and I will be your guide
Do not trust your vision for nothing here is certain
Please pay no attention to that man behind the curtain
Rely on me to tell you what is real
Do not trust your hearing for sound can be deceiving
Do not trust your thoughts and what you think you are
        perceiving
Only I can tell you how to feel

Now if you look out the window to your right ladies and gentlemen you will see the world's largest mountain of industrial waste. We call this mountain: Prosperity. Beautiful, isn't it? A bit further beyond that mountain on the right is another mountain. This other mountain is made from the rubble of bombed out cities. We call this mountain: Victory. Magnificent! Ah, I love the smell of victory in the morning.

If you look out the window to your left you will see a memorial to the dearly departed. The inscription on the stone reads: Irony. Do any of you believe in ghosts?

We are passing through a new world
A hard-to-tell-what's-true world
A world that's less of substance than of mind
A sketchy world where pundits spin
Where in is out and out is in
A world that's quite confusing and you'll find
You cannot trust the experts for they've been bought and
        paid for
You cannot trust your TV for that's not what it's made for
So put your trust in me, your friendly guide
I will tell you what to think
What to eat and what to drink
I'll open up my head, please step inside

Okay folks, I've just been informed that we are approaching the outer limits of the Emerald City, that shining city on the hill, the city of brotherly love, the city of angels. To pass through the city gates we must pay a toll. The admission price is faith. To enter, we must believe. To believe you must suspend all disbelief. The laws of physics have been repealed here. Logic and reason should be disregarded. Critical thinking is not welcome. Surrender your mind and obey my instructions.

Oh, sorry folks. I've just been informed that there will be a delay in our tour due to some roadway construction ahead. We call this roadway: Progress.

Shoppers Unite
by Tracy Deitz

In Walmart an unusual sight arrested me
two Tibetan monks in tangerine tunics
doing a double take
nope—not hallucinating
young Asian men
cropped black hair
gingerbread skin
stood there
right arms bare
respect
an international moment
exchanging currency
at 1 p.m. in a local store
monks' orange clothing flow
into pleated fins of goldfish
contained behind politeness
refrained from asking the Buddhists
about their lives and how did
they like our states united
in commonality exit with purchases
covet the receipt
exports guarded at the gate
red, white, and blue
by a vested company
polite nod and blind eye
toward proof of belonging
from a clipped colonial accent
British English
acquired in India
speaking the quintessential American phrase:
"Have a nice day."

Brake the Fast

by Tracy Deitz

Configured like monoliths at Stonehenge
sausage patties circle the griddle,
leaving room between columns
for druids to dance.

Ancient rite of preparation
anticipates satisfaction
when smoked pork
blends with buttery biscuit
slathered with strawberry jam.

Saturday morning meditation
without the hurry-scurry;
enjoy the simple pleasure
of breakfast at home.

The Stationary Family
by Andrea Reed

We seemed to stay in place.
The extended family came to us face to face.
They came from all directions.
Places to us that were only locations.
In summers we were graced with visits from South Carolina-
Cousins with southern accents we loved to hear them talk.
The mid-westerners hailed from Kansas.
We rode roller coasters and went on brief day trips
with cousins, aunt and uncle.
The Georgian visitors came less frequently,
but still delighted us.
We had a seafood feast for them.
The east coast was represented by visitors from Maryland who
would bring bear hugs, family gatherings
and delightful conversation.
We remained the stationary family,
and reveled in their visits.

Fredericksburg 1727
by Norma E. Redfern

~~~In 1732 Colonel William Byrd visited Fredericksburg five years after the Charter was granted; the town showed great potential for future growth~~~

Faith led the way to the history of our town

Resolutions were drafted by leaders on April 25, 1775

England had increasing troubles with her colonies

Differing views; Parliament ruling including taxes on tea

Envisioning what Fredericksburg would become

Revolt expected in all of the North America Colonies

Independence celebrated in Fredericksburg
    with a Peace Ball

Community leaders were Mercer, Weedon, Woodford,
    Posey, Wallace and Towles

Keeping the town financially stable with Fielding Lewis'
    fortune

Signers pledged their lives and fortunes; arms if necessary

Bold and honorable this country would stand strong

Unity and prosperity flourishing beyond our dreams

Rebellious patriots stood together to make Virginia
    their own

George Washington first led the Army, then the Nation

A Night Out in Fredericksburg (An Artist at Work)

by Michelle O'Hearn

Crafted and intricate,
Bejeweled at every centimeter
The fabric retains an order of elegance
Wealthy enough to hold the most delicate breasts
Soft; moisturized and powdered

Up two feet to the top of the head,
Each strand of conditioned hair placed perfectly and sprayed,
Little wisps to grace the face
Where here, the most care and attention is placed,
A stunning blend of colors to keep one occupied
    during conversation
Details in the eyes and on every lash

Talking to a painting and having the beauty speak in return
The true desire when strolling any echoing museum
Color licked the lips of this spectacle behind the glasses
And smoothed the paintbrush down
To a sequined shoe and sparkling toes
Somewhere between getting lost in the linear extension
    of the legs,
Crafted and intricate, is the perfection of the artist's stroke

Eratosthenes

by Madalin E. Jackson

I wonder what rest
In the stone and marble halls.
Tomes and scrolls from ancient times
Forever lost?
Beta kept them secure
While original thoughts he wove
To Siene at
Solstice time.

A shadow, an angle
A theory took flight.
The proof was calculated,
The ancients knew
What Columbus sailed to prove.
East found west
And a new land was
Born.

Suddenly the distance
Shortened and
The world became one.
Knowledge became power;
Conjecture proven.
Mankind drawn closer
By the meager thoughts
Of a Greek librarian.

Apprenticed to Art
by R. L Russis

The guiding rule of thumb was,
"One over two, two over one."

He said it often and just as often said,
"Once you pick a stone, place it –

there's no sense to handling it twice,
so develop your eye and let it guide you,

size the space, seize the stone and set it in place.
Lift it but the once, more is waste of time."

His movements were spare, lean; nothing extra
here, except the care he gave to what he did.

He was an artisan, in the old tradition, his
hands and eyes honed both by time and stone.

He favored dry-stacked – no mortar and trowel.
He couldn't be bothered, *"More waste of time,"*

he'd say, *"if built right, it will stand firm*
upon the land, time has shown us that!"

And so, like his forebears, he built to last,
built it right, level and straight, squared

and true. And such was the way he built,
what I learned, how he taught me to do.

Observation

by Norma E. Redfern

Out the window
I gazed around
A bald head emerged he
Looked around quickly
Off his shirt came

A half-naked man
What was he doing
At the Salem Church Library?

I was here for a meeting
Was he going to take off more?
Would it be brief, boxers or bare?

All I could think of
Naked man in parking lot
Children all around

To my surprise
Out came a white shirt
Buttoned quickly
Off he went
I wondered where he was going

I watched, mouth agape as
He walked into our meeting
Arms loaded with books

He was the main attraction
Sharing his information about writing
An elegant poet, no longer naked

The Orchid
by Jackson Harlem

He is not a flower.

The penile monster with multiple tongues and glowing stamens
Clouds my judgment with his cocainous pollen
The drug-dealer of flora;
He's a dirty priest breeding seeds with the sun and the rain and I can't breathe it.
I know he's plotting something, though I can't see it.

In the quiet of this winter-colored room
I am nameless; I have nothing to do with literature
I have given my name to the desk clerks and my clothes to my siblings
And my history to the journalists and my books to librarians

Outside of this literary laboratory
Researchers scurry like mice in their white coats,
Pushing their glasses upwards on their noses
While all the books cry out from their shelves
"Pick me!" they exclaim as the spectators crowd my mailbox of a window.

I have let myself go, a twenty-something-year-old poet
Stubbornly performing for the people
They have blogged about me until my stock has sky-rocketed
I have watched my name in headlines, sprawled across newspapers and magazines
Printed little pieces of me with oversaturated verbs
Like candy-infested children procreating in the media.
Yet in this sterile room, with photographers' lights flashing through the window,
I close my eyes to the storm of men outside.
I am a monk now, I have never been so silent.

Silent as the dead I liken this silence to
"Will I join my fellow poets of yore?" I wonder to myself
Lightning flashes from a camera and jars me back to reality
Like Communion juice being choked from a virgin throat.

Loaded guns point from the orchid's mouth who stands
in a vase
on the small white table beside my bed:
The Technicolor monster eats up my oxygen.

Wild and brazen like a Serengeti beast, I cannot tame him
Loud and wide-mouthed, he is a silent violent delinquent
His rapturous ends pistil whip the air
Humans swell and shed tears when he opens his mouth,
but he doesn't care.
A visually vulgar siren blaring freckled expletives
into my retinas.

I protrude my double-edged razor and he does not flinch
He leans toward my tongue of fire
He photosynthesizes
My melanin drips away from my face;
I am sweating poems I've been promising to write.

I close my eyes and bow my head
What kind of ceremony is this?
He opens his mouth and eats me whole, poetry and all.

My reds bleed into his yellows and the pollen powders the oranges
brown.
The brute and I are one.

I am the orchid poet; Fearless and silent.
Silent and beautiful. Handsome and cocainous.
Cocainous and brewing. Brewing and deadly.
Deadly and enchanting. Enchanting and chanting
Rhythmic cantatas about sunlight and scriptures, standing
on a small white table
Beside my empty sarcophagus of a bed.
I pose for mailbox-sized pictures for the carnivorous gluttons

with their cameras.

Lean toward my tongue of fire
Let me speak my opium for you.

Let me speak my opium for you.

Shades of Music
by Tracy Deitz

Front-row seat, middle section
Nose even with the stage floor
Peering beneath the Steinway grand
Saw the pianist's glossy black shoes press pedals
Tips of tux tails dance
But no face
His left thumb twitches on the thigh
Benched below the spotlight
Resting for a moment, hidden
Fingernails closely trimmed
Telltale flick of cuff prior
To next run on keyboard
At an oblique angle
Bodiless fingers pluck strings
Of a harp
One hand white; the other an exact silhouette

Across the stage under another music stand
Slender foot strapped atop high heel
Taps in rhythm
Black fishnet hosiery belies austere gray slacks
White bow tie askew at that view
Red strawberry under chin
From kissing the violin
Prim bows buzz like angry bees

From instrumental *Magic Flute*
In resplendent theater
Concert segues after applause
Outside to cold, dark street
Three youthful black percussionists
Comprise ancient-modern tribe
Beating plastic paint buckets and aluminum trash lids
Inviting, compelling
Elderly, ethereal white hands to note
Melody singing in the shadows

Trepidation turns gold moonlit faces away
Tucks heads in fur coat collars
Oblivious to unsolicited encore of blues.

*Conflicts
Small and Great*

Punctuality

by Larry Turner

I always hate
To get there late.
My wife hates being early,
Creating strife
Twixt man and wife,
And driving us both squirrelly.

From Your Sweet Lips

by Anne H. Flythe

As usual what you say to me
flows like a stream of honey,
slow, sweet, golden;
between a few smooth rocks
of truth that guide the flow
away from outright lies
your tongue savors
the sticky pleasure of evasion.

Twins Anonymous: Support Group for Those Overshadowed by Their Twins

by Larry Turner

1. Iphicles

Hello. My name is Iphicles, and I'm a twin.
I am the son of Alkmene and Amphitryon.
Herakles, my twin, is the son of Alkmene and Zeus.
All my life, when kids chose up teams, they'd choose
Herakles before me. If there was a Nemean lion to be killed,
folks would turn to him. If there was a Cretan bull to be captured,
would anyone think of asking me? At least I never minded
that it was Herakles who had to clean the stables.

You say, "It must have been wonderful having Herakles
to protect you. When those two serpents came into your cradle,
Herakles was there to kill them for you." But that's not
the point. Were it not for Herakles, nobody'd send us snakes.

And girls. Do you suppose girls ever look at me
when Herakles is around? At least while Eurystheus
sent him off to do those impossible tasks,
he was out of my hair and the girls noticed me. No matter.
He came home more famous, more insufferable yet.

2. Thomas

Hello. My name is—Never mind. Nobody even knows my name.
All my life, it's been just "Twin." "Thomas" in Aramaic.
"Didymus" in Greek. And through this nickname, Thomas,
all doubters in the world are called after me.

My twin has always eclipsed me. I even wrote a gospel,
and 2000 years later they still won't put it with the other four.

Pardon me for saying so, Iphicles, but Herakles' father Zeus
did tend to play around, so he had lots of sons. My twin's father
had only the one, so that son is, well, unique.

I am the son of Mary and Joseph. Jesus,
my twin, is the son of Mary and the Holy Spirit.
Imagine how my psyche has been harmed
when half the people in the world believe
my mother was a lifelong virgin.

Homage to the Cardiff Giant

by Larry Turner

And we're standing, Jenny and me,
in front of the Cardiff Giant at the Farmer's Museum
in Cooperstown, New York
What's so great about a fake giant? she asks.
So I tell her that back in 1869
this atheist George Hull got irritated by the Bible literalists
who said there really were giants back in the days
        of Genesis.
So Hull had this statue made, nearly eleven feet tall.
He aged it then buried it on Newell's farm in Cardiff.
A year later, Newell hired two men to dig a well there,
and the workers discovered the Giant.
Newell charged people 25 cents, and then later 50 cents,
to see the Giant. The marvel was so popular
Hull and Newell sold out to a syndicate.

You keep talking about Barnum.
What's Barnum have to do with it?
Barnum saw the success of the syndicate,
offered $60,000 to rent the Giant,
but they said no dice. So Barnum
had a copy made and began to show it.
At one point, both Giants were on display
in New York City, each claiming
to be the only authentic one.
Next time we'll go to
Marvin's Marvelous Mechanical Museum
near Detroit, and see Barnum's copy
among vintage coin-operated machines
and a replica of the electric chair from Sing Sing.

I'm telling her that, and I'm explaining
how Barnum was teaching folks to be skeptical,
just look at the what's there,
draw conclusions for themselves,
not let someone else do their thinking for them.
*And how do I know Barnum ever cared
about teaching the public? How do I know
he just wasn't out to make a quick buck?*
Why shouldn't he take money for teaching?
At their best, that's what the universities should do,
teach you how to evaluate evidence,
not teach you facts.
No facts. No historical facts. No scientific facts.
No facts of any kind.

*What do you mean, No facts?
How can you have science without facts?
How can you have history without facts?*
Facts? What about George Washington?
Did he chop down the cherry tree?
Did he throw a dollar across the Rappahannock?
Did he crush a horse's ribs between his legs?
*You go this way, there's nothing left
of George Washington but his false teeth.
George Washington was real.
And he really did make history.*
Phooey to History.
Phooey to Science.
Phooey to Religion and Government and Advertisers.

Riverside Writers

And Phooey to Love, she says.
If you loved me, we'd go where I want to go sometimes.
It's not enough you drag me up here to see a fake Giant,
now you want to drag me to Detroit to see a fake fake.
Cooperstown is only 250 miles from Niagara Falls.
No, I don't mean I want to marry you—
at least not now. But Niagara Falls is real.
Real water falling down from real rocks.
Oh, I know they turn it off at night,
send all the water to make electricity.
But cascading water filling my field of view,
smelling and feeling the mist,
hearing the roar.
That's real.

A Cake for Josie
by Donna H. Turner

As Chris entered the apartment with Gram after church, the first thing she saw was the empty table. No cake. "Mom, I was telling Gram about the birthday cake I made for Josie, but I don't see it."

"Well, the whereabouts of the cake is a story in itself," Vivian said evasively. "I'll put the tea out, you can put the dishes out, Chris, and we'll have tea and apple pie."

"Yes, but what happened to the cake? When Gram picked me up Friday afternoon, it was right on the kitchen table. And now it's gone."

"Well, to explain what happened to the cake, I'll have to start at the beginning. Friday night after I talked to you from Evelyn's apartment, I came home and went straight to bed. When I woke up Saturday morning and went into the kitchen, there was the cake with 'Happy 11 Birthday, Josie' on it. I realized Gram must have picked you up before you could take it to her. I was sure Josie would love it, and decided to take it to her. Evelyn Engleston answered the door and in her most offensive voice, she asked, 'Well, what do you want?'

"I just stood there with the cake in my hands and started to explain that you made it for Josie's birthday and that my mother picked you up before you had a chance to bring it over, so I thought Josie would like to have it.

"Then Evelyn up and said, 'Why would she make a cake if she wasn't even invited to the party? No gift is needed or desired.'

"'Chris and Jody have been planning this party for a month,' I explained.

"And she said, 'Well, they were wrong. I control who comes to my house, and it's not Chris.'

"So I asked, 'But why? What could you possibly have against Chris? She is as sweet and kind as she can be; besides, she and Josie are good friends. She's never done anything to you or said anything offensive.'

"And darned if she didn't tell me, straight to my face, 'She has you for a mother, and that's reason enough. That's what's wrong with her.'

"Then Evelyn turned around and called Josie. 'Josie, come in here right now. I do not want you playing or associating with Chris at all. Do you understand?'

"'No, I don't. Mom, she's my best friend.'

"Evelyn went on. 'That, young lady, is not a matter for discussion. That is a direct order.'

"She turned back to me. 'So you see, we don't want you or your cake.'

"'Oh, Mom, Chris bakes such good cakes. Can't we even take it?'

"'Really, Evelyn,' I began, 'I'm sorry you feel that way.'

"Evelyn glared at me. 'Let me tell you where you can take your cake and stick it!'

"Then something very strange happened. I felt the cake grow heavier and heavier. Before I knew what was happening, it somehow slipped and fell all over Mrs. Engleson's face, blouse, skirt, legs and shoes. Immediately, Josie's brother was down on the floor, eating it as fast as he could pick it up, and saying through his full mouth, 'Hey, this is good. This is really good.'

"Mrs. Engleson screamed, 'John Michael, leave that cake alone! I'm calling the police!'

"Sweet as sugar, I told her, 'Oh, I'm so sorry, Evelyn. What a waste of a fine dessert. At least John Michael is getting some of it.' He kept shoving tidbits into his mouth.

"I tasted the crumbs of cake left on the plate. Honey, your cake was so good. Then I walked out of the building saying, 'You know where to find me, Evelyn.'

"Darling, I'm sorry your cake was ruined, but I tell you, it couldn't have happened to a nicer lady."

Gram was appropriately shocked. "Vivian, I can't believe you did that. You know better. Especially to someone who dislikes you that much, and might do something about it."

But Chris's laughter was infectious, and soon Gram smiled. Then her smile vanished, and she said, "Well, it must have been fun, but don't be surprised if Josie has been forbidden to play with Chris. And, Vivian, Mrs. Engleson did threaten to call the police."

"I know, Gram," Chris put in, "We don't have to play together here. We can see each other at school, and I just bet Josie was laughing too."

"You know, Mom," Vivian added, "what can the police do? Even if she does call them, they can't prove the cake didn't slip. And I never touched her. Chris, this may not be one of my finest moments, but to tell the truth, it felt great!"

Doris Emmit

by Donna H. Turner

I thought I was terrible when I stole money to pay off Doris Emmett. Doris was two grades ahead of me and twice my size, and when she said to bring a quarter or get beat up, she meant it. My eight-year-old mind figured I had two choices: one, to pay her money or, two, transfer to another school, away from Doris. I reasoned that God didn't really want me to get beat up every day, and there wasn't another school in our area, so it was all right to take the money. I wasn't the only child she threatened, but she could easily pounce on me as an example of what would happen if she didn't get her money. Doris was smart enough not to beat me up during the school day, but she did pound on me after school. She tore my dress, pulled my hair almost out of my head, knocked me down in the dirt, then sat on me. I'd go home a sorry sight. When my mom asked what happened, I'd tell her I was playing too hard and fell in gym. At the time she asked me to be more careful and let it go at that.

There was no way to avoid Doris. We lived in the same housing project and had to go home the same way. I'd beg my mother for a nickel to ride the bus home, to avoid Doris, but there never was a nickel to spare. After several torn dresses and bruises all over, I decided I had to pay Doris what she demanded, even if it meant stealing.

While my mother was asleep, I foraged through her purse to find my extortion payment. A quarter doesn't mean much these days, but in 1945, it was enough to buy a large loaf of Wonder Bread. Mom didn't catch on that I was taking money from her purse, but I felt guilty. I'd never stolen anything in my life. After a few times, Mom mentioned she couldn't find the change she was counting on for bread, and I owned up to what I had done.

To my surprise, Mom wasn't mad at me at all, but just held me close as I cried. When I stopped sobbing, she asked me why I had taken the money, and I spilled the beans about Doris. The next day, Mom called the principal and explained what was happening. She also found a nickel for me to ride home on the bus that day, so I could avoid Doris after school.

Mrs. Grey, the principal, must not have mentioned me as the one whose parent called. Doris was summoned to Mrs. Grey's office, and her mother was called in. The policeman standing by added credence to the seriousness of the situation.

After school, the janitor opened Doris's locker. It was filled with half-eaten candy, cakes and cookies. And roaches. Her locker had become a fast food restaurant for the school roach population. They had to fumigate all the lockers, and for days we couldn't use them.

I never saw Doris again. Kids said she was suspended for ten days, then transferred to another school. When her scam was out in the open, more than a dozen other parents came forward with the same story. I didn't miss being beat up, and I certainly didn't miss having to steal money from my mom.

As an adult, I've often wondered what happened to Doris Emmett in later years. As for me, she affected my life in two indelible ways. First, I'll never forget the healing of my mother's unconditional love. Second, throughout my twenty years as a middle-school teacher, I was always on the lookout for little kids like me who had to face a bully.

A Message for Antoine

by Anne H. Flythe

I used to think you aimed
the damage at your brother
when you blew a hole
in the bottom of the family boat,
not caring if you sank us all.
I now know you shot yourself.
You sank. We still float.
We miss you, mourn you.

Nine Tenths of the Law

by Anne H. Flythe

He put his monogram, initials, name
upon his silver julep cups,
on the linens into which he blew his nose,
both phlegm and fabric his;
even as an alpha wolf pissmarks the margin of its range
to demonstrate possession and to ward off rivals.
His women bear his marks as well
in fading rainbows on bruised flesh
and always, soon or late,
a small tattoo lewdly placed to warn
the imprudent of dangerous trespass.

Beyond the Covenant
by James F. Gaines

Captain Roy Morrison swayed with the corkscrew rhythm of the seas as he made his way towards the bow of the freighter *Mary Foster*, hanging onto the guideline that stretched toward the forecastle. As the passage of a roller pitched the ship up to its crest, he looked northward to the South African coast for the Cape Agulhas light, but saw only the dim confusion of cloud and spray. Too late to turn back now, he thought. At the end of the line he caught at the handle of the hatchway and let himself into the warm, bright refuge of the crew's quarters. But he could smell the rot as soon as he got inside. Billy Barney, the first mate, was in one of the rooms with Coelho. He had cleared it out when the first symptoms appeared and gone inside with his medical kit. Morrison had promised to recommend Barney for his own command if he came out alive. He rapped two short knocks on the door of the room.

"Still here, Captain. No change in the patient. Not for the better anyway. Fever's the same. He bleeds from the ears a little."

"Still got food?"

"Plenty. But you can have someone slip in another pint of rum. It can do double duty because I'm almost out of carbolic."

"Right." Morrison paused, not knowing what to say. "Carry on."

As he turned he saw the chief engineer Petersen in the corridor behind him, puffing on a stubby pipe. The engineer said nothing and peered at him through a slight cloud of smoke.

"Well," said Morrison. "Anything to report?"

Petersen slowly drew the pipe from his teeth and replied, "She's holding her speed pretty well, sir. Of course if we turned…"

"Can we make Colombo?"

"Aye, sir, Colombo and probably Calcutta, too, unless this storm lasts more than four days."

"Then maintain speed," said Morrison, and shoved past the engineer to head back to the bridge.

Petersen walked past the quarantine cabin and into the crowded space beyond, where the next watch was getting ready to go on duty. A sailor named Bellows accosted him, "Hey, Fishy, was that the skipper you were talking to out there?"

"It was," answered Petersen, "Though I hadn't intended to pass the time of day with him."

Bellows drew the Dane closer and looked over his shoulder as though he expected someone to be spying at the door. "Look here, did he go in to see poor Coelho, or did he just knock at the door?"

"Just knocked," said Petersen, poking at the bowl of his pipe, "As usual."

"Old Cappy Ryan would never have let a sailor go deadly sick on board. Die on board and get dumped in the sea."

"That Morrison's no fit man to sail with." The interjection came from an older man with sideburns who had been listening along with the rest of the watch.

"Really, Porter," said the skeptical Petersen. "And what would Ryan have done?"

"Put into Durban. Or Lorenço Marquez, an Allied harbor, or a neutral one, if he was afraid of mines. Any port with a decent doctor ashore. Ryan was a sailor's sailor and never would have let a crewman down." Porter puffed out his chest at the proud memory of the *Mary Foster*'s former master.

"Aye, but it's war now," ventured Bellows. "That cargo of tanks and trucks we took on in Cape Town is under a timed contract for the army in India. I suppose we should do our patriotic duty to get it there."

"Hah!" snorted a clean-shaven fellow in his twenties. "That contract increases the shipper's profit with every day we shave from the delivery. And you can bet Morrison's in for a share of that. A share the forecastle will never see."

"Calm down, Red," chimed in several voices from the watch. "You'd stay under way with a crew full of corpses if you could get into Odessa."

A thin, nervous laugh spread through the cabin, with even Red taking part to relieve the pent-up pressure. Worry about the strange disease that Coelho had brought aboard in Cape Town. Worry about the gale that was blowing in their face. Worry about the unfamiliar captain who had been sent to take over their ship only two months earlier. Worry about the unknown out beyond the storm, on the waves and beneath them.

Petersen calmly lit up his pipe again and pronounced, "Red may be right. The captain seems hell-bent on unloading his cargo on time. At least he knows what he wants. Still, I am going to talk to Cunningham to see if he can convince Morrison into heading for Durban. The Captain would never go to a neutral Portuguese port, where a U-boat could pin him in for the rest of the war."

The watch, swathed in slickers and sou'westers followed him out into the screaming wind and manned their posts.

Back on the bridge, Morrison shook the seawater off his outer clothes and hung them on pegs. He used the new electric communicator to call the forecastle and spoke to one of the past watch just turning back in, ordering the sailor to slip a bottle of rum through the door to Barney. The electric communicators had been installed to deal with the din of battle. For service in this new war, *Mary Foster* had been fitted with a two-inch cannon and an antiaircraft pom-pom gun. When they were firing no normal human voice could be heard. But the communicator served equally well over a Roaring Forties gale. Morrison turned to watch his Second Mate Cunningham at the wheel. The young officer's eyes were riveted to the compass binnacle as he struggled to keep the bow as far into the wind as the course would permit. Morrison cast a cursory glance at the gauges before telling Cunningham that he was taking an hour's rest. The captain's cabin offered a welcome rest, even if it pitched crazily as the rollers struck and ran the length of the hull. A picture of a vine-covered cottage overlooking the Bristol Channel hung on the bulkhead, alongside framed certificates tracing Morrison's career as a merchant marine officer. Secured within the little desk was a book with all his recommendations, each one mentioning his punctuality and dependability. When Roy Morrison entered into an agreement to deliver his cargo at a certain time and place, that was paramount.

Really should have taken medical training, too, thought the captain. Bad luck to have a fever on board this first trip into the Indian Ocean. What could it be? Plague? Dengue? Marsh fever? As if the parasites were not enough, Africa was swarming with every imaginable form of fever and bloody flux! Good thing Barney was on board with a little bush-doctor experience and enough ambition to play nursemaid to that wretch Coelho. Or more likely undertaker. Morrison had seen the livid patches and pustules on the seaman's skin and the blood oozing from his ears and eyes. He was sure Coelho wouldn't last another night, not long enough to make Durban. And if they did, he might die just as the doctor was coming on board to quarantine the *Mary Foster* for a month or more. If Morrison was to continue to collect testimonials to his seamanship, he didn't need forced time ashore. Especially if he continued to chase that secret little dream of his, a true naval command. Officer casualties had already been high and in this part of the world, it was not unheard of for an exceptional master to be offered service on a Royal Navy ship. Perhaps only an oiler or transport, but he would gladly accept any old hulk that flew a naval pennant overhead. He fell asleep dreaming of being piped aboard and reviewing a crew in immaculate uniforms.

Cunningham's forearms were just getting tired from his unending struggle with the wheel when Petersen came onto the bridge. The wrinkled Dane nodded at the second mate and offered, "I'd be willing to stand a while at the wheel if you'd like to break for a cup of tea."

"Gladly! How are things below?"

"Oh, she strains a bit in this sort of gale, but we're good for at least another week before we have to give the engines a once-over."

"That isn't what I meant."

"The human part of the ship is not so easy to keep oiled," responded the engineer.

Cunningham cupped his hands around a mug of strong dark tea that had been steeping under a gray cozy for hours. He looked cautiously at the impassive Petersen, who seemed to be able to draw on his pipe without any audible breathing. "You've been at sea a lot longer than me. How bad is it? How much more will the crew take before they break loose?"

"They're good boys and they know their profession," Petersen nodded. "But we were all attached to Ryan. He made each one of us know we were men, worthwhile in our own right. I suppose we all blame Morrison a bit for taking Ryan's command. It wasn't natural that the old captain should go on half-pay ashore at his age and in the middle of a war. Where do you stand?"

The question took Cunningham aback. Though he had come aboard at the same time as Morrison, he had never known the man before he stepped on the *Mary Foster* and he resented the fact that many crewmen considered him a minion of the new captain. "I stand where I have to stand. As an officer, there's no question of my opposing a skipper of sound mind and body. You must understand that, Petersen, you're more than a common stoker yourself."

Petersen ignored the compliment and stared at Cunningham with intense eyes. "Then, you'd better do something while you still have a choice. You can talk to Morrison. Tell him how the men feel. Tell him about the risks of a two thousand mile cruise past the U-boats with an uncooperative crew. And what if he does get the damned trucks to Calcutta before the deadline? Nothing changes then. Not with the boys in the forecastle. It can only get worse."

"What alternative do we have?"

"Durban is closer than Mozambique. It's protected by planes and patrol boats. No chance of being blockaded there, like in a neutral port. True, we'll have the weather more amidships, at least for a while. But we can be there in less than eight hours, unload Coelho's carcass, swab out and get a clean bill of health, and miss a good part of the storm to boot. We'll raise Colombo a lot faster at twelve knots than at five. No net loss."

Cunningham had already figured out most of the pros and cons himself during his hours at the wheel, but he was nevertheless impressed by the Dane's concise grip of the situation. He had never expected this kind of sharp thinking from a forecastle philosopher. On the other hand, with so much intelligence, Petersen would be a dangerous antagonist if it came to breaking out the side arms against a mutinous crew. "If I were to do my best with the captain..." Cunningham paused, "Would you promise to keep the crew in line?"

"The question is : could I keep that promise?"

"I'd be sticking my neck out to argue with a senior officer on my first assignment. I could be blacklisted in every port east of Suez. I want to get something for my trouble."

"What about your conscience?" Petersen intoned. "Don't you care about Coelho? Maybe you think officers float around on little antiseptic clouds, but had you stepped into a wrong bit of dust and germs, that could be you in there with Billy."

"I took an oath. A binding agreement to obey orders and serve."

"Is the oath more important than the man that makes it?"

Cunningham gulped down the rest of his syrupy tea and stepped to the wheel. "I'd better take over again, now," he said. He really needed time to think out what Petersen had suggested. "Listen, Fishy, don't tell the men too much about our little exchange. I don't say yes and I don't say no."

"You can't fret forever," growled Petersen. "I'll be back in an hour."

Within minutes members of the new watch returned from their errands and took over the wheel. Cunningham made his way along the precarious guideline toward the forecastle and stopped outside the quarantine cabin. He coughed, then knocked, and was answered by a weary Billy Barney, "Yes, what is it?"

Since the door didn't open, the second mate reluctantly came closer and spoke louder. "It's me, Cunningham, how's he doing, Billy?"

"Won't die," Billy shot back, "But he's not alive by very much either. Tough little bugger, I suppose. If he ever gets out of this, he'll think he's indestructible."

"Billy, listen, the men are pretty hard against Morrison."

"I can imagine. One reason I'm not sad to be in here instead of out there with you. I don't imagine they'll come storming in to take it out on me."

"You knew Morrison before. Can I appeal to him? Is he likely to put into port if I convince him of the danger?"

Barney thought a long moment. "Morrison's like granite. He very seldom changes his opinion on anything. He has the confidence of the owners. They hand-picked him to replace Ryan because they thought the old man was going soft and costing them dividends."

Cunningham's hopes were fading. "What if I held the owners up against him? Wouldn't he be afraid it might change their minds if the crew made trouble?"

"He has an iron-clad contract," Barney blurted out. "First of its kind. Full salary for six years even if he's ashore. Engraved in stone by God the Father himself. You'd best make up your mind to stand behind him. Or find a nice quiet place for the storm to blow over and hope he doesn't survive."

Cunningham started to walk back to the hatchway and turned again. "Will you come out and help? Will you raise a pistol against our own crew?"

"Don't think so. You see, I've sealed this cabin pretty well with some glue I brought in. I'm starting to feel not so well myself. Think I'll lie down. Don't bother sending in another nursemaid." There was a silence that seemed very long. "It seems I've chosen badly."

Petersen met Cunningham on the way up to the bridge. "The men in the engine room have started to set aside tools and hatchets. Hidden under a tarp here and a box there. But close at hand. You don't have long. Make it good." Then he disappeared down the corridor.

Cunningham went to the captain's cabin and knocked until he woke up Morrison. Bleary-eyed, the skipper opened the door and once he recognized his second mate, he waved the young man into his quarters.

"What's the cause of all this commotion?"

"Sir, I have to report that the first mate is becoming ill and I respectfully request that we put into the port of Durban with all possible speed."

"Hmm. Well rehearsed. Surely you didn't come up with that all by yourself. I smell a Dane behind it."

"Sir, some of the men have talked with me. They don't want to challenge you, sir, but this just doesn't seem right... to them."

"And what about you?"

"Personally, sir, I, I... well, with two crewmen sick and the others on the brink of disorder, I think the only prudent thing is to put into Durban."

"Or become the victims of mutineers?"

"Er, yes, so it would appear, sir."

"I'm not worried!" declared Morrison.

"But the ship, sir, as officers, we are responsible...."

"Perhaps I know something you don't." When Cunningham could only stare quizzically back, Morrison suddenly grabbed a set of keys and lurched down the corridor, stopping at Billy Barney's cabin. He unlocked the hatch and invited the second mate to have a look. Inside were a half dozen Royal Marines with submachine guns lounged in various attitudes of half-sleep around the compartment.

When Cunningham looked incredulously back at Morrison, the captain was lighting a cigarette in a very self-confident manner. "You see, these fellows were down guarding the munitions in the holds, but with the storm I suggested they spend the night up here. Especially since the first mate was otherwise occupied. Are you still worried about a few grease monkeys armed with wrenches?"

"No, sir," blurted Cunningham. "But that doesn't change the fate of the men who are ill. Don't you care about them? Leaving Barney sealed up in that plague cabin like a tomb just about broke my heart. Is it so great a delay just to see them into safe hands or into a decent grave?"

Morrison looked more serious. "This is war. Many men will die, but we can't let ourselves go all to pieces with the first sign of bloodshed. These men signed on to this ship promising to give all in return for their wages. The pledge will be honored in full. I will see to it. I promised to get these munitions to Calcutta in time for them to be used by the Indian Army. That promise will be honored in full. Need I remind you of your own engagements?"

"I know I promised to obey and I will. But you are captain, sir," objected Cunningham. "Look, everyone acknowledges that you are master of this ship. While we are at sea, no one, not even the owners can countermand you or call you into question. And these men ask nothing more than the chance to serve you with some respect. What in God's name is to stop you from showing a little judgment, a little mercy, a little consideration for those two up in the forecastle?"

"I am. I hold myself to judgment. I am also able to stop myself from doing anything so foolish. Because it is not what I have promised to do. Now go explain to Petersen what the situation is. Tell him about the Marines. Can't keep that surprise forever, anyway."

Cunningham descended ladder by ladder down into the engineer's realm. A place of percussion and vibration, where enormous forces were pressed into a discipline of thermodynamics and mechanical precision and channeled into the whirling blades that invisibly propelled the *Mary Foster* through the ice-cold seas. Down in that humid and strange-smelling forest of cams and pipes and valves, Cunningham found the Dane, as imperturbable as ever, smoking his pipe and waiting. He seemed to know the bad news before the mate could open his mouth.

Cunningham made profuse apologies. Then he told the engineer about the Marines.

"Don't worry, lad," consoled the wizened sailor, "You've tried your best. Made your plea for humanity and it failed. After all, it wasn't in the contract. Somehow, that kind of thing never is. Time now to think of the rest of the crew that are still alive."

Suddenly a group of seamen appeared at the foot of the stairs, looking like a Viking raiding party. Red and Bellows carried axes from the fire stations, Porter hefted an enormous pipe wrench, and Cho Sing, the cook, held his Chinese cleaver. Some of the others had nothing more than folding knives or marlinspikes. Petersen could not help chuckling when he saw them and muttered to Cunningham, "As the novels would say, a lubberly lot of scoundrels." The Dane went over to the little force and told them it was no good, the boss had a detachment of heavily armed Marines aft, ready to mow them down, and they'd best behave themselves until they got to Calcutta. Cunningham was surprised by the way Petersen closed his little speech.

"....and as for me, I'm going to turn myself over to Captain Morrison as the ringleader of this little Kaffeeklatsch and sit for awhile in the brig. In any case, he would have me arrested if I did not. That should keep him happy for the rest of the trip."

Petersen's surrender, pronounced in such a magnanimous way, did not fail to elicit claps on the back and a few tears from his fellow crewmen. As calculated, it completely disarmed them. Petersen followed Cunningham back up the ladders to the bridge. "I do have one last idea and plan to use that as a bargaining chip with the captain. Since he can't resist the power of a covenant, perhaps I can still find one last way to get Coelho and Barney some medical help."

"What do you have in mind?"

"Maybe a way to save something without giving up the word of the law. A move I learned from an old herring fisherman back home. The trick will be to make him believe he thought of it himself. But then, he is so vain, perhaps that will not be such a trick after all."

"What can I do for you, Petersen?" asked the mate, feeling guilty that he would survive this nasty business while the engineer was to be brought up on charges in Colombo or Calcutta. "Can I talk to a consul for you? Is there anyone you know?"

Petersen answered slowly. "You know, there's not much of Denmark left any more, right now. This ship is all the home I have. Still, it's better than staying behind in occupation with no choices left at all. Don't worry about me. I dare say I know enough about machines to draw some pretty easy time in the clink."

When they reached the bridge, the Dane motioned for Cunningham to stay behind and he went to confront Morrison alone. A few minutes later, he emerged with a smile on his face and nodded to the mate as a Marine ushered him aft towards the damp little compartment that served as brig and cable locker on the *Mary Foster*. Beaming, Morrison hurried forward, almost bumping into Cunningham.

"Ah, there you are. Up to the radio shack and send out a message to any allied shipping inbound toward South Africa. Tell them we seek a ship's doctor to see to two sick men."

He said it as though it were his own idea.

A half-hour later, Cunningham knocked on the door of the captain's cabin. "I managed to raise a Dutchman out of Batavia bound for Cape Town. *Hoogenboom's* got a surgeon on board and can rendezvous with us in about four hours. He offered to bring them to Durban."

"So you see, Cunningham, I was right. If everyone holds up his own end of the agreement, everything comes out right."

"Yes sir. Still, lucky the Dutch freighter was willing to care for a couple of helpless devils." He could not prevent himself from adding, as he went out the door, "Not even their own people, either."

Morrison took a second to get the point of the remark, then considered calling the mate back, but instead lit a cigarette and settled down with a copy of Royal Navy regulations. As night was falling, he lit an extra light in his cabin. Might be dealing with new rules very soon, he thought.

The rays of light went out the porthole and penetrated into the murky mixture of sea and air that cascaded around the ship. They split up and scattered and spread over the gray-green water and some entered a metal tube and reflected in two mirrors and emerged in the periscope sights of U-323. Oberleutnant Schilling recorded the bearing and turned to his commander. "Same course, sir. What orders?"

Kapitän Ballauf looked him in the eye and shot back, "What would your orders be if you were in command?"

"Well," Schilling paused, "At this point in the conflict, we should not waste our torpedoes. We are far from our re-supply point. But the seas right now do not permit an attack with the deck gun." Ballauf was nodding slowly to encourage the young submariner, but he threw up his hands when his protégé concluded, "So we should wait a few hours and then surface and open fire with the cannon."

"Kvatsch!" shouted Ballauf. "Who knows whether the seas will be calmer then? And have you forgotten the message we intercepted about their meeting with the Dutchman? Do you suppose that even a Hollander will just stand around while you shell the English ship, waiting for its turn? You have to learn to be creative with any situation."

Ballauf turned to his navigator. "Have you calculated the course to the rendezvous point with *Hoogenboom*?"

"Yes captain. All ready. All in order."

"So now," Ballauf said to Schilling, "You know what to do."

Schilling went to the communicator and ordered the forward torpedo tubes to load one. Then he looked to his captain, who was frowning.

"We don't have time to play around, lieutenant!" He held up two fingers.

Schilling added a second torpedo to the order and prepared the periscope to sight the launch. One! Two! Two obedient metal fish, very heavy with doom. Hot, straight, and normal. *Mary Foster* broke in two from the force of explosions in the cargo holds and the two ends of the ship sank instantly, quelling the fevers and ambitions of all aboard, ending all confinements and all anticipation. Loosening all bonds.

Aboard U-323 Schilling and his captain headed back to their tiny compartments to fill out the reports contractually required of all German Navy officers. On the threshold of his cabin, Schilling whispered to Ballauf, "Thanks for not scolding me in front of the men."

Ballauf smiled benevolently. "I always take care of my crew."

Loaded Sabers
by Rod Vanderhoof

The battlefield turned quiet as the Rebel cavalry led by General Thomas Rosser withdrew beyond a large grove of pines, yellow poplars, sweet gums, and oaks half a mile away. The Yankee cavalry remained in place since they had reasonable cover, at least for the moment. The blasts of the horse artillery, the whack of rifle shots, the metallic clash of sabers and the blood-curdling war yells had stopped. Smashed caissons and supply wagons smoldered. A low, smoky haze drifted across a cornfield littered with the carcasses of mules, horses and men. Choking dust clouds and the acrid smell of black powder settled back to earth as the air cleared. Swarming turkey vultures hovered in silence over a nearby orchard and eyed choice morsels of mutilated flesh among the carnage. Even the moans and cries of the wounded seemed to abate as if awaiting some momentous event.

Corporal Charles Smith of Company C, Sixth Michigan, sat astride his gray steed in the front rank of the regimental formation. His forage cap, ornamented on the top with a cavalry insignia of crossed sabers, was pulled low over his forehead to keep the sweat from his eyes. He wore the signature red scarf of Custer's brigade and had yellow cavalry stripes down each leg of his trousers. His blue wool uniform was already too hot for the day. Above all, he was exhausted from ongoing fighting that started just after daybreak.

Smith, like the other enlisted men, knew the situation to be perilous. Earlier, his regiment had been cut off from the rest of the Union force and was now surrounded by Confederate cavalry. The entire brigade, consisting of the First, Fifth, Sixth and Seventh Michigan regiments, had been stretched for miles along a narrow forest road. The Rebels made a surprise charge from a side road, piercing the long, blue column and isolating the Sixth Michigan. Now they were alone and low on ammunition. Smith wondered what Custer's next move might be, but he knew that Custer would never surrender.

Smith gazed across the cornfield and saw two Confederate riders approaching. The first carried a guidon with a white flag fluttering and snapping in the gusting wind. On the man's sleeves were the chevrons of a sergeant. The second rider rode easily on an aristocratic, golden-tan palomino with white mane and tail. Judging from the second man's well-tailored gray uniform and confidant demeanor, he was an officer.

Brevet Brigadier George Custer sat atop his horse at the head of the Union formation with Old Glory and the Michigan colors close at hand. Corporal Smith was not thirty feet distant.

The date: Thursday, June 9, 1864. The place: a farm in mid-Virginia near Squirrel Creek Station on the north-south Virginia Central Railroad.

"Hold your fire men," yelled Custer, a command echoed by his company commanders along the line.

The Confederate emissaries halted in front of Custer. On instructions from the first sergeant, Smith dismounted, handing his own reins to a Michigan trooper next to him. He hurried forward and, as the Rebel officer alighted, Smith grasped the palomino's reins and kept the animal in place. From there, he could hear everything.

The officer stood before Custer and saluted. "Suh, Colonel Johnston at yo' service. I have a message from Gen'l Rossah with his compliments."

Custer returned the salute, climbed down from his mount and accepted a brown, official-looking envelope.

"You're pretty young to be a full colonel," observed Custer.

"Gen'l, you're pretty young yo'self." Custer ignored the Southerner's comment and opened the envelope.

Cavalrymen on both sides are young, Smith thought. Cavalry fighting is a young man's game. Custer was said to be twenty-four and was a combat veteran who defied the odds. Many horses had been shot from beneath him. Even after being unhorsed and sent sprawling on the battlefield, he always arose, found another mount and returned to the fight.

Today, General Custer seemed edgy and impatient. Skirmishing had been heavy. A spent rifle ball staggered him this morning, knocking him cockeyed and leaving a lump on his head. "I thought they threw a rock," Custer said. He regained his senses after a few minutes.

Custer was respected and admired by the men in the Michigan Brigade. He led each charge and his saber, as often as not, was the first to draw enemy blood. The Michigan men wore scarlet neckties because Custer did. He sometimes had a brass band in the front ranks playing "Yankee Doodle" or "Garry Owen" to inspire them. Today, however, with the brigade split, the band was back somewhere in the maze of wagon roads through the dense forest. Suddenly, just for an instant, Smith thought he heard the strains of "Yankee Doodle." He held his breath so as to catch any sound, no matter how faint, but heard nothing further. *Must be my imagination,* he thought.

Smith and the other Michiganders knew what was likely to happen that very afternoon. At the opportune moment, General Custer would raise his saber toward the enemy and holler, "Come on you Wolverines!" The Michigan men would cheer loud enough to drown out even the famous Rebel yell. They would start their horses at an easy trot, but as they neared the enemy, they'd move into a full gallop with weapons raised. They'd become wild men hurdling low walls and dead horses. Custer would set the example with his blond hair streaming in the wind. They'd tear the enemy ranks asunder, chopping and slashing with sabers and firing Colt revolvers and Spencer carbines at point blank range. Custer's trademark was being in the thick of the heavy fighting and that's where he'd be today, you could count on it.

Custer tore open Rosser's letter and began to read. Then he looked at Colonel Johnston and said, "General Rosser wants me to surrender."

"Yes, suh. Gen'l Rossah told me."

"Does he really think I'd surrender my troopers just because we're surrounded?"

"Apparently, suh."

"Tom Rosser and I were roommates at West Point. We were like brothers. He should know me better than that."

"Yes, suh."

Custer continued reading and commenting. "He claims he'll destroy us with his horse artillery, but he's bluffing. His troops are on all sides. If he fires, he's just as likely to overshoot us and kill his own men."

"Yes, suh."

"He's even offering me bacon, eggs and real coffee, if I come over with a white flag flying. Can you imagine that?"

"No, suh . . . I mean yes, suh.," he stammered.

"So the answer, Colonel, is no."

"I need that in writin', suh."

"What's wrong, Colonel? Is the message too difficult for a Southern gentleman to remember? Just tell him no."

Colonel Johnston's face reddened at the inference of being thickheaded. "Of couhse, suh," he snapped.

"In fact, tell General Rosser I shall see him in hell before I surrender."

"Suh, he knows yo' must be low on cahtridges."

"Ah, but he doesn't know for sure does he? Tell him to remember this: if we run out of cartridges, our sabers are loaded. You tell him exactly that, Colonel Johnston."

"Yes, suh."

"Our sabers are loaded!"

As soon as Colonel Johnston and the flag bearer departed, Corporal Smith returned to the formation and remounted his gray. Custer turned to his adjutant and said, "Ride down the line and tell my company commanders to get ready. As soon as the white flag is out of sight, we're going to make a saber charge right into the teeth of the enemy. I'll take Rosser up on the bacon, eggs and coffee, but on my terms, not his."

As the white flag disappeared beyond the woods, Corporal Smith again heard the strains of "Yankee Doodle." This time there was no doubt. The music was directly behind Rosser's position and coming nearer. A trooper next to Smith yelled, "It's our guys! They're coming for us!" Excitement rippled up and down the cavalry line. A tingling surge engulfed Corporal Smith. He was ready. He'd follow Custer anywhere.

Custer heard the band, too, and turned his horse to face the regiment.

"Men, we've got Rosser and the Rebels front and back, right where we want them!" He drew his saber and thrust it skyward. "Come on you Wolverines!" he yelled. The Michigan cavalrymen drew their sabers, too, and cheered.

"Bugler!" Custer commanded loud and clear, "Sound the charge!"

The Fountain
by Juanita D. Roush

Tears ran down my face as I walked from marker to marker, reading the names of soldiers, both men and women, who had lost their lives in service to our country. I thought of all the unrealized dreams, the families for whom life had become a wound that never heals.

I noticed the wives' names, buried afterward with their husbands, his name facing East, hers facing West on the same marker. I thought of sons who never came home, of husbands whose wives were left alone and of fathers whose children became fatherless.

The trail meandered upward as I slowly climbed the hill as the breeze blew gently waving the tree branches. When I arrived near the top of the hill, I found a flame. The caretaker stopped pulling weeds from the crevices in the granite and looked at me. He said, "It is an Eternal Flame. This flame has come to mean freedom and the passion for freedom." I looked around at the words carved in stone that were so much now, a part of our history, "Ask not what your country can do for you, but ask what you can do for your country…" I thought of a time of innocence in our country when the presidential administration was called Camelot, and the day in Dallas when it all came tumbling down.

From there, I looked upward at the Lee mansion, and thought about all that it symbolized, a great man who loved this country, but came to lead a faction that, for a short while, became a nation. And our land was at war with itself, brother against brother. Restoration came to the nation in the years after the war but families were scarred and some hurts were never healed.

From there, I turned and looked back down the hill to the silent headstones of Arlington Cemetery. My cheeks were wet with tears that flowed unchecked down my face.

The land came together, regrouped, recommitted and stood side by side to fight again in World War I, and we have stones to prove it. It was going to be the war to end all wars, so the loss of life should have been worth it, shouldn't it? But of course, it didn't end war.

White stones stand as witnesses to the wars that came after that war, World War II, Korea, and Vietnam. So many young men came home in flag covered coffins. Some returned alive but so different from the person who had left home that they never overcame addictions and nightmares that never allow them rest. And then there were newer stones, which tell the tale of recent wars in faraway lands, Bosnia, the Persian Gulf, Afghanistan, and Iraq. And the mothers and fathers cried.

Amid the daily flow of tears, we realize that there is no war that will end all wars until the coming of the Lord. As long as men play games, building bigger and better, and ferociously guarding what they build, we will have war.

As I stood there, my heart was broken. I looked around at others who were so touched. I saw veterans there to pay tribute to their friends with whom they fought. Their lives are forever changed by the loss of their brothers in arms.

The old caretaker has seen the tears of millions. I see him watching me and I turn away. I feel a hand upon my shoulder and I turn and look up. He says, "Come, I have one last thing to show you." We walk past the Tomb of the Unknown Soldier. The caretaker said that a soldier from each war is interred there, a young man whose body sleeps in the crypt and represents all the families that will never stop looking for their soldier to return to them. The guard is vigilant, day and night, changing every ½ hour. He makes that slow march, back and forth, standing guard so that no more harm comes to those who have given all. The caretaker and I stand and watch as the guard changes, a solemn ceremony that takes quite a while. The bell tolls for those who have fought and died and were unidentified.

The old caretaker takes my elbow and we walk on to a copse of trees – and as we travel toward it, I see that it is dark. It is a little forest all alone in this great cemetery. We go into the trees. It is not as well taken care of as the rest of the cemetery…a forgotten place. We go deep into the forest and suddenly, I see sunlight and I walk towards it. The light streams through the trees. There is a meadow in the midst of the forest and in the center is a fountain. The water sprays upward and then comes down into a pool at the base. The spray causes a rainbow to arch over it. I look with amazement. It is a beautiful place.

Silently, the caretaker leads me to a stone. It lies flat on the ground and is embedded deeply in the soil. He stoops down and lovingly clears grass from its surface. His wrinkled face looks up at me as he brushes it. I read the words inscribed there, "Dedicated to the people who have lived all of their lives, broken, hurt, in pain. This fountain is lovingly created to honor those tears shed through the ages for our warriors, those who never came home, and those who came home broken, shattered, living lives that cannot be put back together. To the mothers whose sons never again knew what it was like to laugh and be carefree, to the fathers, who have unshed tears just below the surface…this fountain is dedicated to you."

"What does this mean?" I ask him.

His shaky old hand points up to the fountain, and he said, "Don't you know what this is? This is a fountain made with the tears that have been collected from loved ones. It never runs dry; there is always a fresh supply of tears, for the soldiers who lie here are not forgotten. They have families, sweethearts, children whose lives are forever bound to this place. This fountain was filled with tears."

"But why is the fountain so far away from everything else, here alone in the trees?"

"Because the tears you see are only a shadow of what takes place in the dark of night when pillows are wet and faces stained. Most tears are never seen. This fountain is created only with those that we see, and yet it is as eternal as the flame. If all the tears shed were brought here, there would be an ocean in this place; instead, there is only a fountain."

The caretaker took my arm and we turned and walked away, back towards the gate that surrounds this humbling place. So many stories are buried here. We walk silently in reverence of what we have seen. I see another woman walking towards me, tears flowing down her face. Her eyes meet mine and instinctively I can see in her eyes that we share a bond of grief. The caretaker releases my arm and takes hers and escorts her up the hill.

A Time of Restlessness
by Madalin E. Jackson

It was a time of restlessness,
A time of wars and sorrows.
We strummed our songs on six gut strings
And sang of bright tomorrows.
But time slipped by while we grew old
Brightness gently faded
Peace allusive; time slipped by;
Our ambitions now belated.

Wars persisted, oh, that's true,
But our eyes failed to see
With overdue bills and hungry kids
Housework and mounting laundry.
The guitars gathered dust alone
No one remembers now.
Optimistic smiles and laughter
Replaced by lines upon our brows.

But hope remained; a young voice spoke;
A small hand touched my side.
She saw the strings, the dust, the wood
And smiles I could not hide.
What's that mom? Can I touch it please?
She placed it in my arms.
I strummed, I tuned, I sang
Of poetry and peace, of families and farms.
I sang the dreams we dreamed
Of wars we won and lost
Of times long forgotten
Of freedom's frightful costs.
Now we fight for others
Their freedoms we must win
For women's rights and children's lives
And years of selfish sins.

Swept Away

by Larry Turner

This dome: so well constructed that it stood
while everything on acres all around
was swept away that dreadful August day
when from the sky there fell a single bomb.

Terms like Mesozoic and the like
were judged too hard for grade-school kids to learn.
And so the textbook gave them simpler names;
it called them Era of the Ancient Life,
of Middle Life, of Modern Life. With these,
our teacher Mrs. Keck said we must now
include Atomic Age. How did she gain
a wisdom giving her so clear a view?

The very air above Hiroshima
was torn in two, and so was history.
Along with buildings and the people there,
the blast obliterated rationale
for war as instrument for policy
and claims of sovereignty by any land.
What Mrs. Keck so quickly grasped back then,
the leaders of the world have yet to learn.

For the Love of Words

The I
by Dan Walker

> **The lamb entreats the butcher: where's thy knife?**
> **Thou art too slow to do thy master's bidding,**
> **When I desire it too.**
> (Shakespeare: *Cymbeline*. III.iv.103-105)

The "i" doesn't have much knowledge of any sort.
It doesn't know, for instance, if it's long or short,
only that it's after a "b" (let's say)
and before a "d," as in "bid."
But the letter to come after that *could* be an "e," which, if it did,
would make the "i" long, of course.
But what if there were in fact another "d"?
Then things would have to go on, and assuming the "i" *could*
really see
through that first unfriendly "d"—
to find a space or the end of a word, such as "bidding,"
Well, that would settle the shortness once and for all,
but un-settle something else, if you get my meaning.

It would raise, would it not, the question of intent:
who put that *"bidding"* there at all, and why?
And the lower case of the "i":
was that some fortunate (or unfortunate)
fall from grace, requiring some repentance?
And if there really is this something called a sentence,
of which the word is a part,
designed to be read—if so, by Whom?
And is that text just exposition,
or a kind of recreation, a kind of art?

And then there's this:
does the "i" just have one size?
Or are there others—? Other fonts? In fact, other "i"s?
In other sentences? And (assuming there are such things)
by other Authors?
And what if the sentences were part of a book,
on a shelf with other books, in a building packed
with other shelves…?

How much more or less, then, would it matter—
that secret, secret question:

Could it ever change, could it be italicized?—
or even (just imagine!) be capitalized?

Cannot

by Patricia A. Moton

I'm a writer. I love words.
I love other things—
The seashore, water birds.
But . . . I love words.

I take offense when words are wronged,
Be it in a poem, be it in a song.
And, when words are attacked, like "cannot" now is,
Well, I fight back! That's just how it is.

That's what I'm doing now.
I've given it a lot of thought.
And, at this defining moment,
I'm defending the word "cannot"!!

"Cannot" cannot defend itself,
So I'll step up to the plate.
I'll strive to be successful.
I pray I'm not too late.

It's ONE WORD, people. No, it's not two.
It's ONE WORD, people, and it has work to do.

There's no reason to kill the word,
Or, by ignorance, bring it down.
It's ONE WORD, people.
And it wants to stay around.

It has its own purpose, and it wants to live.
It has its own purpose, and it wants to give
Meaning to sentences, though negative, it's true.
But . . . It's ONE WORD, people.
ONE WORD for me; ONE WORD for you.

So rally with me to the cause, save this word from desecration.
It's ONE WORD, people. Please don't change its derivation!

Words

by John M. Wills

Words can be welcome
Touch our hearts
One may be all we need
One may be all we can bear

Powerful and hurtful
Insightful and reassuring
Words inspire and inflate
Too often full of hate

Like a bullet from a gun
Never to return
Uttered too quickly
A scar in place for some

Be careful when choosing
Be careful what you say
Words live on forever
And define beyond the grave

Blackmail. Noun, Verb, Adjective

by Larry Turner

It's called blackmail because in past times it was written on black stationery. It was important that the recipient immediately notice such a letter among the advertisements, charity appeals and other junk mail received every day.

In smaller towns, a stationery store would have a section of such stationery. In larger cities, there were stores that specialized in stationery for blackmail: writing paper and envelopes, expensive or cheaper depending on whether the blackmailer wished to stress his seriousness or his desperation.

And silver ink. Because such ink was very thick, it tended to smear, and the blackmailer had to practice writing with it. Even a person being blackmailed for the first time could tell whether the blackmailer was a beginner or an experienced professional. If the recipient disobeyed orders and took the letter to the police, some officers had enough experience to recognize the blackmailer by his handwriting, though it was considered bad form to use this information to track down the blackmailer.

Then as now, the Post Office required mail to have a return address. Blackmailers, as you can imagine, did not want to comply. So mail in black envelopes was exempt. In exchange, there was a higher postage rate for blackmail letters, with special stamps bearing the picture of a vulture.

Wo Ist die Post? Learning a Second and Third Language

by Donna H. Turner

When I first started Carnegie Tech, I signed up for beginning German. I thought, *What's so hard about languages? I study hard; I listen in class, take good notes, and am motivated.* So I started class and studied hard, took good notes, and found I was indeed motivated. The only fly in that ointment turned out to be two flies. One, I couldn't hear any differences among the sounds, and two, the instructor was prepared to teach students who already knew a lot of German, not me, who had learned only a few swear words from my grandfather. Well, not "All's Well that Ends Well" as my friend Shakespeare would say. I struggled hard but at the end of the year, I knew how to say, *"Wo ist die Post?"* and that's about it. In 1960 there were no audio tapes to listen to, so I had to work on my own. I didn't fail the course but it wasn't a shining moment either.

Years went by and I forgot I had ever taken German. My husband and I had moved from Pittsburgh to Richmond, Indiana. I was raising three children, but started taking courses at Earlham College. After several years I had nearly enough credits for an Earlham degree.

Suddenly the fly in the ointment turned into a bee and stung me very hard. I had to have a year of foreign language to graduate from Earlham. *Okay,* I thought, *I'll take something else, maybe French.* But we had now moved to the small town of New Concord, Ohio, where Muskingum College had abolished its language requirement that very year. As a result all the other students were rejoicing while I thought, *What do I do now?* By the early seventies, audio tapes were available to students, and the college was offering beginning French. I felt pretty lucky. I went to my first French class and found there were only two of us in class. One was a young Romanian woman who already spoke five Romance languages; I was the other. After the first quarter ended,

Kathy was speaking fluent French, and—remember the two flies? They came back. In the bleak midwinter, I studied hard, took good notes, was certainly motivated—I had to pass—and yet, I could not hear differences in words, even with the tapes. Nor could the instructor get down to basic *le* and *la*. He and Kathy were talking to one another in fluent French.

They did provide a lot of help to me, though. Kathy became my tutor, and the instructor was kind. He hadn't a clue as to why I was having such a hard time, but he assured me that if I worked hard all year, he would find some way to get me through. That seemed more than fair. Later on I realized that with only two students in the class and language study now optional, the powers that be would notice if half the class failed.

But I did work hard all year, and he did pass me, so I got credit for a year of French, and soon afterwards, a Bachelor of Arts degree from Earlham College.

So indeed, now I may say, "All's Well that Ends Well"—at least as long as I stay away from learning languages.

In a Rush

by Patricia A. Moton

Have you ever been in a hurry?
Have you ever been in a rush?
I've got five minutes to write this poem,
Because then my lunch hour's up!

Some people have time to ponder,
And to search their mind and soul.
Well, I have just five minutes,
And that can take its toll.

I really like writing poetry,
But not in such a hurry.
I'll probably leave something important out,
And then I'll start to worry.

Oh, well, that's my five minutes.
I'll try to polish it later.
If I didn't have a full-time job,
Well, hell, it might have been greater.

If You Must Write
by Laura R. Merryman

If you must write,
Write with imagination,
Find the joy in your heart,
Or the anger
Write because there's something in you
That needs to get out,
Peel back a vent, and let it ripple onto the page.
Write to push back the nothingness,
The desolation,
The three a.m. fears.
Write because there's something inside
And you don't know what it is
--a lost love, beloved pet, a life you will never live.
Write with the ripeness of warm strawberries squishing
In your mouth.
Write with the labor of old age.
Write because there's music in the air
Or a storm rages on the horizon.
Write of attractions and passions
Others will never know,
Unless you tell them.
Write, you see, because
There's a swirling collage of words in your soul,
And if you don't catch it,
It will flee this very instant and re-form.
Write because you must,
Not because I made you.
Yes, write because *you* must.

And so I write this for you.

Eventually

by Patricia A. Moton

Eventually I'll take a stand,
For the kind of poet that I am.
I'll explore the possibility,
Of sharing laughter with you, eventually.

I'm not a poet of death and medical woes,
Though I've experienced more than my fair share of those.
I'm not a poet of battles, or street crime, or strife,
Not a poet enjoying upsetting your life.

No, I like to spread mirth and laughter whenever I can.
This began long ago when I became a fan
Of the poetry authored by one Ogden Nash.
This man of such insight, hilarity, panache!

I read his first poem in high school, 'twas just two lines long.
"A rose is a rose is a rose"— it sounds just like a song.
Then Nash quickly slaps you right square in your face—
"But a caterpillar is a tractor," and . . . he does it with grace.

So, at this time of my life, I'd like to play with my craft.
I'd like to touch your emotions, but then make you laugh.
I'd like to show you life can be fun, and perhaps even silly,
And I'm sure that I'll do that, eventual Lilly.

What Not to Do
by Tracy Deitz

Never, never, *ever* compose ideas and go on and on about something or another or anything, in fact, to the point where your audience gets exhausted and needs to take a nap in order to decode the content streaming from the pen that you hold in a death grip, which conveys the intensity of a life-or-death situation requiring emergency concentration so that there will be no casualty in determining what, exactly, a run-on sentence is blabbering about. And forget dangling prepositions too.

The Pontiff of Poetry
by Jackson Harlem

The uncontestable kingship of his words
makes all the notebooks bow down.
When he performs, his lips are adorned
with English jewels & a star is born.

His robe is non-fiction and the wardrobe changes
when he performs.
He speaks white collar poetry with a crown of thorns.

When the king makes the honeybees kneel,
their minds are opened and their mouths are sealed.
When the court is silent, the king will sing.
Every time he performs onstage, a poet gets his wings.

Harlemese
[feat. the royal court]

by Jackson Harlem

Who's that cat that's writing back?!
I'm a duffle bag poet with a duffle bag mind
Gotta kilo reefa tongue, cat, and I'm always sniffin' lines.
Get back Jack! I writes back. I'm the apple; I cuts 'em all.
Tuxedo poet. Call me Michael cause I be all up
    off the wall.
Moonwalk peola; the Rock'nRolla. I got your change.
    Keep hope alive.
Obama my phone number and translate all this hep jive.

Who's that cat that's writing back?! JACK!

Kill me, baby. Take off your threads. Knees. Prey. Hands. Head.
I gave man fire. Call me Prometheus. Rocks. Paper. Wine. Bread.
Poets call me Dada; I be like Fatha cuz I keeps the sharks
    all fed.
Hunt. Fin. In. Swim. Din. Eat. Slay. Red...
Knocked the trophy, collared the crown.
At least that's what headlines read.
I'm a killer-diller writah and I puts the lanes to bed.
Who's that cat that's writing back?!
JAAACK's the one that lays'em dead.
JACK's the one that schools the poets alive
    and makes them be well-read.
JACK's the one the two, the three, the five,
the white, the brown, the red.
JACK's the one who eats the beasts and beasts
    on microphones and gets ahead.
JACK's the one that gets the head.
I John the Baptist your Pontious Pilate.
I spit rhymes so fly my poems get high and I put them
    on autopilot.
My words so hep sometimes they skip and I just say,

"Oh, the 'H' is silent."
I put the "arlem" in Parliment and I get the whole House excited.
I beat Obama; I'm the Poet's President
And I won by a landslide.
You voted for me cause I was Black--History.
Now translate all this hep jive!
Who's that cat that's writing back?!
I-I'm a duffle bag poet with a duffle bag mind.

*Reaching Out
    Reaching In
        Reaching Up*

The Rainbow Pin
by Larry Turner

After Martha entered the tea shop and greeted Jolene, she handed her a small box. Surprised, Jolene asked, "What's this all about?"

"Open it." Inside was a lovely pin shaped and colored as a rainbow. Jolene took the pin from the box and turned it around, examining it from all angles.

"But, why?"

"Remember, the Bible says that after the Flood, God put a rainbow in the sky to tell Noah things were going to get better?"

"Yes, but—"

"Well, this is to remind you that after the flood of troubles you've lived through, things will get better." They both remembered that during the two painful years Jolene had lived with Tom, he had undermined her self-confidence and driven away all her friends except Martha.

"It's too much. You shouldn't have."

"Don't tell me what I shouldn't do. I saw the pin in a shop and decided you needed a constant reminder that your bad times are behind you. Here, pin it on your blouse."

As she walked home afterwards, Jolene saw a young woman look at her pin and smile. The woman spoke. "A son or a daughter? I hope you're proud of him or her."

"I don't have a son or daughter. I'm not married." Jolene was surprised she had revealed so much to a total stranger. Even more surprised that putting it into words had lifted a weight from her shoulders.

"Oh, then this pin is for you." The woman moved close to her and looked into her eyes. "Was it hard getting to the point you could let people know?"

Jolene couldn't stop herself. "Yes, it was a struggle. But now I'm finally free to be myself." Was this new openness all she needed to make a new friend? Tom never had missed an opportunity to call her unlikable. Except for Martha, whom she had known since childhood, she had never confided in anyone about her troubles. And here she was opening up to this total—but so approachable—stranger.

The woman moved closer still and asked, "How about stopping at Starbucks for tea or coffee?"

"Sorry, I just had tea with a friend."

"Then can we meet sometime? Let me give you my phone number."

Jolene was suddenly quite ill at ease. "I am sorry, but I'm late and I really have to go." She turned away and hurried down the street.

Halfway down the block, Jolene slowed almost to a stop. *Funny, a man with similar intentions would have frightened me.*

But she did find me attractive. She glanced at her reflection in the shop window she was passing and lifted her head high. She chuckled. *Well, what if?* At the thought, Jolene almost laughed aloud.

Margaret Dillard
by Tom Higgins

I first met Margaret at Carriage Hill Nursing Home. One of our Special Friends Sunday school staff, Margaret Ingram, had been told there was a person living there who might want to join us. Our class worked with special needs folks of all ages.

I went and met the nursing home director who introduced me to our potential new student. Margaret was a short, small framed, gray headed lady, probably in her sixties. She was sitting at the activity table with several other people using crayons to color a beautiful lady training two circus horses to stand on their hind legs. I noticed that she was very exacting in her coloring inside the lines, and that she used more than one color crayon. The director and I sat down at the table with her and asked her if she would like to come to Sunday school and church. She said in a loud voice "yes!" It was then I realized that she was hard of hearing. I told her that I would pick her up the next Sunday.

That Sunday came and I pulled up to the front of the nursing home in my small VW Diesel rabbit and walked into the nurses' station. I spotted Margaret in a beautiful blue dress with a Bible tucked under her arm.

With a smile on her face she said in a loud voice, "I wait for you!" We told the nurses goodbye and walked out to the car. I opened the door and Margaret sat down slowly in the front seat. She placed her knees together and carefully pushed the dress down well over the knees. I told her that she looked very nice. She beamed.

We came to Sunday school and she had no trouble fitting in with the rest of the folks. I was not surprised to see that she did the best coloring. At ten minutes to eleven, I walked her up to the church entrance.

We went up the steps, received our church bulletins and walked into the sanctuary. Margaret was in complete awe of the size of the Church. She said in a loud voice, "Lotta people in here!" Heads turned. I whispered to her that we needed to be quiet.

We continued walking up the aisle to the front where Special Friends were sitting.

Margaret was well behaved and at first a little apprehensive. She held on to my hand and Margaret Ingram's, who was sitting on her other side. Our new student, being a small person, could not put her feet on the floor. After relaxing a little, while still holding our hands, she began to swing her legs back and forth. I was reminded of my children when they were small in church swinging their legs.

I picked her up for three Sundays in a row. I especially remember the third Sunday when our lesson was about Daniel and the Lion's Den. We again went up to Church services and sat together. We were halfway through the service when a small elbow hit me firmly in the ribs. It was Margaret with a big smile on her face, and her large Bible opened up to the Book of Daniel. I was flabbergasted. I didn't know that she could read or knew that much about the Bible. I found out later from her family that was all she talked about that week.

The following Thursday the social director at the nursing home called and told me that Margaret had died quietly in her sleep as a result of a heart attack. I felt very sad.

On Friday I went to the funeral for her viewing and met her brother and other members of the family. I went up to the open casket to pay respect to that dear lady. She was dressed in the same blue dress I had seen when I picked her up on that first Sunday. In her hands was her Bible, opened to the Book of Daniel. The tears came.

Today, thanks to the social director, I have that piece of paper with the beautiful circus lady and horses- all colored inside the lines.

Alexander's Legacy
by Madalin E. Jackson

It sits there
Alone.
If it weren't for the
Telemarketers
And their solicitations
Ridiculous and invasive,
It would never make a sound,
A beep, a ring, a jingle.

When it finally comes alive
The voice answers.
Robotically expounding
To leave a message.
The voice stops.
There is no message,
Just deafening
Silence.

She rocks back and forth
Listening. Waiting.
But no one who cares, calls.
She reaches over and
Touches the one button
She knows to push.
And hears the cheerful message
That echos in her head.

Hey, Lady

by Margaret Rose

"Please, can anybody help me? I need to get me a ride." The sound of that pleading voice had a haunting effect on Martha as she walked past the customers browsing through the book displays and the people lined up to wait for the bus stop in front of the bookstore. She turned to see a woman calling out in vain to anyone who could hear her. Martha's eyes met the dark eyes of the abandoned woman who cried out again, "Please, can somebody give me a ride? I need to get me a ride to the DMV."

It took only a few seconds before Martha remembered where she had heard that voice before. She turned away, tightened her hold on her purse and walked straight toward her car, determined to get as far away from this woman as possible. She thought back to that rainy night, several years ago, when she had first heard that voice. In spite of the sun that warmed the day, she shivered as she recalled that night. She experienced a wave of anxiety when she remembered how she had let herself become the target of this same voice and resolved that she was not going to get taken in again.

*   *   *   *   *   *   *   *   *

"Help me! Can't somebody help me? I got to get outta this rain! I'm gonna die if I don't get outta this rain. Hey lady! Lady, can you take me in your car?"

Martha was thankful for the umbrella which she pulled out of her purse, shielding herself from the driving rain and from the loud, pleading voice which confronted her as she left work at the office. She had a long walk up the hill to her car so she left the bags she was carrying just inside the doors of the office building, planning to come back to pick them up in the dry safety of her car. The wind blew her coat open, drenching the lower half of her body and skirt.

When she got back down the hill and was putting her bags in her car, the woman with the loud voice reappeared. "Hey! Hey lady, can you help me? I need a ride. I can't stay out in this rain. I gotta get to the church. Please help me. I'm gonna die if I don't get outta this rain."

Martha looked around the parking lot area. Walking toward her was a disheveled, wild-eyed woman dressed in torn jeans, a jacket, and flip-flops--no umbrella, no coat, no hat. Did anyone else hear this plea for help? Martha had stayed late tonight to get things set up for an early meeting the next day. The parking lot and side streets were empty and dark, absorbed in the blackness of the rain. She was cold, hungry and thinking about how she was going to get home, let out the dog, and get to the church by 7 p.m. She opened the trunk of her car and walked toward the covered entrance where she had stowed her bags. It was impossible to avoid splashing in the puddles of rain that accumulated in the street where she parked.

"Please lady. It's just down the road. The people at the church, they tell me they give me some help but I can't get there in this rain. Can't you help me?" Her voice grew louder with each successive plea.

Martha was desperate to get home, out of her wet clothes and shoes. Why did this woman have to be here on this night of all nights? If only I had left a few minutes earlier, I would have missed her, she thought to herself. Then it dawned on her that if she was so cold and wet in spite of the substantial London Fog raincoat she was wearing, this woman must be equally so—and all she had on her feet were flip-flops. And she was asking to go to a church, after all. Probably some soup kitchen, she thought. The Catholic church was just around the corner less than five minutes from where they stood. She picked up one more box of binders, awkwardly juggling the umbrella, her purse and box, as she tried to stay dry, pack up her car, and figure out how to safely handle the dilemma of the lady in distress. Her mind was in overdrive. She saw no relief in sight.

Part of her wanted to help the woman. However, she was in a hurry to get home and then to a meeting, not to mention she was alone and all rules of common sense pointed to the fact that you don't pick up strangers. In her 50 years of living and driving, she had engaged in such risky behavior only twice, and that was when she was young and foolish and hitch-hiking in Europe with her husband. Those were different times and circumstances. Now she was older and accustomed to using more discretion when interacting with strangers. It was one thing to want to help someone. It was quite another thing to deliberately put oneself in jeopardy. However, turning her back on a woman in distress didn't seem quite right. She herself had two children who were starting out, living day to day on meager paychecks. What if they were stuck and needed help? The woman was circling her, as if zoning in on a target, as she loaded up her car.

"Where do you need to go?" Martha asked.

"Right down that road over there." She pointed vaguely to the north. "The people at the church, they promised they'd help me till I get paid on Friday. I ain't got no money. I ain't eaten all day. Please take me. I got to get outta this rain." Her voice continued to rise. Martha feared the woman was verging on hysteria.

"OK. OK then. I'll take you to the church." As soon as her passenger entered the car, Martha felt a surge of adrenaline pump through her body like that of a child who has been told to not cross the street but who goes ahead and crosses the forbidden street, frightened but determined. She drove out of the parking lot and peered into the dark road ahead. She got in the right-hand turn lane which would take them to the Catholic church she knew was just several hundred yards further.

"No, no, not that way," the woman interrupted. "Here, just stay on this road, right here. You go straight through this light. It's just down this road."

Martha headed down the road as directed, starting to regret her "good Samaritan" decision. She was not familiar with this road. She made a mental inventory of all the churches she knew in the area. She drove through the blackness, searching for signs of life, other people, the church, even a policeman. After what seemed like an eternity but which in reality was probably only about the distance of one mile, she saw a small white building on the left side of the road.

"This is it. This is it. This is the church. Stop here."

Martha's heart dropped at the sight of the vacant parking area outside of the plain building. There were no markers, no stained glass windows or crosses that one would expect to see at a church. Other than one single street light, there were no lights in the building; no people; no cars.

The woman got out of the car, ran through the rain to knock first on one door of the building, then another. She waited a few minutes, then returned to the car. "They promise me they be here tonight to help me."

Martha panicked. Her heart raced. I've taken her this far, she thought. Now what do I do with her? Do I just leave her here and say—sorry, I've got to get home?

Her passenger got back into the car. "I'm Florida, like the state. I work at the nursin' home out in the county."

"Do you have a place to spend the night?" Martha asked.

"No, I got no money. I can't go back to that hotel where I stay last night. I don't get paid till Friday."

"Have you tried the homeless shelter in town?"

"I can't go there. They won't take me in. I got me a job and they don't take people who got jobs."

Thinking to herself that this didn't sound like the shelter she knew, Martha asked, "Well, where did you spend the night last night?"

"I stay at the Ra'al Hotel on down the road here."

"The Ra'al Hotel? Which one is that?" Martha drove this road everyday. She knew that there were no hotels on this road between the spot they were now and the middle of town, at least ten miles away.

Martha's mind turned involuntarily toward all of the horror-story scenarios that she had heard about people who pick up strangers. What if she has a gun or some other weapon? Maybe she thinks I have a lot of money. What if she has friends waiting in the church? We are out here in the middle of nowhere. Of my own volition, she thought, I have driven with a total stranger to an abandoned parking lot in the middle of nowhere. Have I lost my mind?

Out of desperation and a looming sense of panic, she turned the car around and headed toward town. She strained to see into the darkness ahead of her all the while trying to keep an eye on her passenger. She noticed the puddles of water at Florida's feet on the floor mats of the car. Martha's fingers fumbled as she tried to find the heat dial on the dashboard. It didn't help her nerves that the windshield was fogging up.

"Just keep going on down this here Route 1. It's right in town."

As the two women rode together in the darkness, Florida rambled about her job. She said she had no family in the area although she was born in a neighboring county. Martha wanted to ask questions, but she was afraid of appearing to be too nosy or too judgmental. They drove on a few miles, seeing no hotels, motels, inns of any kind on either side of the road. When they approached a major intersection, Florida spoke up, "You know, I think I rather not go back to that Ra'al Hotel anyway. Why don' you just turn right here and I know another place right down this road. Turn right here."

Florida's voice and demeanor had gone from that of the hysterical, needy woman in the parking lot to that of a passenger who was giving orders to her personal driver. To herself, Martha thought, there is no way I am going to go down any more unfamiliar roads or side streets. Aloud, she said, "I think we should just stay on route 1 and locate your hotel from last night. How many more miles do you think it is?" The muscles in Martha's shoulders and neck were stiff; her head was throbbing. Was it fear? Fear for her physical safety? Or fear that she was being taken for a ride? In her own car? Who was in control here?

As they drove on, she realized that the hotel must be on the south side of town in the midst of a series of strip malls and old Route 1 motels. She decided to continue in that direction, praying that they would get there soon. Finally they arrived at the "Ra'al" or Royal Inn. "Royal" it was not. They went into the so-called lobby which, with its very short hall-way and glass window through which she spoke to the clerk on duty through a microphone, reminded Martha of the visitor's area in a jail. Oh well, just a few more minutes, and it would be over. She had already decided to pay for the room for one night for Florida. This was something she could afford to do and was a small way to help a woman down on her luck.

Her hopes were crushed. Instead of getting Florida checked back into her hotel, the clerk informed them that Florida was no longer welcome in his establishment because last night she had trashed her room and the owner was forced to call the police. Florida's face showed no expression. She said nothing. Martha's sense of despair rose. She looked across the road and saw a Motel 6. "Let's try this one across the street," she suggested.

"No, I can't go in there. My son came in there and broke the lamp. They don't want me there no more."

Martha couldn't believe what she was hearing. This was much more than she had bargained for. Florida had not been honest with her. Should she confront Florida about her dishonesty right now? What did she owe her anyway? Talk about a lady in distress! Martha was beginning to feel like the distressed person in this scenario. As Florida became calmer and more sure that her needs would be meet, Martha's confidence level plummeted. Her good deed had turned into an endless nightmare. She was starting to feel trapped inside of her own car.

Suddenly, she spotted a Ramada Inn further down the road. Without a moment's hesitation, she decided that Florida would be spending this night in the Ramada Inn, provided she hadn't already worn out her welcome there also.

When they entered the reception area at the Ramada, Florida headed straight for one of the large sumptuous black leather couches in the lounging area. Martha explained to the clerk that she would like to pay for this woman's lodging for two nights, saying that she was helping her because she had fallen on hard times. She hesitated as she pulled out her credit card. Two nights would get Florida through until Friday and would at least provide a warm breakfast each day. The clerk asked for Florida's identification. Florida poured through her big floppy purse. She pulled out paper after paper. Martha prayed, oh God, please let her have an ID of some kind. Finally she produced a document which passed the scrutiny of the clerk and then headed for the free coffee machine.

The clerk handed Florida the key to the room. Martha handed Florida a pair of gym shoes that she kept in the car. "I hope these will fit you. It looks like you could use some warm shoes." She paused and added, "I hope that things work out better for you by Friday." With a blank stare, Florida walked down the hallway toward the elevator, without turning around to say goodbye or to utter a word of thanks. She punched the elevator button and waited in silence, holding her bag, cup of coffee and the shoes that Martha had given her.

Emotionally drained and confused, Martha walked out of the hotel and returned to her car, feeling like she had just been held hostage and then released with no explanation. She opened the car door and looked around to see if she had been followed. After less than an hour of time shared in the car with Florida, she could not shake the feeling that she was being pursued. The disturbing sequence of so many false starts and misleading bits of information left her feeling that she would never be free of this woman. The hysteria that she had observed in Florida at the beginning of the evening had passed contagiously into her own psyche, infecting her with fear and self doubt.

When she was safely seated in the car, with her doors locked, she slumped forward against the steering wheel and thanked God for bringing her through this encounter safely. She didn't understand why she felt so bad after doing what she thought was a good deed. She balked at the realization that she had not acted wisely, not only for her own safety but also for the long-term welfare of Florida and she was embarrassed about that. Had she been an enabler for Florida? Was she really doing anyone a favor by booking a room in a nice hotel for a woman who had a reputation for "trashing" rooms? It had all started out so innocently; giving a woman a ride to a church. She shivered with cold and with nagging self-doubts about just who had taken whom for a ride. She couldn't rid herself of the cold vision of Florida turning away from her without even a thank-you.

Later that night she shared the story of what she called her "close encounter" with her friends at church. She was grateful for the opportunity to process the evening's strange turn of events. Some called her choices unwise. "But aren't we supposed to help those who are in need?" she asked through the tears which gushed from her troubled soul. "Why does it have to be so hard to do a good deed? I was so scared and now I just feel plain stupid." Her friends responded by pointing out that, not unlike a soldier who instinctively reaches out to protect his comrades because of his unquestioning loyalty to his duty, she had either consciously or subconsciously, done what she thought was right. She had followed her convictions, however wise or unwise her behavior may have been, and isn't that the way we want to live?

The following day, she couldn't help but relive the night's experiences as she crossed the parking lot at work. Once back to her desk, she tried to focus on the day's pile of assignments waiting for her. After her morning meeting, Martha did her daily email check and saw that one of her friends at church had written to her. The subject line said, *"No such thing as coincidence, Martha."* In his reading that morning, her friend had come across a paragraph that was uncanny in its timeliness. The author was Dean Koontz and the book was From the Corner Of His Eye. The words were a soothing tonic to Martha. With each sentence she read, her spirits were raised. Her muscles relaxed, her questions were answered, and her heart was profoundly moved.

"*Not one day in anyone's life is an uneventful day. No day without profound meaning . . . because in every day of your life there are opportunities to perform little kindnesses for others, both by conscious acts of will and unconscious example. Each smallest act of kindness reverberates across great distances and spans of time, affecting lives unknown to the one whose generous spirit was the source of this good echo. Kindness is passed on, and grows each time it's passed, until a simple courtesy becomes an act of selfless courage years later and far away. All human lives are so profoundly and intricately entwined that the fate of all is the fate of each, and the hope of humanity rests in every heart and in every pair of hands.*"

She wrote back, "Mike, is this just another weird coincidence that you are reading this particular passage in this particular book on this particular day? What a salve for my psychological and emotional wounds! If you are implying that my brief encounter with Florida started some sort of chain reaction, then I guess it was worth it. What I did may have followed the courage of my convictions, but was it smart or safe? Or is that the wrong way to approach life, to always be safe? I wonder what I will do the next time I run into a Florida, or a Georgia or a Virginia. Which of my instincts will prevail? In any case, one thing I know is true. Your kindness in taking the time to share with me this morning has provided much needed solace and a reason for celebration as I strive to find meaning in my experiences. You are a blessing for which I am truly grateful."

Note to the reader: The passage quoted from Dean Koontz has originally been attributed to H.R. White from a speech entitled "The Momentous Day" but remains unverifiable, according to all research I have done. I have used the Dean Koontz source since that is where it was originally pointed out to me.

Enlightened?

by Anne H. Flythe

The distance between smart and wise is vast;
even in increments it compares
to distance measured in light years.
The past, replete with victory and defeat,
is best stored in a childproof bottle
in a cool dry place safe from light.

Probing memory is irresistible,
painful as exploring the socket of a missing tooth
for the oddly reassuring taste of blood and iron.
Pain and pleasure coexist.
If life lasts long enough, sort the detritus
of a lifetime into manageable bytes.

It's unwise to leave the evidence
in the open where it can trip you up,
smart to get on with whatever time is left,
wise to give each moment of the present tenure.
The past is best stored in a cool dry place safe from light.

Imagination Lost
by Juanita D. Roush

Little pixie dancing
on tiny spritely feet,
now laughing and charming
the people that she meets.

Fluttering the breezes
with little tiny wings,
listening and skipping,
then the little sprite sings.

Dancing, dancing, dancing,
charming the group en masse,
while keeping to the beat
of wind upon the grass.

Tiny little pixie,
dancing without a care,
wish I still had the heart
to see you dancing there.

All We, Like Sheep

by Dan Walker

All we, like sheep— I hate that comparison.
Not that we're too good for it, you understand.
We're just not like anything
with a plural the same as its singular—
all those wool-lined gloves, inside out,
and standing around on their finger-tips.

No, we're more like that wolf pack off in the hills,
howling at the Government
and *wishing* we had a shot at those accessories.
Or even like that dog out on patrol,
hoping if the inventory comes up short
it won't be on his watch.

I wouldn't be that dog for anything,
and certainly not the pack leader.
But I might be running along the side,
trying to hang my tongue out like the rest
and taking notes for a documentary,
hoping to be in some of the footage.

But you see what I mean:
Whatever I am, and we are,
sheep is not it.

Inside the Bubble
by David Mitchell

I'm feeling quite secure here inside my little bubble
Protected from that frightful world outside
There's nothing I should fear here
There's never any trouble
I always have a place where I can hide
I am the king of my own realm
I am the captain at the helm
Everything I need is here inside
Inside this shell there's no bad news
I'm shielded from upsetting views
Inside I always have my sense of pride
I love my bubble doubly for now my life's so bubbly
It's the safest feeling I have ever known
They tell me there's a world out there
But honestly why should I care?
In here I have a world all of my own

Magic Glasses
by David Mitchell

I just got this new pair of glasses.
They were giving them away for free,
and with these new magic glasses
I see just what they want me to see.
When I look through these new magic glasses,
I see how easy my life can now be.
For with these new magic glasses
I see just what they want me to see.
Gone now is all that confusion
that was playing tug-o-war with my mind.
For with these new magic glasses
to contrary views I am blind.
It's like looking at the world through a tunnel
that leads only to that which is true,
and life is just so much easier
when you only have one point of view.
So go do yourself a big favor,
and go get yourself a free pair.
You'll find that life is just so much easier
when there's just one point of view
we all share.

Monster in Her Room

by David Mitchell

Little Rosie Bloom
had a monster in her room.
He was lurking in the darkness
cloaked in shadow and in gloom.

"Go away!" Rosie said,
as he sat upon her bed.
"I really do not like you,
because you make me feel afraid."
But the monster would not heed her cries
and in her room he stayed.

"Perhaps you'll disappear
if I pretend that you're not here.
To make you go away
I'll just close my eyes and pray."

The monster merely laughed, and said,
"Oh, you silly fool
That trick only works with an imaginary ghoul.
You can cower in your bed
with your blanket up over your head,
but when you pull it down, my dear
I think you'll find that I'm still here.

"Oh, no, you cannot be true.
Everybody tells me I should not believe in you.
You're just a fanciful creation
of my wild imagination,
a waking dream delusion,
an optical illusion.
So go away now please, you big old scary creep.
It's getting rather late, and I really have to sleep.
The monster did not leave, he just sat there and smiled.

He must somehow prove his existence
to this disbelieving child.
And so he said
as he sat upon her bed,
"The people who created me will stubbornly insist
That I am really not so bad, or that I don't exist
They want you to ignore me as if I am not here
And will try to reassure you, I am nothing you should fear.
But as you see, I am real- I simply can't be missed
Do not believe their lies, my dear. Monsters really do exist."

Rosie still could not believe that monsters do exist,
for she was young and innocent, if you get my gist.
She wanted only good in everything that was,
and could not comprehend just what it is a monster does.

And so she said
to the creature on her bed,
"Perhaps you're just misunderstood
Perhaps deep down inside there's good
Good that others cannot see
Perhaps you need a friend like me
To melt that monstrous heart of ice
And turn you into something nice
I can change you, you shall see
I'll teach you about civility
I know- we'll have a tea party!
Just think how splendid that would be-
a social tea for you and me!"

The monster had to give Rosie credit for trying.
He could say his heart was touched,
but then he would be lying,
for you cannot touch a heart that really isn't there.
A monster is a heartless thing that simply doesn't care.

"You may invite me to your social teas
and delight me with your pleasantries
You may dress me up in fancy clothes
and teach me manners I suppose-
but all of that would be a sham.

You cannot change this thing I am."

"Is there nothing I can say
to make you go away?"

"If there was, why would I tell you how to rid yourself of
   me?
If I did, what kind of self-respecting monster would I be?
To be nice is just preposterous;
for I am nothing if not monstrous."

Rosie began to comprehend
that this fiend was not her friend.
He was a most unwelcome guest,
a horrid thing- a pest.

"You're like a really bad dream.
You make me want to loudly scream.
In fact I think I will.
I'll scream and scream and scream until
I scream so long and horribly loud
I start to attract a curious crowd."

At this the monster seemed concerned
and from this little Rosie learned
that monsters are actually rather shy
and do not like the public eye.
It was the monster's turn to react with fright
and Rosie was emboldened by this sight.

"Now I know just what to do:
I'm going to tell the world on you!"

The monster stood up from his seat,
his head bowed low in his defeat.
"Okay, Rosie, today you win.
I'll go out as I came in.
However, you should know
a simple truth before I go:
While I may vanish from your sight

I'll still be out there in the night.
Monsters come in different guises
and are known to pull some rude surprises"

A monster is that thing you fear when you turn out the light.
He's that nagging apprehension that keeps you up at night.
You want to just ignore him and erase him from your mind,
but the more that you ignore him the more you'll come
        to find
that monsters thrive on diffidence
and prosper from your ignorance.

To make a monster go away
you must expose him to the light of day,
make his presence widely known
and his bad intentions clearly shown.
Monsters flee when they're uncovered
And their true nature is discovered

Rambling Thoughts in Panic Mode
by Madalin E. Jackson

Rambling thoughts in panic mode
Careen inside my head.
Fear of failure,
Criticism,
Deathly stares
And pangs of guilt.

Take a breath.
Close your eyes.
Let serenity surround
With calming words
Like Chamomile
The mind relaxes now.

What Might Be?
by Norma E. Redfern

Dreams of flying to the moon,
traveling around the world.

That's not what I most desire.

A trip to a spa, something
I have only dreamed about.

Making changes to my body,
feeling renewed and refreshed.

Oprah, please give me a break,
make my wish come true.

The Truth about Truth
by David Mitchell

Truth has become, well…subjective
It is a matter of one's personal perspective
You may declare it as true
If it agrees with your view
And if not you can deride it with invective
Reality can be what you wish it to be
You can choose facts to use from the news on TV
For the television news presents differing views
And your mind can just see what it wishes to see
Now forget what your science has shown
For I've got some scientists of my own
Who, for a nominal fee
Will concur only with me
And dispute what was previously known

Goodbye, Alceste

by James F. Gaines

The Misanthrope and I have parted ways.
There was a time when I could not contend
With people who continually spend
Their sum of life on delicate displays,
But now I've learned that delicacy pays.
The world's not black and white as some pretend;
Instead it's filled with moral shades that blend
Into a vast infinity of grays.
I find a new relief in common sense
That sifts the marvelous from useless dross.
No longer I a stranger to pretense
If mild deception thwarts a greater loss,
And I can let love lull my carping mind
If death and loneliness are left behind.

The Study of Logic in Vienna, a poem to Frank—not the cat

by Kathie Walker

He calls himself Vampire of Vienna, Virginia,
slayer of spiders,
available for fantasy
and dragons,
but only while wearing orange,
perhaps. Equivocation on this
point is entirely
possible.
He jests
He jokes
He warps his words into
fine lines of logic.
And he has things perfectly
under control.
He thinks.

About what,
he doesn't say.
He is and he isn't.
Panera Bread makes
good sandwiches
or so it's said.
This isn't about
logic—
It's chemistry,
being or not being,
holding hands in the rain, and
what of lovers, kissing while eating ripe peaches
instead?
We'll see. Even a player
falls in love—After intermission.
Words
between the acts?
Entr'acte.

As for me, I just keep standing
in the rain, reading.
Trying in vain to understand (in)completeness.
The logic of Kurt Godel.
Paper and ink.
Theorems in the rain,
getting wet.
I think.

And so, this need:
Godel studied logic in Vienna
and so do we.

Inconsistency and Remedies

by James F. Gaines

Some call the unfairness of life immense.
Rather I'd say too impartially dense,
Distributing bonanzas and booby gifts
Without consulting common sense,
Much less our personal Christmas lists.

In the universal lottery
It is often the priest, poor fellow,
Who wins the night at the bordello,
But has to sit and drink his tea
And ruminate on chastity,
While wracked by lusty throes.
And the motorcycle goes
To the chair-bound amputee,
While the firm of loin and the fleet of foot
Must be content to just stay put
And moan, "Not I. Not I. Not I!"
But what if we could rectify
This math of careless destiny
Rebalancing foul with fair, stale with fresh?
The limbless might swoon in the pleasure of flesh
And the vicar could, with angel speed,
Streak to the site of spiritual need.
Simon of Cyrene, the ox,
Incurred no loss
For having borne the cross
A few short city blocks.

Dancing in the Rain
by Juanita D. Roush

Puddles of liquid spotlight
highlight my feet as I dance;
Slowly turning, twisting, bending
listening to music that only I hear;
Internal music playing its gentle rhythm
water running down my face,
Lips, wet with the rain,
linger on your lips
as we part and come together again.
Artificial memories,
but we could have been
Dancing in the rain.

The Music Plays
by Diann Brunell

The music plays.
I keep walking through the heavy storms.
I keep writing through the darkness.
I keep witnessing through the turbulent years.
"Rebuild, for I am with you."
Still the music plays...
I hear it, on my journey to my eternal home.
God is my beautiful music.
I can hear Him now.

Big Bang Take Two
by Tracy Deitz

Microcosm of the universe
in a yellow dandelion flower
rooted to the ground
but heading to seed.
Perennial parachutes preparing
to launch, balancing upon a breath,
to spread colonies far and wide.

Crowned atop a sturdy scepter-stem
rises an elaborate dome,
crisscrossing high-rise beams,
constructed of silky white cow eyelashes.

The complex infrastructure
resembles a spherical space module
poised to disseminate
pods bearing life,
traversing currents of air
and dispersing
into new habitats.

One scientific theory states
that the Big Bang began—
at random, you see—
causing planetary existence.
An alternate proposal:
God sneezed.

His Hand

by Tracy Deitz

How does one measure the universe?
No clue, myself—
but an astronomy club
explored the topic.

"I presume this calculation
is not a completed study,"
one guest said.

"I've seen all the way to Pluto,"
said another, touting his telescope.

Me, too, with a textbook.

Michael, not the angel, recited
a brief history of human efforts
to track the starry Host:

Finite fingers in the Egyptian plateau
matched pyramids of Giza
to stars buckling Orion's belt.

In Athens around 632 B.C.,
Meton tracked eclipses
in 18.61-year cycles.

Can we compute our own demise?
Ancient Mayan temples foretold,
through snakes crawling
along the spring equinox,
that the world would end in 2012.

Such calculations hurt my brain.
Locate astronomical positions?
I can't find my glasses half the time.

Archimedes counted grains of sand
to estimate the mass of the cosmos,
while Erastosthenes traveled on a camel
to determine the earth's circumference.

The supernova in 1572
flared for Queen Elizabeth,
ending the notion that stars
remained stationary.

A short time later, Galileo
rotated to the sun for the center,
gaining himself a reputation
as a heretic with the Inquisition.

Each era's evolving ideas
circle inside the orbits
of planetary perceptions
and loop-de-loop around truth.

Mortals' see only an arc minute.
What is constant?
Dustlings on Earth gaze upward,
seeking a peek at eternity.

So when our celestial bodies shake
or quake, we take comfort
knowing that the breadth
of The Maker's hand,
which marks off the heavens,
will pillow our fall.

God alone determines the number
of the stars and calls them—
as He does with us—
each by name.

(Special thanks to Michael Masters and the Rappahannock Astronomy Club for the presentation about historical facts of astronomy. Bible verses referenced include Genesis 1:16, Psalm 8:3, Psalm 147:4, Isaiah 40:12, and Matt 24:29.)

The Poet's Prayer

by Jackson Harlem

Poets, which art imprisoned,
hallowed be thy heart's flames.
Thy wisdom comes, from trials you encounter
on route to heaven.

Give the world this day thy sacred gift: Thy words
To warm and nourish the world with your courage,
knowledge, and wit.
And let us speak no evil.

Keep thy word and thy passion
As true as thy Father's.
For it is He who hath brought us such Gifts.

Restake thy claim in history
As our predecessors have
Until we become the predecessors of the future
beacons of light.

And lead us not into silence
For Our Father's gifts are within us.
Thy gifts shall guide us
And shall deliver us from the valley of darkness
as we deliver our people.

For God's Kingdom is the Power and the Glory
And as we worship the King, with our pens in hand,
Our lives shall be blessed in Jesus' name
Forever.

Apen.

Courtney's Miracle
by John M. Wills

I picked up the phone. "John . . . CC's on her way to the hospital!" My wife, Chris, cried as she tried to force the words out between sobs. "CC fell and hit her head; she's unconscious; Tina couldn't revive her. She and CC are in an ambulance . . ."

I could hardly believe what I was hearing. CC was our three-year-old granddaughter. Tina, our daughter, had named her Courtney, but I nicknamed her CC when she was born. It seemed to fit her well, since she was so tiny. She was the sweetest little girl; she had no trouble capturing all of our hearts with her exaggerated smile.

"Chris, please calm down. What happened?"
"It's horrible."
"What's going on?"
"Please come!"
"Okay, I'll meet you at the hospital."

That conversation changed everything. Sunday morning had begun so well, highlighted by a deep blue sky, featuring a brilliant sun, it promised to produce the perfect day. A gentle breeze cooled me as I ran under beautiful elms and oaks that shielded me from the sounds of the city. Chris and I typically used this day to recharge our batteries from the prior work week. I was in the practice of starting each day with a run on our local exercise path. It was an ideal activity for reflecting on the past, planning for the future, and talking with my best friend, Jesus Christ.

I seldom carried my cell phone with me—too much in my pocket—I really didn't want my solitude interrupted by phone calls.

On this day, I carried my phone. I didn't realize it at the time, but there was a reason I had changed my routine. About a mile into the run my phone rang—it was Chris with the bad news about CC. I absorbed what she told me, quickly hung up, and ran as fast as I could back to my truck.

My heart ached for our little angel. Although not knowing how serious her injuries were, my only thought was that we couldn't survive without her in our lives. She and her brother,

Colin, had become the focal point of our lives. We relished our role as grandparents, and looked forward to seeing them each day. As I ran, I lifted a prayer to Jesus asking him to please leave my side and hold CC's hand. *Dear Lord, you made the blind see and the deaf hear, please don't let us lose our beloved granddaughter.* I implored Him to hear me, but knew it was His will that ultimately would be done.

As I made my way to the hospital, all the while continuing to pray, I asked Him to give me a sign that CC would be okay. *Dear Lord, please . . .* Within a few seconds a sense of calm washed over me, my anxiety disappeared, and at that moment, I knew He had just told me she would be fine.

Arriving at the emergency room, I saw my wife standing outside. She was tearful and very distraught. I went to her and hugged her. "CC will be okay—she's fine. The Lord gave me a sign; He answered our prayers."

Then as the ambulance pulled into the ER loading area and backed in, Chris and I went over and waited for the doors to open. When they did, we saw CC and her mother, lying on the stretcher. When CC saw us, she cried, "Nana, Papa!" and gave us a big smile.

Our little girl spent a long day in the ER. After multiple tests, a CAT scan, and much observation, it was determined that CC suffered no permanent damage. The doctors assured us she would be fine, although they were unable to explain fully why she lost consciousness. I, however, am confident that on this day the hand of God touched our family.

Years ago, if I heard a story such as this, I'd be skeptical about its veracity. Today after experiencing this incident with my granddaughter, it seems perfectly believable. I start each morning asking our Lord to walk with me; during the day, I often speak with Him—it all seems quite normal. I know He will always answer me, sometimes quickly, other times slowly. I know He has a plan for me; I know He will use me as He pleases.

One thing is certain: He is with me each day. He always speaks to me, and all I need do is listen to hear His voice. If I ask Him to walk beside me, He will. With Him, I am on the road to Eternal Salvation. Without Him, I will surely lose my way. CC's miracle brought me closer to God. I already knew He loved me, but His quick answer to my prayer for my granddaughter made me love Him even more. Thank you, Lord, for the gift of faith.

Contributors

Diann Brunell served five years in the Marine Corps. She now resides in Fredericksburg, Virginia with her husband and three children. She wrote "The Music Plays" during her son's piano lesson. As her thoughts of human suffering were overcome by the music, she was inspired to not give up. She looks forward to discovering her third career.

Tracy Deitz, a Spotsylvania resident for seventeen years, dabbles in gardening, painting and poetry writing. Meter is her nemesis; she avoids sonnets and haiku like influenza.

Anne Heard Flythe, a navy brat, attended 16 schools and won the senior prizes in art and poetry. Her poems have won second in the Mid-Atlantic Writers Conference, first prize in the Virginia Writers Club Golden Nib contest in 2008 and third in 2010. While all of the Riverside Writers anthologies include her work, she is proudest of the one dedicated to her in 2008. She studied art for one year at the Corcoran and Phillips galleries in Washington DC. In 1947 she produced a weekly TV show sandwiched between Jimmy Dean and the Washington DC based WMAL evening news. She crewed and cooked on a 75 ft. schooner for a year from Maine to Granada via Bermuda. Married Bill, a newspaperman, in 1959, she has two sons and one granddaughter. Widowed, Anne lives on and manages "Rebel Yell", a Loblolly plantation in Spotsylvania County. Surprised to reach 85, she remains fascinated by the beauty and complexity of life and people.

James Gaines is a professor in the Department of Modern Foreign Languages at the University of Mary Washington, where he teaches courses in language and literature, including courses on piracy and Germanic mythology. He has published poetry in French and English and is especially interested in translations, ranging from medieval to modern. His first collection of poetry, "Downriver Waltz," is now in preparation, and he is also working on a collection of prose tentatively entitled "Priests, Ghosts, and Pirates." He dedicates his story, "Beyond the Covenant," to the men from ports all over the world who gave up their lives in the Second World War.

Elaine J. Gooding spent most of her life in New York until joining the Marine Corps as a musician. Waiting to enter boot camp, she won 1st place in a song writing contest, and would later write more songs to include two which appear in this anthology. With a BS from Regents College (now Excelsior University), and a MALS from Mary Washington College (now the University of Mary Washington), she jokes that her high school also changed its name--twice! She wrote about "Mastery Learning" in "The Marine Gazette." Having taught as a substitute for many years, she currently tutors from her home. Recently, she received second place from the Riverside Writers for "Memorare," which is based on her recollections of life in a Catholic school. Married nearly 34 years, Elaine and her husband are blessed with two sons, two grandchildren, a church family and an awesome God.

Jackson Harlem is the unequivocal Renaissance man. Growing up, Harlem thrived onstage and through sketching menswear and writing poetry, all from the age of nine. After publishing his first work at thirteen, Harlem began frequenting poetry clubs across the country during his book tours. While studying opera privately at Tougaloo College, Harlem became the college's first poet laureate and later won a slew of poetry competitions and talent shows. In 2009, Harlem won the Riverside Writers' 2009 Poetry Festival Slam. Harlem has published two successful collections of poetry, *My Southern-Fried Affair* (2006, Medea Publishing) and *Black Boy Juice* (2008, Medea Publishing) and is an entertainment journalist for the Jackson Advocate newspaper as well as a menswear designer. The works submitted to this anthology reflect Harlem's versatility and purpose. From romance and religion to social commentary, poems like "Harlemese", "Yew", and "The Pontiff of Poetry" expand the ideals of modern poetry through educational and highly emotional content and performance.

Thomas J. Higgins has lived in Fredericksburg, Virginia his whole life. With a B.S. Degree in Business Administration from Virginia Tech, he worked for the Department of Agriculture. After seven years he left and opened a gift and florist shop in Fredericksburg with his wife Anne, where they stayed twenty-five years. They then became supervisors of two group homes for the mentally handicapped owned by Fredericksburg Baptist Church, retiring in 2006 after sixteen years. Tom has taught a Sunday school class for the mentally handicapped at that church and done other service for folks from the Sunday school class and others from the community. He wrote "Margaret Dillard" in 1991, and after retirement began writing his autobiography about working with the mentally handicapped. In 2010 the Fredericksburg Jaycees presented him with the Distinguished Service Award and the Rappahannock Community Services Board presented him with the 2010 Distinguished Intellectual Disability Volunteer Award.

J. Allen Hill (pen name of **Judy Hill**) was born in downstate Illinois but now considers herself an "east coaster" having lived not far from Atlantic beaches for over forty years. She has written to keep body and soul together as a Fairfax County School administrator, a Pentagon based training and documentation Project Manager and MENTOR's data manager. There have been many delightful paid and volunteer interludes involving writing, the arts and history: crew for Signature, a Tony Award-winning regional theater; usher at Arena Stage in Washington DC; docent for James Madison's Montpelier; Toastmaster governor; participating editor of many organizational newsletters, including Fairfax County, VA Parks. Currently she concentrates on short stories, a little poetry and a just completed literary novel. Encouragement and support has come from family, friends and membership in The Writer's Center, Bethesda, MD, Playwright's Forum, Washington, DC, Riverside Writers, Fredericksburg, VA and Virginia Writers, Inc.

Chuck Hillig was born in Chicago and has two Masters degrees. He has enjoyed successful careers as a naval officer, social worker, college instructor and county probation officer. After living in Ohio, Missouri, Rhode Island, Virginia and Pennsylvania, he moved to San Francisco during the late 1960's. Between 1978 and 2006, Chuck worked as a state-licensed psychotherapist in California. His five books, combining eastern philosophy and western psychology, are currently available on Amazon.com. Last year, Chuck was interviewed for the movie *Leap! Finale.* His writings and interviews have been published in nine languages, and he has been a guest on many radio and TV programs. Chuck travels frequently to speak at conferences and to conduct workshops about his books. Written almost 47 years ago, "The Boy Who Had Waited" was Chuck's very first work of fiction. He invites you to visit his website at: www.chuckhillig.com

Madalin E. Jackson (Madalin Bickel) was born and lived most of her life in West Virginia. She has a BS degree in Education and English and an MA in Gifted Education from Marshall University. She completed post graduate work at numerous institutions including WVU. She has taught over 38 years at the elementary, middle, and college levels. Her writing career spans over fifty years including prose, poetry, nonfiction, and music. Many of her articles have been published in professional journals including the WV Gifted Associations' Journal *Aegis*. Her first professional published work was *Discovering Astronomy* for DOK publishers. She is currently pursuing the publishing of numerous literature and educational units. She is a member of the Poetry Society of Virginia, Virginia Writers Club, Riverside Writers, and the Stafford, Virginia, and National Education Associations. She is the Resource Teacher for Gifted Students at Stafford Middle School and the newly elected president of Riverside Writers. This is the second Riverside Anthology to include her writings.

Laura Merryman is a high school English teacher and college instructor. Her professional activities include: reviewing for the *Rappahannock Review*, teaching courses in mythology, creative writing, science fiction and fantasy, and film studies. She has published in scholarly journals and conference proceedings and recently was selected to attend the 2010 Orson Scott Card Writing Bootcamp. Although raised in King George, Virginia, she considers herself a deep southerner at heart. Along with her husband, Stephen, she has raised four children and a menagerie of creatures.

David Mitchell arises at the crack of noon each day and devotes his full energies to pondering the great mysteries of life, such as why soft snacks turn hard when they go stale while crunchy snacks turn soft. David has lived most of his life in Massachusetts where he was well known as a visual artist specializing in paintings of sad clowns on velvet. He has recently ventured into writing poetry, because, as he puts it: "That's where the real money is."

P. A. Moton was born in Washington, D.C., and has lived her entire life (so far) in the D.C. Metropolitan Area—mostly in Northern Virginia. An honor graduate from George Washington High School in Alexandria at the age of 16 (she skipped a year of school), Pat began her love of poetry and of writing while in high school. She has spent a forty-year career with the Federal Government—three years with the Department of the Interior and the remaining years split between the Food and Drug Administration and the National Technical Information Service (NTIS) of the U.S. Department of Commerce. Pat currently serves as the Customer Advocate for NTIS, and as such created and still writes and edits the *Customer Advocate's Corner*, a quarterly newsletter distributed to over 600 subscribers.

Michelle O'Hearn is employed in business administration while pursuing her love of the arts, earning a degree in Culinary Arts and Business. Born and raised in Virginia, Michelle began singing/writing as a youth with recognitions in school writing and art competitions. She authored several eulogy poems, as requested by co-workers and acquaintances in her 20s while writing/performing with various rock bands. Michelle published three chapbooks (2007-2010) with Polican Publishing and a music CD, *Try to Relate*. Another music collection, *Peace and Quiet*, is digitally released under pen name, MiCKi. Recent writings earned recognition from Massachusetts State Poetry Society, Charlottesville Area Transit, VWC's Inside Back-Cover Poetry, and others. "Reduce, Reuse, Recycle" has been performed at litter and "green" events with her collaborator, Earl Dixon. MiCKi hosted open-mike performance venues from Orange, Virginia to Bozeman, Montana as an outreach endeavor to promote artistic expression of the "everyday man and woman".

Diane Parkinson grew up in the San Francisco Bay Area, joined the Navy at nineteen and has written and edited free-lance since high school. She writes book reviews for the *Historical Novels Review* and worked as a historical editor for The Wild Rose Press from 2007 to 2010. Her first novel, (written as Diane Scott Lewis) *The False Light*, a historical adventure with romantic elements, was released in April 2010. She lives with her husband and dachshund in Locust Grove, VA.

Mr. Kelly Patterson is a vibrant sixty-seven year old poet and writer. The majority of his work as a poet deals with much of his own experiences like the poem "Paper Boy," which is a true story. His keen wit and ability to assemble words paint a vivid picture in the mind of his reader. Often his peers call him an entertainment writer, and from the quality of his work this is true. Kelly loves beautiful women, animals and good coffee. His secret ambition is to become a novelist but feels that his work must be accepted by a publisher on its own merit; vanity publishing is out of the question. He was owner of Southern Home Company for twenty years, worked in the rocket and electronic industry prior to that. Kelly doesn't drink or smoke but he does everything else. His latest distinction was a letter of appreciation from Senator John Warner thanking him for his poem "The Soldier."

Norma E. Redfern was born in Shreveport, Louisiana in 1943. A military brat, she moved from Shreveport to Japan, Georgia, Alaska, and at last to Virginia, where she lived with her family at Ft. Belvoir. Norma met her high school sweetheart when both attended Mount Vernon High School. They were married in December, 1961. Norma worked for the government for five years after high school. After having three sons, she and her family moved to Fredericksburg, Virginia. She went to work for the government in Quantico, Virginia in 1978 as a military pay clerk, later promoted to military pay supervisor, verifying and auditing all facets of pay and allowances. Norma retired after twenty five years in the pay field in June of 2003. She joined Riverside Writers in 2001. She writes poetry and short stories.

Andrea Williams Reed is a member of the Riverside Writers Group; her writing experience began with writing and developing curricula for Work Ready Workshops and Work and Family Studies school curricula. She now enjoys writing poems and short stories. A native of Gloucester County, Virginia, she now makes her home in Fredericksburg with husband John.

Margaret Rose is recently retired from a 34-year career as a French teacher and a specialist in world language teacher training, which took her numerous times to France and also to professional conferences throughout the US and to China. Since her retirement, she has sought out opportunities to catch up on all the books and movies that she did not have time to enjoy while she was working and raising two sons. She is a devoted animal-lover and mom to a seventeen-year-old Siamese cat named Coco Chanel. Margaret's essay,"The Save Pile," first appeared in the May 2010 issue of *Front Porch* magazine." The story "Hey Lady" is the result of an assignment in an online writing course that she took through the University of Wisconsin. Margaret rejoices every day at the pleasures and challenges that she has encountered and invites readers to share their views on what she calls "the third phase of her life" in her blog at www.womenofacertainage2.blogspot.com.

Juanita Dyer Roush's love of writing was instilled in tenth grade English. Then, in senior English she had a teacher who would play music as they walked into class. Students would immediately put their heads on their desk and listen—and then write where their thoughts took them. Suddenly, writing became more personal. Nita didn't get serious about writing until she was diagnosed with genetic Meniere's Disease with a prognosis of total deafness. Suddenly it was important to write her thoughts. Rather than just journaling, she began to formalize her writing into poetry. When her son went to Iraq, Nita joined an online writing group to keep her mind busy. She has received much encouragement there. After some years of writing poetry she was encouraged by friends to try short stories. Last year she tried her hand at NaNoWriMo (National Novel Writing Month) writing a 50,000 word mini-novel in a month. Someday Nita hopes to have her novel published.

Ron Russis's first profession was as a U.S. Marine, retiring as a Master Sergeant after twenty-three years of service. Following retirement he renewed his formal education, graduating first from Mary Washington College with a B.S. (Psychology Specialization) and then from Goddard College with a MFA in Creative Writing. His writing typically addresses topics of rural interest.

Elizabeth Hessman Talbot's work in the anthology intertwines history and fantasy. "Loved by All" is the story of a struggling college instructor who takes an inadvertent trip back in time to the

Great Depression. A tour in Panama led by a "Canal Zone brat" inspired "Collateral Damage," a poem describing an emotional reunion set against the history of the Panama Canal. "Whiteout" is based on the pre-Christmas blizzard of 2009. Busy with raising children and a legal career, she did not start writing in earnest until after joining the Riverside Writers. "The feedback keeps you going." The group encouraged her to submit one of her first poems, "I am Rappahannock" to the West Virginia Poetry Society's 57th Annual Contest, which then won second prize. Her goal is to find a wider audience for her work.

Stanley Trice has had a dozen of his short stories published in national and international small press magazines in addition to several essays and over a dozen book reviews published locally. The story "Pane Glass Window" came from a small graduation party where, looking outside in, the graduates were framed against a pane glass window and thin blue flowers on the windowsill. Stanley is currently looking for publication of his science fiction book about monsters who may be no more than different looking people.

Donna H. Turner and her husband Larry moved to Fredericksburg in 2001 to be closer to their three sons and their families. She has a BA from Earlham College in Music, Art and Drama and an MA in Theatre from Northern Illinois University. She taught English in middle school and worked as a professional director for community and professional theatre groups in America and England. Currently she is directing for a dinner theater and teaching English as a Second Language at Peace United Methodist Church in Fredericksburg. Her essays appear in four published books as well as numerous literary magazines and have been translated into several languages, including Japanese and Turkish. Her children's book, *Thanzaloria Sticks Her Neck Out*, was published in 1996 by University Editions. She has written dozens of short dramas used in church services, some of which have been published.

Larry Turner moved to Fredericksburg after retiring from a career in college physics teaching and research in the USA and England. His poetry has appeared in many magazines including *Kansas Quarterly*, *The Lyric* and *Spoon River Quarterly*. Arbor

Hill Press published his first book of poetry, *Stops on the Way to Eden and Beyond* in 1992, and Infinity Publishing, his second, *Eden and Other Addresses* in 2005. He edited this anthology and the two previous ones for Riverside Writers. He has just completed a term as president of Riverside Writers. Earlier he was president of the Illinois State Poetry Society and regional vice-president of the Poetry Society of Virginia. "Blackmail," "Swept Away," "Song of a Continent," "Homage to the Cardiff Giant" and "Punctuality" have won prizes in national contests. "Bomyr's Leash and Tycy's Collar" won second prize in the VWC Golden Nib Contest.

Rod Vanderhoof grew up in the Puget Sound region of the Pacific Northwest. He studied economics at the University of Washington and was named Distinguished Military Graduate, Air Force ROTC. He earned a Stanford MBA, served twenty years in the Air Force, and retired as a lieutenant colonel. He traded bonds and stocks for nearly twenty years with Dean Witter Reynolds, Inc. in Washington D.C. Rod authored a novel, *The Cry of the Shidepoke,* plus numerous short stories, and wrote short comedy pieces published in the June and July 2009 issues of the *Virginia Heritage Gazette.* He was coeditor of several literary anthologies. Awards include the Riverside Writers Best Fiction, 2008, for his short story, "I Send My Regrets," and the Best Nonfiction, 2010, for his essay, "The General Who Saved Gettysburg." He won the Virginia Writers Golden Nib Prize for Poetry, 2009, for his poem, "Yellow Heat."

Dan Walker is the author of the novel *Huckleberry Finn in Love and War: The Lost Journals* (PublishAmerica.com, 2007), *Teaching English on the Block* (Eye on Education, 2000), and numerous poems and stories. He currently teaches English at the Commonwealth Governor's School in Spotsylvania County. Dan has also taught at the University of Mary Washington and at the Virginia Summer Residential School for Humanities and has worked as a seasonal park ranger at both Shenandoah National Park and Fredericksburg-Spotsylvania National Military Park. Dan and Mary, his wife of thirty-eight years, live on a small farm in southern Spotsylvania County, with nine cats, four dogs, three horses, two graveyards, and one pear tree—with no partridges (yet). About writing, Dan says "I enjoy it. I'm not smart enough to be humbled or intimidated by it. Once I thought I was a serious writer, but I got over it."

Kathie Walker lives in rural Virginia with her husband and their dogs, cats, and chickens. She is working on a memoir and a non-fiction book about antique photographic images of cats.

John M. Wills writes fiction and non-fiction, publishing more than one hundred articles in various law enforcement magazines and websites, relating to police training, fitness, officer survival, and ethics. He is a monthly contributor to Officer.com, the largest web portal for law enforcement, and is a former Chicago police officer and retired FBI agent. His latest novel, *Targeted*, to be released in Spring, 2011, is the third book in John's exciting series called *The Chicago Warriors Thriller Series*. He is also an award-winning author of short stories, many of which have been published in anthologies such as Randy Sutton's *True Blue to Protect and Serve* (St. Martin's Press), and *Stories of Faith and Courage From Cops On The Street*, part of the *AMG Battlefields & Blessings series*. He is an authorized NCAA speaker on the topic of steroids and dangerous drugs. John writes book reviews for the *New York Journal of Books*.

Index

Bickel,	Madalin	See Jackson, Madalin E.
Brunell,	Diann	Music Plays, The, 309
Deitz,	Tracy	Big Bang Take Two, 310
		Brake the Fast, 216
		His Hand, 311
		Oasis, The, 126
		Shades of Music, 225
		Shoppers Unite, 215
		Thwarted, 139
		What Not to Do, 275
Flythe,	Anne H.	Balefires, 5
		Enlightened?, 294
		From Your Sweet Lips, 229
		Manic Implications of a February Thaw, 169
		Message for Antoine, A, 240
		Nine Tenths of the Law, 240
		On the Wisdom of Allowing Wine to Breathe, 70
		Personal Equinox, A, 175
		Saudade, 71
		Slow Food, 172
		Something Old, 27
		Undeliverable Condolence, An, 73
		What You'll Get, 69
Gaines,	James	Beyond the Covenant, 241
		Goodbye, Alceste, 305
		Inconsistency and Remedies, 308

Gooding,	Elaine J.	Overtime, 86
		Butterfly Song, The, 97
		It's Not Original, 29
		Memorare, 119
		Twelve Haiku, 180
		Whiplash Takes a Ride, 160
Harlem,	Jackson	Harlemese, 276
		Orchid, The, 223
		Poet's Prayer, The, 314
		Pontiff of Poetry, The, 275
		Yew, 31
Higgins,	Thomas J.	Margaret Dillard, 283
Hill ,	J. Allen	Menudo, 44
		Mice Christmas, A, 162
		Panic at Milepost 42, 90
Hill,	Judith	See Hill, J.Allen
Hillig,	Chuck	Boy Who Had Waited, The, 34
Jackson,	Madalin E.	Alexander's Legacy, 285
		Eratosthenes, 220
		Mature Love in Words Only, 42
		Poe, 89
		Rambling Thoughts in Panic Mode, 303
		Time of Restlessness, A, 259
		Urn, The, 76
Merryman,	Laura	Crocheting Class, The, 91
		For Ollie, 143
		If You Must Write, 273
		On Stephanie's 16th Birthday, 136
		There is a Sweetness in Country Life, 194
Mitchell,	David	Fifty-Cent Tour, The, 213
		Inside the Bubble, 297

		Magic Glasses, 298
		Monster in Her Room, 299
		Substance of Youth, The, 111
		Truth about Truth, The, 304
Moton,	P. A.	Cannot, 267
		Eventually, 279
		I Miss You, My Friend, 93
		In a Rush, 272
O'Hearn,	Michelle	Blue Collar Shadorma, 86
		Footprints in the Grass, 170
		Night Out in Fredericksburg, A, 219
Parkinson,	Diane	Islands, 12
Patterson,	Mr. Kelly	My Boy Rex, 145
		Yo, Paper Boy, 133
Redfern,	Norma E.	Brimstone, 72
		Cassie, 30
		Fall, 179
		Fishing with My Dad, 128
		Fredericksburg 1727, 218
		Observation, 222
		Pain, 88
		Rebirth, 171
		Spring Rain, 170
		Three Haiki, 179
		What Might Be?, 303
Reed	Andrea	Stationary Family, The, 217
Rose,	Margaret	Hey, Lady, 286
		Save Pile, The, 83
Roush,	Juanita D.	Dancing in the Rain, 309
		Fountain, The, 256
		Imagination Lost, 295
Russis,	R. L	After Fieldwork, 140

Riverside Writers

		And Us Almost Done, 193
		Apprenticed to Art, 221
		At Twelve, 131
		Between the First and Second Milkings, 197
		Closer to Scratch, 118
		Dog Days, Snake Days, 174
		Early Widowed, 41
		Favored Sayings—and Sage Advice, 132
		Lady, King, Queenie, Max ..., 142
		Meditation on Winter's Solstice, 184
		Our Valley, 173
		Question of Horse-Power, A, 196
		To Me It Was Magic, 141
		Visiting Home after Long Absence, 200
		Watch! Watch!, 199
Talbot,	Elizabeth	Collateral Damage, 201
		Loved by All, 204
		Whiteout, 185
Trice,	Stanley	Pane Glass Window, 98
		Summer Discoveries, 6
Turner,	Donna H.	Best Friends Forever, 114
		Cake for Josie, A, 235
		Doris Emmit, 238
		Gift of Grace, A, 127
		Late Romance, A, 64
		Wo Ist die Post?, 270
Turner,	Larry	Baby in a Box, 107
		Birds and the Bees, The, 112
		Blackmail. Noun, Verb,

		Adjective, 269
		Bomhyr's Leash and Tycy's Collar, 146
		Century for Freedom, Century for Peace, 23
		Homage to the Cardiff Giant, 232
		Morning in the Twi-Lite Motel, 40
		Never Mind, 18
		Pajamas, 33
		Picture of Guilt, 20
		Punctuality, 229
		Rainbow Pin, The, 281
		Swept Away, 261
		Twins Anonymous, 230
Vanderhoof,	Rod	Genghis and the .55 Magnum, 151
		I Send My Regrets, 55
		Loaded Sabers, 252
		Yellow Heat, 3
Walker,	Dan	All We, Like Sheep, 296
		Black Spruce, 178
		I , The, 265
		Land Bridges, 176
		Marks, 182
Walker,	Kathie	For Dave, 27
		One Fish, Two Fish, 159
		Study of Logic in Vienna, The, 306
Wills,	John M.	Courtney's Miracle, 315
		Nightstand, The, 74
		Words, 268